The Secret Life of Sarah Hollenbeck

Center Point
Large Print

BETHANY TURNER

The Secret Life of Sarah Hollenbeck

CENTER POINT LARGE PRINT
THORNDIKE, MAINE

ISBN: 978-1-68324-581-0

Library of Congress Cataloging-in-Publication Data

Names: Turner, Bethany, 1979- author.
Title: The secret life of Sarah Hollenbeck / Bethany Turner.
Description: Center Point Large Print edition. | Thorndike, Maine :
    Center Point Large Print, 2017.
Identifiers: LCCN 2017035081 | ISBN 9781683245810
    (hardcover : alk. paper)
Subjects: LCSH: Christian women—Conduct of life—Fiction. |
    Women—Religious Life—Fiction. | Women authors—Fiction. |
    Christian life—Fiction. | Large type books. | GSAFD: Christian
    fiction. | Love stories.
Classification: LCC PS3620.U76 S43 2017b | DDC 813/.6—dc23
LC record available at https://lccn.loc.gov/2017035081

Now to him who is able to do immeasurably more than all we ask or imagine, according to his power that is at work within us, to him be glory in the church and in Christ Jesus throughout all generations, for ever and ever! Amen.

Ephesians 3:20–21

1.

The Next Emily Dickinson

If you're willing to admit it, you probably know me as Raine de Bourgh. Yes, *that* Raine de Bourgh. Did you blush at the mere mention of my pen name? Yeah. So did I.

Three and a half years ago, I certainly had no intention of ever becoming Raine de Bourgh. I was simply Sarah Hollenbeck. Or maybe I was still Sarah McDermott? No. Sarah Hollenbeck. Sarah McDermott was the product of an empty, loveless marriage, and I was doing all I possibly could to prove—at least to myself—that I wasn't the shell my marriage had reduced me to. But did I even remember Sarah Hollenbeck? The girl I was *before* I met the guy? Could I become her once again?

The answer had to be yes, so that Monday evening in June, three and a half years ago, I hoisted my Kate Spade messenger bag a bit higher on my shoulder, straightened my Stella McCartney blazer, wiggled my toes in my Christian Louboutin pumps, and took a deep breath. As I reached for the doorknob of the high school library, I noticed a slight tremble in my hand. I didn't understand what was causing the reaction. I'd been faithfully entering that library each week for two months, and it was, after all, just a book club.

Until a couple of months prior, my life had consisted of the duties of a trophy wife, proudly—though often resentfully—supporting my husband on his rise to the top of a Fortune 500 real estate conglomerate. *His* Fortune 500 real estate conglomerate. But suddenly, from the moment Patrick sent me a text message that said "Bringing Dan for dinner. He's gluten-free" followed by a thumbs-up emoji, my life as I knew it was over. Well, I suppose that wasn't the moment. The moment came later that evening when I caught Patrick making out with Dan's wife, Bree, in the room I had dreamt would someday be a nursery.

The dissolution of my marriage left me with a lot of free time. There were no gluten-free dinners to plan, no charity events to attend, no bigwigs to schmooze. We had been together since high school, and while the last few years certainly hadn't been fulfilling or happy, I didn't recognize my life without Patrick by my side. I didn't recognize *myself* without Patrick by my side. All of our friends were actually Patrick's friends, it turned out. I couldn't blame them, really. They were social-ladder-climbers, and I was most definitely a woman whose social status was experiencing a free fall.

Every job search came up empty. Apparently no one in the tough Chicago job market was interested in hiring someone who hadn't worked since college, where she'd earned a degree she'd never once put to use. I'd had one career and one career only, and I'd been forced into early retirement—and I never was able to figure out how to list my job experience as "Mrs. Patrick McDermott" on my résumé.

I was a social pariah desperately in need of something to do, but for a depressed, newly divorced woman with more money and time than talent or skills, finding the right hobby is a surprisingly tricky thing.

Traveling meant traveling alone, and that wasn't something I knew how to do.

Quilting took too much patience.

Community theatre took too much confidence.

Painting took too much effort.

Book clubs? Book clubs could work.

I joined seven book clubs in the Greater Chicago area simultaneously. Seven. And that meant I was reading seven novels simultaneously. I thought that was the perfect solution—after all, doing that much reading, when would I have time to think about the shambles of my life? Yeah . . . that sounds good in theory, but every book reminded me of what I'd lost—or worse, what I'd never had. A fulfilling marriage. A life with some-one who considered me his best friend. Children.

Every book, from *The Picture of Dorian Gray* to *Eat, Pray, Love*, from *Lord of the Rings* to *The Hunger Games*, somehow reminded me of my misery. When my Dark American Romanticism book club started reading *The Scarlet Letter*, I knew I'd had all I could take. I quit all of the book clubs except for the one on Monday night, because that was the one that met closest to my house. I decided that Monday night book club would be my primary hobby and exclusive social circle.

And I approached that social circle the only way I knew how—with all of the rules and safeguards that had been so necessary for self-preservation in the highfalutin world of the snobs and blue bloods, into which I had made every effort to feel as if I belonged. I would dress for success and speak only when I had something monumental and memorable to contribute. I would hide my scars and shortcomings, and only put forth the most impressive version of myself. I would keep everyone at arm's length so that if I eventually fell out of favor with them, I would not be impacted.

It would be just like any other social gathering I had ever attended, apart from one striking difference: my last name was no longer McDermott, so I wouldn't be viewed as nothing more than an accessory from the moment I was introduced.

And with all of the extra time, once I had whittled the book club list down to one, I would write a book of my own. Then I could be in control of the content. Then my emotions wouldn't be putty in the hands of authors who had probably written to escape their own misery, with nary a care given to the feelings of the miserable divorcée who would one day read their work while attempting to bury her pain beneath enough cheesecake to bestow diabetes upon a small village. I'd never written anything before, but I'd certainly done more than my fair share of reading.

How hard could it be?

My first attempt was a book of poetry, and while I waited for the call from the president asking me to accept the post of Poet Laureate of the United States, I decided it was time to share my gift with the world. Or at least the Monday night book club. Though I couldn't ever remember their names, the ladies in that circle were, after all, my closest friends. No, I hadn't known them very long, and yes, our conversations had never plunged any deeper than whether we'd preferred Jim Caviezel as the Count of Monte Cristo or Jesus, but they were the constants in my life of upheaval, and I knew that our bond was true and indestructible.

I'd been walking into that high school library every Monday evening for two months, but that first Monday evening in June was the beginning. That Monday evening represented a fresh start.

That Monday evening was the first book club meeting of the rest of my life.

"Excuse me." I raised my hand and smiled as the ladies began gathering their things to go, having exhausted all possible thoughts, feelings, and debates over *Northanger Abbey*. "If you could all spare just a few more moments of your time, if it's not too much to ask." I blinked sweetly, conveying humility so well in that tried and true manner I had watched Patrick employ for so many years.

I rarely spoke in book club, so I wasn't surprised that everyone stopped in their tracks.

"Of course, Sarah. What can we do for you?" asked the leader of the book club, whose name had slipped my mind. And by "slipped my mind," I mean I hadn't bothered to learn it.

"I value each and every opinion in this circle. You each present such witty and insightful views, and that, I believe, is what I as a budding poet need in order to develop my craft." I saw them take in my rehearsed speech, and they responded with enthusiastic support. Once I was fully convinced that they were the eager demographic I was seeking, I meekly proceeded. "You are all just the best. If no one would mind . . . may I?"

I opened the leather-bound binder in my hands and pulled out the crisp linen stationery on which I had lovingly transcribed each poem by hand over the course of the past several days and began to read.

> Lights flicker. Kerosene?
> Perhaps.
> The man in suede wishes me well,
> But I doubt his sincerity.
> Never you mind.
> Suede and kerosene. The two don't mix.
> Boom.

I read poem after poem after poem and, as expected, I was rewarded with stunned silence. They were clearly overcome with emotion and overwhelmed by the power of the lyric. I smiled at them all and gave them a moment to collect themselves. I cast my eyes downward, not wanting to impose upon their deeply intimate moment.

"Thank you, Sarah," Book Club Leader Lady said after clearing her throat. "That was truly . . . something."

"Yeah . . . wow . . ." random women in the circle said in unison.

I was so very full of myself that I took it as true, sincere praise.

"Thank you all so much." I beamed condescendingly. "It was an honor sharing my work with you."

"I'm sorry," a woman I had never noticed before said softly. "Can I be honest?"

You want me to take over the book club? You think I'm the next Emily Dickinson? You're a Hollywood producer who wants to adapt "Lavatory Purgatory" for the screen?

"Of course." I smiled and gestured to indicate I would allow her to proceed. "Please."

"Well, I don't want to be rude, but this group is about honest analysis of the quality of what people write, and it's also about the way what we read makes us feel. So, I just have to say, I have some issues with your poetry that I would be happy to elaborate on if you would allow me to do so."

Convinced that she couldn't possibly be referencing anything more than a rhyme she didn't like or, more likely, a long-buried emotion within herself that my words had unwittingly brought to the surface, I nodded that she had the floor.

"Okay," she began, sitting up a little straighter. "I think there is a pretty decent chance that you've actually got some writing talent, but let's face it—poetry isn't where you need to be. And what's with the subjects? It's like you just flipped through the yellow pages until something jumped out at you. What's next? Exterminators?"

I looked down at the papers in my hands and sheepishly shuffled "Insecticide Nuclear Winter" to the bottom of the stack.

The critic pressed on. "Look, I didn't feel any emotional connection to any of it, and that's fine. I don't feel any connection to Jane Austen, either." Every other woman in the room gasped, which made her smile, I noticed. "But the problem is, I don't think you felt any emotional connection to any of it. That is what it is, I suppose, and if you're running from something or trying to avoid feeling, well, that's your decision. But please don't subject the rest of us to it."

The others in the circle seemed not to breathe, anxious for, and yet dreading, my reply. I knew she was right. Of course I knew she was right.

And that was the moment. The depression and the hole in my heart and the suffocating sadness couldn't be pushed to the background any longer. I started crying like in an old *Looney Tunes* cartoon—you know, where the tears shoot out horizontally with the force of a garden hose. Actually, I think it was kind of a combination of *Looney Tunes* and *I Love Lucy*, because I think I actually made that "Waaaaa!" sound.

All of the women in the group—the nameless women for whom I hadn't taken the time or made the effort to develop true respect or affection—gathered around me and hugged me and said generic things like "There, there" and "It's going to be okay." I was so touched by that moment. So much so that I told myself I was going to make brownies for them all and bring them to next week's meeting. They may be the only thing I know how to bake, but my brownies really are amazing, so that was a big gesture for a social pariah allowing herself to feel again.

2.

The Speaker of Painful Truth

The next week in book club, it wasn't until after I had soaked in all of the praise—this time undoubtedly genuine—for my brownie-making skills that I noticed something. Each week, I sat in a circle of fifteen women—all ages, body types, hair colors—and saw nothing of any of them apart from their ages, body types, and hair colors. Skinny Redhead with Freckles sat just to the left of me each week, and on the other side of her was Boob Job Bonnie, as I had mentally named her. Across from me sat Coke Bottle Glasses, Dorothy Hamill Hairdo, and Granny. Each of them stood out to me as a caricature, apart from Book Club Leader Lady, who I was so grateful was the leader of the group, since she seemed to possess no other defining visual characteristics whatsoever. There were visitors to the circle once in a while, but I didn't even bother to glance at them until I knew they would be around awhile. But on brownie day, for the first time I noticed someone was missing.

"Hey, where's . . . umm . . ." I began before quickly realizing I had no way of describing her apart from Plain Girl I'd Never Noticed Before

She Dashed My Poetic Delusions, and that didn't seem like a nickname that should ever be allowed outside of the confines of my mind. I pointed my eyes and chin toward the one empty chair in the circle and hoped that she, like the rest of us, sat in the same spot each week.

"Hey, guys, sorry I'm late," a voice called out from the door as the speaker of painful truth herself walked into the room and took off her coat.

"Hi, Piper!" Barbra Streisand Nose said in greeting. "Sarah was just asking about you."

Piper. Okay, so I knew a name, but I couldn't help but wonder how other people knew it. I really didn't remember ever seeing Piper before the previous week. Does it tell you how self-centered I was back then that I never for a moment wondered how they all knew *my* name? Of course I was Sarah, and not Perfectly-Coiffed Camille, or Princess Prada, or any of the other names I probably would have come up with if I saw myself on the other side of the circle.

"Hi, Sarah. Are these the famous brownies?" Piper smiled at me as she took one from the pan and carried it with her to the empty chair between Botox and Way Too Old for Pigtails.

For a brief moment I wondered which friend Piper and I had in common, and I was obviously flattered—though not terribly surprised—to discover my brownie-baking reputation preceded me. I smiled in response to the flattery and was just about to say something like, "Famous? I doubt that. Though they are quite legendary in the wives' lounge of the Beverly Country Club," but all of a sudden I had what felt like an out-of-body experience. I could see clearly, as if I were floating above the scene in the moment of my mental breakdown from the week prior. I had thought the promise of brownies had been only a silent, mental one. A note to self, if you will. But, no. In the moment that had been half Porky Pig, half Lucille Ball, and just a little bit Marlon Brando in *A Streetcar Named Desire*, I had wailed, "I'll bring you my secret recipe brownies, because I love you all!"

I felt as if I could see what they had all seen, and I was mortified. Absolutely mortified. I looked around the room and examined the eyes, all of which were planted on me, and realized for the first time that, while my brownies were indeed delicious, the emotion being conveyed by all of those sets of eyes, and Pirate Patch Patty, wasn't appreciation or awe. It was pity.

"Excuse me," I mumbled as I bolted out of my seat and ran into the hallway.

I stood there with my tear-ridden face buried in my arm, which was propped up against a row of lockers. *I have never been so humiliated in my entire life,* I thought for one brief moment before the onset of the sad realization that there was no truth in that at all. As bad as that moment was, it had been a year of moments that were far worse.

"Are you okay?" Piper asked as she approached quietly and carefully, no doubt fearing that the wild animal might attack.

I turned around, humiliation not mattering much at that moment. "Is it possible that upon the dissolution of my marriage to my high school sweetheart, the only emotion I am truly *feeling* is embarrassment? Can that really be what my life's reduced to?"

For the record, I was very proud of my epiphany. I felt very mature and profound for figuring that out—but that's not to say that I was proud of the way I was feeling, of course. Nevertheless, I expected at least *some* marveling at my diagnostic skills, but Piper didn't marvel.

" 'Upon the dissolution'? Is that really how you talk?"

I stared at her for a moment, willing myself to be offended, but in the end all I could do was laugh. "I don't know!"

And she laughed with me, though neither of us really understood the joke.

"What do you mean, you don't know?"

"I mean, I don't really know how I really talk. I haven't been just me for a very long time."

Understanding and kindness shone in her eyes. "Stay here," she commanded kindly, and then she walked into the room where the circle of ladies had become more of a parallelogram as they all wiggled and stretched to get a view of whatever was going on in the hallway.

Within seconds, Piper was back with her backpack and my Louis Vuitton purse, Kate Spade messenger bag, and Williams Sonoma brownie pan.

"Let's go get some coffee," she said as she handed everything to me.

"Okay," I said, not fully understanding why we were going to get coffee but not opposed to the idea. "I just have to run back in quickly. I left my pen with . . ." Oh, here we were again. I had to refer to someone in the group, and I had no idea what her name was. I sighed, embarrassed once more.

"Eh, don't worry about it. I have plenty of pens. I'll loan you one."

I didn't move from the spot.

She sighed. "Is your pen a designer too?"

I blushed. "Montblanc."

"Okay, I'll go get it. Who has it? Marilyn?" she asked. I scrunched up my nose, trying to act like I was just having a mental lapse. "Shawna? Rachel? Cynthia? Shaniqua?"

I did an involuntary double take and then tried to hide it. Of all those laced-up white ladies, which of them could possibly be named Shaniqua?

"Umm . . ."

Piper started laughing. "Come on, Sarah. We know that you don't know our names. Just describe her."

Oh, how the embarrassment grew. And yet, it was funny. Piper made it funny.

I mumbled, and when she couldn't understand me, I said a little more loudly, "Mullet Marie."

"Got it. Be right back."

I watched out of the corner of my eye as she went right up to Mullet Marie and got my $400 pen.

"Thank you," I whispered when she handed it to me, a smirk on her face.

"You're welcome. Let's go."

Over coffee and scones, I told her my sob story. I was surprised and saddened to discover that my entire adult life could be relayed in about ten minutes. I met Patrick at the end of our junior year of high school and never looked back. We went to DePaul University together because that's where he was going, and I couldn't bear the thought of being separated from him. DePaul, of course, is a Catholic university. I wasn't Catholic, but Patrick was, and that was all that mattered. We graduated and decided to stay in Chicago so that he could work for his dad—a dreadful bore of a man who wouldn't allow me to call him anything other than Mr. McDermott. Patrick worked during the day and went to classes at night in order to earn his MBA. We didn't see much of each other in those early days, but that was okay, because it was all temporary, I thought. It was what was necessary in order to achieve the American dream. On our fifth wedding anniversary, Mr. McDermott died of a massive heart attack, and Patrick was suddenly the man in charge.

I was so proud of him. I really was. But that doesn't mean that life was everything I wanted it to be. For every perk of our life, there seemed to be twice as many drawbacks. Yes, we had money, but I was usually left to spend it alone. Yes, we had use of a private jet, but the only vacation we ever took together was our honeymoon. Yes, we had a huge house in Near North Side, but the empty rooms were filled only by echoing silence during the day and the cold business talk of colleagues and clients at night.

And then there was Bree.

She wasn't his first mistress, but it was the only time he ever dared to bring one of them into our home. That was the night I realized what we'd become, and on some level what I had become, though of course I was still trying to figure that one out.

I stopped there and sat back in my chair, exhausted.

"This is the story you should write, Sarah," Piper said, speaking for the first time in several minutes. "You're on this journey, trying to figure out who you are now. This is stuff you know, and stuff you feel. Patrick, his dad, Bree . . . all of it. That's what you should write about."

I hadn't had a conversation this intimate with anyone in a very long time. I thought for a moment, trying to remember the last time. It certainly wasn't with Patrick, or my mother. Ah, that's right. Father Horatio.

Father Horatio is my favorite priest. I never really got into the whole church thing, but I still had to act like a good little Catholic wife for appearances' sake, so I would go to confession. But only to Father Horatio. My first confession to Father Horatio, two weeks after Patrick and I got married, was that I didn't believe in God.

It wasn't true, of course. I didn't have a lot of faith, and my actual spiritual life was pretty nonexistent, but I'd always believed in God. But I figured that telling a priest I didn't believe in God was a pretty good litmus test for how he'd handle all of my other sacrilegious baggage.

"Excuse me?" Father Horatio asked through the lattice, and I smiled before continuing solemnly.

"Yes, that's right, Father. I don't believe in God."

"No, dear, I wasn't talking to you," he said in reply.

What? Was someone in there with him? I was new to Catholicism, but I was still pretty confident that was somehow against the rules.

"Who are you talking to?"

"Actually, I was talking to God. He was wondering why I was sitting here in an empty booth. Turns out he doesn't believe in you either."

I laughed so hard, and so did Father Horatio, and from that moment on I was completely honest with him. With Father Horatio, I could be myself. He was the only one.

Well, until now. I knew nothing about the woman sitting across the café table from me, but I was more comfortable with her than I was with people I had known my entire life.

"Can I ask you something?" I was about to look like a self-centered jerk once more, but I knew it was unavoidable.

Piper nodded that I could as she took a sip of her coffee.

"What made you feel so free to say what you said about my poems?"

She grimaced. "Come on now, Sarah. Aren't you being a bit generous by calling them that?"

I laughed. "Yes, yes, I know. 'Kerosene Boom' was pretty bad."

"Well, hang on a minute. I actually thought that was one of the better ones."

"Oh, that's a sad statement!"

She quoted a few choice lines from "Air Freshener Catharsis" to demonstrate her point, and tears began running down my cheeks, I was laughing so hard.

"I think that 'Ernest Hemingway Was Never So Young as a Chimpanzee in School, Part 2' is actually rather profound," I deadpanned. "One might even say enigmatic and enthralling."

She shook her head as she began laughing every bit as freely as I was. "And what was the one about the spleen?"

"That one was called 'Spleen,' I believe."

"Oh, of course."

I rolled my eyes. "Trust me, I know they're bad. And I'm not for a moment suggesting you shouldn't have said anything. I mean, you were the only person with the guts to tell me the truth, and I appreciate that. You didn't tell me anything I didn't know, really, on some level. It's just . . ."

"I don't know." Piper sighed. "I'd just been watching you for weeks, and it was plain as day that you were going through something. I thought you deserved the truth. Don't we all deserve the truth?"

And then it poured out of me. "Okay, here's the truth: I never even noticed you before that day. Not once. When you spoke up, it was like you had just wandered into the room. So that was pretty shocking."

"It would be, wouldn't it?" She frowned. "You'd never noticed me at all?"

I shook my head.

"I wasn't even a Mullet Marie?"

"Nope. Everyone in that room has a nickname,

but not you. I never noticed you. I don't even know how that's possible, actually." I pushed away the momentary consideration that she was a ghost or an angel, though that made as much sense as anything else I could come up with. But somehow, Piper knew exactly how to explain it.

"From the first day you joined the book club, it was so unbelievably obvious that you were searching for something."

I didn't ask her what she thought I was searching for. I think that even then I knew I wasn't ready for the answer.

"You seemed like you needed a friend," she continued. "I watched you, and I noticed that you never made eye contact with anyone. You went out of your way to avoid it, whether you realized it or not. I didn't know why—I still don't—but I knew I was right. So, never being one to back down from a challenge, my quest each week was to get you to make eye contact with me. So I watched you all the time."

I couldn't believe it. "Did you? I didn't notice."

"Of course you didn't notice." Piper laughed. "I was the only person in that circle who was willing to meet you head-on. I think everyone else is almost as bad as you are. Everyone is running or hiding from something. It took three months to get Alisa to make eye contact with me." She started laughing again as she stood to throw her napkin away.

"Who's Alisa?" I asked, no longer embarrassed by my lack of knowledge.

"Hmm. Let me think. How would you know her? Surprised Sally, perhaps?" That didn't trigger anything other than a smile. "You know," she continued, "she always looks surprised. Or startled, maybe. Her eyebrows are always . . ." She used her fingers to push her own eyebrows as high as they could go, and I started laughing loudly as realization hit.

"Botox! That's Botox!"

Piper covered her mouth to try to keep the laughter from being too loud, but she failed shamefully, which just made me laugh even more.

I couldn't think of the last real friend I'd had. I suppose Patrick was the last. That's sad, isn't it? But there was a time when he was my friend. My best friend. And then we got married.

Piper and I talked for hours, and it felt like, well, hours. It didn't drag on because it was an excruciating experience I couldn't wait to walk away from. Not at all. And it also wasn't a giddy, slumber party–esque gabfest where the time flew by as we talked about boys and hairstyles and ate cookie dough. We laughed and bonded and just genuinely enjoyed our time together.

It was very real, and very impactful. And the time that we spent together was perhaps my first dance with reality, at least since reaching adulthood. I wasn't carrying on a conversation with the sole purpose of impressing a client for Patrick. I wasn't laughing at jokes and flashing my pearly whites, hoping that I didn't zone out during all of the boring stock market talk.

For the first time in a very long time, I was just *me*. Piper helped me remember what it was like before I ever became Sarah McDermott. I was once again Sarah Hollenbeck from the south side of Chicago—a girl who may not have grown up in an affluent neighborhood, a fancy house, or even a happy home, but she was genuine.

From that point on, I was committed to the belief that there was no one else I needed to be, ever again.

That was a good thought, in theory.

3.

Raine, with an E

I took Piper's advice and started writing what I knew. But what did I know, really? I knew who to call if you ran into a landscaping emergency at 10:00 in the evening. I knew which items from Burberry's previous collections were timeless and which to pass off to consignment. But none of that seemed like enough to fuel a novel, so I realized I would have to dig deeper.

I dug deeper for about the same length of time as the *Frasier* rerun I was watching, and then I decided, instead, to write what I knew nothing about. Not in the Yellow Pages poetry way, which had failed so horribly for me. No, it was time for something more. It was time to have fun. It was time to dream and pretend and conjure up a working hypothesis of what I thought it might be like to be half of a loving, functional couple.

Something I knew nothing about.

Loving, functional couples always fall in love at first sight, right? At least that's how it usually happens in the films and books I had filled my head with. And they can't keep their hands off of each other, even when the moment is less than appropriate. And tempers and passions continually flare, usually stemming from or leading to misunderstandings that could have been cleared up with simple questions like, "Is that your ex or his twin brother whom you've never mentioned?" or comments like, "The lady I'm going to the party with tonight is my dying aunt and not a rich benefactress you assume I'm sleeping with."

I wrote *Stollen Desire* over the course of about six weeks, while sustaining an unhealthy—and rather disgusting, in retrospect—diet of hot wings, quinoa, and Merlot. It was the story of Alex Stollen, a rich, successful, celebrity chef, and Annie Simnel, his young sous-chef. It was unrealistic and schmaltzy, and both of my lead characters' last names were types of baked goods. But she made him want to be a better man, and he made her feel whole again. And they got to throw a lot of flour around during their love scenes.

I'm not exactly sure why I decided Alex and Annie's sex life needed to be written about in such graphic detail. Then again, I suppose it's not that difficult to connect the dots, considering I spent every day blaming my ex-husband's infidelity on my own apparent sexual inadequacy. I had no real reason to suspect that Patrick had been dissatisfied with the physical aspect of our relationship, apart from the fact that there had been no physical aspect at all for a very long time. "Experts" would most likely hit on something more profound and insist that our separate bedrooms and his infidelities were symptoms of a deeper wound, but it was much less painful to confront the idea that he turned to Bree and the rest of them because of who I was in the bedroom, rather than who I was as a person.

So maybe I wrote certain scenes certain ways in order to confront what I was dealing with inside my head, or maybe that's what I was trying to avoid. Or maybe I was just tired of watching *Frasier* reruns. Regardless of why the book was written, *who* it was written for was never in doubt.

Me. Only me.

And no one would have read it if I hadn't been distracted, and thoroughly amused, by the disbelief, shock, and horror every other woman in the circle was exhibiting as Piper explained why she just didn't think Mr. Darcy was "marriage material."

"How can you say that?" asked Mullet Marie, whose real name was Mullet Cynthia. I mean, just Cynthia, of course. But who are we kidding? The mullet just cried out for an identity all its own. "The entire book is literally about how Mr. Darcy is marriage material. He's the very embodiment of the phrase, Piper."

Piper scrunched up her nose, and when I caught the mischievous wink she directed toward me,

I knew she was in her element. I didn't want to miss a moment of it. So when Moira, previously known as Barbra Streisand Nose, asked if she could borrow a piece of paper, I didn't bother to take my eyes off of the evening's Austen debate.

Clearly not paying attention to my own actions, I inconveniently picked up my Kate Spade messenger bag by its leather base rather than the leather strap. Everything came tumbling out of the bag. It was kind of like it all happened in slow motion—I focused on the bag in horror, taking just a moment to verify that I had indeed lifted it by the wrong end and that there wasn't somehow a hole or tear, before setting it back on the floor beside me. All at once, Moira picked up my notebook and tore out a sheet of blank paper before slipping the notebook back into the bag while Cynthia retrieved my Austen anthology and handed it to me with great care—as if the very lives of Mr. Darcy, Colonel Brandon, and Captain Wentworth were entrusted to her.

It wasn't until I saw Shawna, with the aid of her Coke bottle glasses, trying to make sense of the coffee-stained 8½-by-11 sheet in her hand, that I began to fully understand the magnitude of the moment.

"Hey, Sarah, what's this?"

A few pages of my very private story were

scattered all across the floor, but the question came from Boob Job Bonnie, who I instantly renamed Bad News Bonnie (her name is actually Alma). In her hands was a stack of papers about an inch thick, covered in coffee stains throughout. I reached out to grab it from her hand as she flipped through the pages, but she wasn't holding the manuscript as tightly as I'd thought. The papers flew from her hands and mine and rained down on the group. Instantly, everyone—graciously and annoyingly—started helping to pick up the pieces of paper, and as they did, they spotted certain words.

Words that couldn't help but grab a reader's eye.

The room went quiet as all of the ladies read what they held in their hands. I was powerless to stop it, and then I didn't want to. There were near-silent teeters and sighs and a few rosy cheeks as they picked up additional pages to read them.

"What *is* this?" said Pirate Patch Patty (who actually is named Patty, as it turns out). And then the room erupted into unabashed giggling.

My name wasn't on the manuscript—after all, I wasn't seeking publication or even proofreading from anyone. The only person I had intended to share my work with was Piper, who by then was without a doubt my best friend. Although, let's face it: she had become my best friend the moment she became my friend. The best among one. But don't let that undermine the depth of our friendship.

"Oh, it's just something a friend of mine is working on," I lied.

"This is . . ." Granny, whose name I hadn't yet learned, paused, and I shuddered, preparing for the shame that I knew was about to flood my soul. Which adjective would she choose? Sickening? Reprehensible? Smutty? "Amazing!" she finished.

The other ladies excitedly chimed in.

"I only read a page, and I don't want to put it down!"

"I should feel guilty reading this, but I actually don't."

"I need a cold shower!"

"Who's your friend, Sarah?" Jane, aka Book Club Leader Lady, asked. "Do you think she would let us read her book? I think all of the ladies would love that." She blushed.

I saw the enthusiastic nods and grins, and I thought, *What the heck! What can it hurt to tell them that I wrote it? My ego could use a boost anyway, and it might help take away some of the residual pain of "Kerosene Boom."*

"Well, actually—" I began quietly, but before I could go any further, Piper cleared her throat.

"Not all of the ladies, Jane. You know, it's not really my cup of tea. But if you all want to read it, go ahead, and I'll just pick back up with you the next week."

Jane frowned. "Oh, are you sure, Piper? We certainly don't want to exclude anyone."

My best friend smiled sweetly. "I'm sure. Really, it's no big deal. I'll just continue through the monotony which is the complete works of Jane Austen."

I smiled at the twinkle in her eye, fully aware now that while her lack of love for Austen was genuine, she regularly played up her distaste to get a rise out of the rest of the group.

"But I certainly want to hear more about your friend, Sarah." Piper's eyes were on me, and for the first time in many weeks, I wasn't comfortable maintaining eye contact with her.

So books like *Stollen Desire* weren't her "cup of tea." That wasn't harsh criticism, certainly, but if it wasn't the cup of tea of the one person whose opinion mattered to me, I didn't have the confidence to confess that the creation was mine.

"Oh, she's just an old friend from college," I fibbed. "She just asked me to proofread for her. No big deal." I smiled nervously as I gathered as many pages as I could—the pages that weren't caught in the death grips of the ladies—and stuffed them back into my bag. The thought of letting the group read what I had written had faded quickly under Piper's penetrating gaze.

"I just don't think I've heard you mention her. What's her name?" Piper asked.

I knew that Piper *knew* she hadn't heard me mention her. Or any friend.

"Her name is . . ." I looked around the room, trying to piece together a good name for a writer of steamy romance. The rat-tat-tat of raindrops hitting the roof, a constant reminder of the wall of humidity that would hit us the moment we stepped outside, stole my attention. "Raine. With an *e*," I stammered. *Was the "with an* e*" really necessary, Sarah?* "Raine de Bourgh."

One pair of eyes stayed focused on me, and I'm sure you can guess which pair that was. Every other pair, and Patty, looked down at the book they held in their hands or their laps. *Pride and Prejudice*.

"Oh. Like Lady Catherine de Bourgh?" Moira asked sweetly.

Good grief. Had I really just chosen a name from the very book that my entire book club had been poring over for three weeks? The very book that every woman in the room, apart from Piper, had practically memorized? The very book that had inspired near-weekly debates as to whether or not Colin Firth had ruined the role of Darcy for any other man, because no one else would be considered worthy ever again?

"Oh!" I laughed nervously. "Well, yeah . . . wow, what a coincidence."

Piper knew. I knew that she knew.

"That's funny," she said, but she sure didn't look amused. "I mean, we've been reading this drivel, and it never once occurred to you, in the course of all of the reading and discussions and debate and Darcy-love, that your friend from college, whose manuscript you have in your bag, shares a last name with Darcy's aunt? Hmm. Funny." She was daring me to lie directly to her, and I didn't want to do it, but I also didn't see any other way out.

"But however insincere you may choose to be, you shall not find me so. My character has ever been celebrated for its sincerity and frankness, and in a cause of such moment as this, I shall certainly not depart from it."

Those words from Lady Catherine de Bourgh herself applied very nicely to Piper Lanier, I realized with a mixture of awe and fear. And suddenly it was a battle of wills. I met my best friend's eyes with my own, prepared to "fake it till I make it" in regards to confidence and the story I had to create.

"Well, it's a pen name, of course. She doesn't want her real name out there—"

"I can't say I blame her," Piper said softly, but I heard her loud and clear. And while just a couple of weeks or, let's face it, hours earlier, I might have been devastated by what I viewed as her unfair passing of judgment, the interest and

38

appreciation of the rest of the group gave me a confidence in my work, and myself, that only fueled the fire.

"You see, she's written some other works of literature that don't fit into the genre of this particular work—"

"Poetry, perhaps?" Piper muttered under her breath.

I stood from my chair, allowing my copy of Austen and my Montblanc pen to fall to the floor. "What is your problem?"

She looked surprised at my outburst, but not nearly as surprised as the rest of the circle. Well, those who were paying any attention, that is. About half of them were trying to get the scattered pages of *Stollen Desire* back in order and were completely focused on their illicit reading activities.

Piper cleared her throat, and for the first time, she refused to make eye contact with me. "Nothing. Nothing at all. I'm sorry." She started gathering her things, and I felt like a creep. "Forgive me, everybody. I'm really just not feeling like myself today."

"It's probably the thunderstorms," Answer for Everything Abby contributed, most unhelpfully.

Piper had all of her possessions in her arms and was ready to walk out of the room, but she stopped to say, "No, not the thunder. Just the Raine."

She didn't have to say, "Raine with an *e*." It was understood. And it hurt.

I should have gone after her and we should have had the argument right then. There was no need for it to stretch out as long as it did—none at all. But I was angry and offended, and I wanted to get back to basking in the praise that had made me feel so happy just a few minutes earlier.

The rest of the group sat, afraid to move and unsure of what had just happened. I understood their confusion.

"She's a Christian, you know." Answer for Everything Abby finally broke the silence as I stared across the circle at the suddenly vacant seat.

Of course! She's a Christian! It all made perfect sense. Except it didn't make any sense at all.

I sniffed. "What's that have to do with anything?"

She didn't have an answer to that—or at least not one she was willing to share with me, I suppose—so she just shrugged and turned her attention back to the other ladies, whose attention was gradually returning to the few pieces of paper they had managed to hold on to.

Soon, the pages that had been hastily stuffed back into my bag were distributed freely, and Piper was seemingly forgotten by all as the discussion turned back to Alex, Annie, and their various food-oriented escapades.

I finally completed the story of my friend's pen name in my mind in case I was asked again— "Lady in Red" by Chris de Burgh was the last song she danced to with her husband before he died—but it was no longer of any concern to anyone. Right then they didn't care who Raine de Bourgh was, they just wanted to read the tawdry tale she had written.

What happened next feels, when I look back on it, like one explicit whirlwind after another. Over the course of the next couple weeks, the book club read *Stollen Desire* and loved it. A week later, Jane gave a copy of the manuscript to a friend who was married to someone in publishing, and seemingly before I knew it I had an agent, a book deal, and tons of new best friends to replace the one I hadn't heard from in six months.

In all that time, Piper hadn't been back to book club.

Once or twice I thought of calling her, but what was the point? She had made it very clear how she felt about "Raine's" book. I didn't understand it. I mean, even then I knew it was smutty and I understood that it truly wouldn't be every woman's "cup of tea," but was there any need to storm out of book club and out of my life?

So maybe I didn't have the most thorough understanding of what Christianity actually was, but I thought Christians were supposed to be understanding and compassionate. And they were supposed to turn the other cheek. And always be honest about their feelings and put the needs of others above their own. And walk on water. And never, ever storm out of book club and out of their best friend's life.

If Piper was a Christian, she sure had a funny way of showing it.

My book deal was for a trilogy, so as soon as the deal was inked I started working on the next two books in the Desire series—*Rising Desire* and *Kneaded Desire*—and exited the book club to focus on my newfound career. Yes, the women in that circle had been there for me when I had no one. Yes, the first book never would have been published if not for them. Yes, I knew it was wrong to turn my back on them and act like I was too important for them all of a sudden.

But I thought I was too important for them all of a sudden.

Nine months flew by as I got lost in Alex and Annie, and the next thing I knew, Raine de Bourgh's first novel hit bookshelves and, more importantly, very private e-readers. Readers who may not have wanted to be seen purchasing such a risqué book didn't have to worry about that, and book sales exploded. By the time *Rising Desire* was released another nine months later, and *Kneaded Desire* six months after that, I was well on my way to becoming a millionaire. And it was my money. It wasn't Patrick's or Mr. McDermott's. Suddenly I had to hire a team of people to take care of me and my affairs, and I had constant requests for interviews and appearances.

Well, that was a problem. For a while, I was able to avoid it all, because my publishers thought it wise to keep the author of such a salacious book shrouded in mystery. Raine de Bourgh. Say the name aloud. Seriously, right now, say it aloud. What image comes to mind? Probably one of two things: a tall, voluptuous blonde in four-inch stilettos and a leather dress, or a distinguished, octogenarian Barbara Cartland–type, though maybe a little less Phyllis Diller in her style.

Chances are the name Raine de Bourgh does not evoke images of a 5'7", midthirties brunette who hasn't been to the gym since her divorce. I'm not unattractive, but clearly I'm not Bree, either.

So, the shroud of mystery was nice. The added bonus, of course, was that a group of ladies sitting in a circle in the library of Northside College Preparatory High School would never know that the author of their favorite book had in fact lied to them and been in their midst all along.

I could have kept it a secret forever, probably.

My team of people had to sign legally enforceable and binding confidentiality agreements. Beyond that, the mystery actually fueled the fire, and more and more books flew off the shelves, digitally and otherwise. As long as that was the case, my agent wasn't going to go to too much effort to get me to agree to a sit-down interview on television.

I was the one who made the decision to go public. Patrick called to tell me he was getting married again, and I lost it. Completely lost it. He wasn't even marrying Bree. I think if it had been Bree I could have at least convinced myself that there was only one other woman, no matter how untrue I actually knew that to be. Her name was Kimberly.

Of course it was.

Kimberly was a dental hygienist who was going to give up her career to be the perfect supportive wife that he needed. And she was amazing in every way, and her dream was to be an interior designer, which was so fantastic because Mike and Deb Lorenzio were looking for someone to add some new life to their condo. And they planned to start a family right away. Well, as a matter of fact, Kimberly was ten weeks along, and they weren't really telling a lot of people yet—until after the wedding—but he thought I should know. Oh, and she was twenty-four.

Of course she was.

I hung up the phone after speaking to Patrick and immediately sent a text to Sydney, my assistant.

What's the highest profile interview request we've received?

The mood I was in, there is a pretty good chance the text also included the red dancing lady emoji and a snake emoji. And maybe that "100" emoji that I've never understood, but I can't say for sure.

Tonight Show

Hmm. That wasn't too shabby.

Second guest.

I stared at my phone, somewhat deflated by her follow-up text. Suddenly the text was covered as Sydney's name popped up and my phone began ringing in my hand.

"Do you want me to book it?" she asked as soon as I answered.

"Second guest? That's the best we can get? What about Oprah?"

"What *about* Oprah?" she asked.

"Wasn't *Stollen Desire* on *O* magazine's guilty

pleasure list, or whatever? Doesn't she want to interview me?"

"You're an author, Sarah. Not a Kardashian."

I sighed. "Yeah, but this will be Raine's first interview. The first time anyone finds out who she is. Isn't that pretty big news?" *Even if all I am is an author,* I thought with a somewhat resentful nod to the Kardashians.

"Yes. It is big news. That's why they want you on *The Tonight Show.* Second guest," she added once again.

I wasn't sure if she thought second guest was a good thing or if she was trying to keep me humble, but I instructed her to go ahead and book it.

Kimberly may have been twenty-four and perfect and having my ex-husband's baby. And she probably fully understood the entire emoji language. But her novel wasn't making women all over the world blush every time they baked bread, was it? *Kimberly* wasn't about to be a guest on *The Tonight Show.*

Second guest.

4.

Now What?

One Monday evening, after Sydney had left for the night, I was just about to pour myself a glass of wine and drink and cry myself to sleep, as I had begun to do most evenings, when the phone rang.

It took three rings for me to realize that I was going to have to answer it myself. I didn't do that sort of thing much anymore. I was hesitant to answer it at all, certain it would either be my mother, making her daily attempt to get back in my good graces now that I was someone, by her standards, or another Hollywood director, begging for the film rights.

"Hello?"

"They're making me read *Sense and Sensibility*. Again, Sarah. How many times does this make? Please come back to book club tonight. I really don't think I can go through it alone." I sat in stunned silence for a full thirty seconds before she added, "It's me. Piper."

"Oh, I know." I smiled as I wiped away the tears that had formed in my eyes. "I'm just confused. I mean, I thought you *loved* Jane Austen."

"I'm sorry. Maybe you misheard me," she deadpanned. "It's Piper. Piper Lanier."

I wiped away a few more tears of joy as I cracked up laughing and began slipping on my shoes. "I'll have you know I was in book club for six months without you, and we didn't read a single Austen. It must be you . . ."

"Well, I've been back at book club for a year without you, and we've read *every* Austen, so you may be right," she said with a giggle.

"I've missed you." I laughed, though I was fully aware I had never been more serious about anything I had said in my entire life.

"I've missed you too." She sighed. "Sarah, I'm so sorry."

"It's okay," I began instinctively, even though I knew nothing about any of it had actually been okay.

"No. It's not okay." She took a deep breath. "I never should have stormed out of there."

"Well, I never should have let you."

"And I never should have let that come between us. I was just so disappointed—"

"In me?" I choked out. I'd been working under that assumption for more than two years, but hearing her say it was more painful than I could have anticipated.

"No," she answered, before quickly adding, "Well, yes. But only at first. I don't think I'd made it all the way to my car before I realized that I was the disappointment. Whether I agreed with your choices or not, it was so stupid for me to just walk out of your life—though, in fairness, I had no idea at the time that's what I was doing. But the more time passed, and the more ashamed of myself I became, the more difficult it was to figure out how to fix any of it."

"I know." I nodded as I blew my nose. "I felt the same way."

"And then I saw you on *The Tonight Show*, and I didn't feel any bitterness, and I wasn't resentful about your books, and I wasn't even overwhelmed by the regret I'd been feeling for so long. I just missed you, Sarah. And I wanted to tell you how great your hair looked and ask you why you wore flats instead of heels—"

"Martin Freeman," I interjected.

"That's what I figured." Piper laughed.

"Yeah, when I found out he was going to be the first guest, I figured I'd look like an Amazon next to him."

"It was the right call," she agreed.

"I wish I'd had the guts to call you first, Piper. My life became more and more about the books, and—"

"And I certainly hadn't given you any reason to believe that I'd be a part of that life. I really am sorry."

"Me too. So sorry." We sat in silent contentment for a few seconds until I added, "Can you believe

I couldn't even get Martin Freeman to give me Benedict Cumberbatch's phone number?"

"After you were so considerate to make him look taller on TV?"

"I know!"

"You know, to the best of my knowledge, neither of them has ever appeared in an Austen film adaptation. That's probably why I like them so much . . ."

I laughed. "Nice segue."

"Thank you," she replied with a giggle. "Now are you coming or not?"

I told her I was on my way, and then I dug out my Kate Spade messenger bag, Montblanc pen, and Jane Austen anthology, and drove to Northside College Preparatory High School for the first time in two years.

We parked our cars next to each other in the parking lot and walked in together, as we always had. Of course, we walked in much more slowly than we ever had before, catching up as we went and stopping occasionally to hug each other. In so many ways, it was as if no time at all had passed.

There was something very different between us, though. In her presence, I was embarrassed by the Desire books, though for the rest of the evening we didn't even acknowledge the *New York Times* bestseller-sized elephant in the room. That wasn't her doing, it was mine. She asked me questions about my life, and I skirted the issue.

She asked if I was working on any new projects, and I made a joke about Spielberg hounding me for the rights to *Kerosene Boom! The Musical*, but I said nothing of the actual lunches, drinks, and dinners I'd had with Hollywood directors and producers. She asked if I had heard from Patrick, and I told her only of his call to tell me about Kimberly and the baby—not the incessant emails and phone calls that had been occurring in the last week.

The incessant emails and phone calls had begun on the day after my *Tonight Show* appearance aired. On the very day he learned that I was Raine de Bourgh. But he didn't call to congratulate me, and he certainly didn't call to chastise me. You see, Patrick wanted to have an affair with me. I think it is important to note that my ex-husband didn't want me back. He just wanted me. Thankfully, I was smart enough to see it for exactly what it was. If my first (and to that point only) love had actually wanted me back, if he had realized he was still in love with me, I may have been tempted. I may have at least considered putting the past behind us. Not because I wanted him, and certainly not because I had forgiven him. But at that point, being the emotional wreck that I was, surrounded by a world of strangers telling me they loved me, if I thought that the man I once loved did actually still love me, well . . . that might have created an appealing diversion. But that clearly was not the case. I was rich, famous, and, if my novels were any indication, possessed a creative approach to sex that I had not had during our time together. Or at least I had never allowed him to see that side of me.

I couldn't really put my finger on why I didn't share these things with Piper, who was without a doubt my best friend—still, after all that time. She was the one person I *should* have confided in, since Patrick got custody of Father Horatio in the divorce. I avoided the idea that it was because she was a Christian, because to admit to that as the reason I felt uncomfortable would be to admit that I had something to be ashamed of. So instead I reasoned it out in a million other ways. "I don't want to appear like I'm gloating," or "Piper isn't by any means poor or unsuccessful, but if she understood my true level of wealth and success, she might feel uncomfortable," and, of course, the easiest one to make myself believe—"This book was the subject of a big blowup between us, and it is best to just let bygones be bygones."

So I put on my rose-colored, high-powered glasses of oblivion and prepared to dive headfirst into the always-entertaining torture of my best friend, caused by the re-reading of the trials and tribulations of Jane Austen's Dashwood sisters.

It wasn't until Piper and I were about to walk through the door of the high school library that

I realized there was a very good chance that Patrick and Piper had not been the only people in Chicago watching *The Tonight Show* that night.

"Piper." I grabbed her arm just before she opened the door. "They probably all saw me on *The Tonight Show*. Do you think they did? I mean, maybe not. Do people keep watching after the first guest? They may know. Do you think they know?"

"Of course they know." She smiled. "Did your agent trick you into believing no one watches late night television?"

"No. But they probably hate me. I didn't mean for them to find out that way." My eyes darted through the window of the door to see if there were any burning effigies in the fiction section.

"It's okay, Sarah." She laughed, though her face expressed nothing but love. "We all found out that way—"

"You already knew," I argued, finally stating what I had long suspected to be the case.

"Yes, but only because I know you. But it took officially finding out on national television, just like everyone else in the world, for me to realize how well I really do know you. And guess what? Those ladies in there? They're super-proud of you. And you don't have any idea how excited they're all going to be when their favorite author walks through this door. I mean, you're Raine de Bourgh." She winked. "This is bigger than when

Mr. Bingley moved to Netherfield, and we're still talking about that one ad nauseam."

The rest of the group did, in fact, welcome me back with open arms and no small amount of awe. I have to admit: I felt some seriously mixed emotions when I realized that they were totally fine with the fact that I had not only lied to them when I told them about my "friend" Raine but had also abandoned them the moment I had something more important to do.

"Of course you didn't tell us you had written the book. It was too early in the whole process to reveal that mystery, wasn't it?" Suzanne said with a mischievous, and slightly unsettling, twinkle in her eye. I was so glad I had learned Suzanne's name. As enthusiastic as she always tended to be about the Desire books, it somehow just wouldn't seem right to keep calling her Granny.

"Well, of course you couldn't just keep coming to book club each week like you weren't one of the most successful authors on the planet!" Botox—I mean, Alisa—said with a giggle.

"We're just glad you're here now, Sarah." Piper beamed at me, truly glad to have me back, I knew.

I didn't understand why, but all of their declarations of friendship and understanding were suddenly making me angry. None more so than Piper's. But I did know that I wasn't angry with them. I was angry with myself. The entire week after that first Monday back, I was unsettled, though I had no idea why. And then the next Monday, I stewed in my own discontent for the entire hour of book club. Why did I care? What did I even care about? Why was I beginning to feel that my success was a bad thing?

"Okay, everyone. Have a good week," Jane said at the end of book club that second week. "Remember, we'll be wrapping up *Sense and Sensibility*, so be thinking about what you would like to read next."

"And if anyone suggests *Pride and Prejudice*, I will scream. Literally scream," Piper muttered to me under her breath.

"It's been a while since we read *Persuasion*," Moira called out.

Piper sighed. "Got me on a technicality." She looked at me with an indulgent smile, but my mind was quite obviously elsewhere. "You okay?"

"Patrick wants to have an affair with me," I blurted out. That was it. That had to be it. That was what had me in such a bad mood and what was making me feel so conflicted. Right? I just needed to talk that out.

Piper's eyes flew wide open. "Patrick?" she whispered. "Ex-husband Patrick?"

"No, Patrick Dempsey. McDreamy and I are running away together. Yes, ex-husband Patrick!"

She smiled and said good night to various ladies as they walked past us before finally looping her arm in mine and walking me swiftly toward the door.

"You're not going to—"

"Of course not!" I exclaimed. "No. Absolutely not."

We reached the door of the high school and exited, but it wasn't until we reached our cars, parked side by side, that she dug deeper.

"Isn't he getting married? I thought you said he was getting married. Kiki."

"Kimberly. But yeah . . . getting married, baby on the way. All of that." She looked more shocked by the second, so I added, "This is Patrick we're talking about, Piper. None of this is shocking."

She nodded, as if remembering every story I had ever told her about my disastrous marriage. "Okay then. So what's bothering you?"

"I just told you!" I shouted, all of the pent-up anger from the previous week finally making its way to the surface with unexpected force. "Sorry." I immediately retreated, tears in my eyes. "I'm not mad at you. I don't know why I yelled. It's just that he didn't want me before, you know? He's not allowed to want me now, just because I'm rich and famous."

"Okay." She nodded comfortingly.

"And I'm not really even all that famous. It's Raine. *Raine* is famous. *Raine* is the one *The*

Tonight Show wanted. And even she isn't as famous as Martin Freeman."

"Okay . . ." she repeated, though her tone was less full of comfort and more laced with confusion.

"The first guest. I was just the second guest." I groaned. "Sorry. *Raine* was just the second guest. Raine was the one they wanted. Raine is the one Patrick wants."

Tears sprung to my eyes, and my best friend hugged me—yes, to comfort me, but also, no doubt, because it was easier than trying to sort through whatever absurdity I was spewing at that particular moment.

When the tears had finally ceased, and I felt absolutely ridiculous but also completely safe, there in the presence of the one person who loved me and understood my ridiculousness, she asked, "So are you going to tell me what's really going on?"

The rest of this book could be a detailed testimony of how my best friend led me to the Lord that day. It's a good story, and I could happily detail to you every word of the prayer that we prayed in the parking lot that evening— the first sincere prayer I had prayed since I was a little girl praying with my grandmother, the only person of faith in my young life.

But that isn't the story I need to tell. This is the story of my feeble attempts to make sense of my life, and those attempts began moments after I prayed and asked Jesus into my heart.

"Now what?" I asked Piper with excitement and anticipation and through the tears. The tears had begun in anger and then transitioned to shame and sorrow, but by the time I had completed that prayer, the tears represented nothing but joy and gratitude.

My heart was ready to live for God, but I had no idea what that meant. Did I need to go to Africa and spread the gospel to impoverished children? Did I need to donate all of my worldly goods to charity?

I should pause right here and inform you that apart from my grandmother, everything I knew about religion I basically learned from movies— and more often than not, *The Sound of Music*. To me, it seemed perfectly logical to think that the next step was to donate all of my clothes, like Maria did when she joined the convent. And then someday, when I was ready to return to the world, after God had closed a door and opened a window, I would wear my one ugly dress that the poor hadn't wanted.

I didn't really think that was how it would go, though that made as much sense to me as anything else I could think of. Looking back, I don't know what I was expecting, but I knew that Piper would direct me. Obviously God had placed her in my life, like my own personal

Christian Mr. Miyagi. I didn't have knowledge or vocabulary for it at the time, but I don't think I would have been all that surprised if, before the night was through, she had assigned me my spiritual gifts and set me on my road of ministry.

"Now what?" she repeated back to me as she laughed, wiping away a few tears of her own, no doubt sensing the anticipation in my eyes. "Now . . . coffee!"

We went and drank coffee and ate scones, as we had almost three years prior when she'd been only Plain Girl I'd Never Noticed Before She Dashed My Poetic Delusions. And, surprisingly, we talked about some things other than the commitment I had just made. We talked about *Sense and Sensibility* (which Piper confessed she didn't actually totally hate, but she made me promise not to tell the rest of the group), and we talked about what books might be coming next. We talked about some of the more noteworthy emails and phone calls I had received from Patrick, and wondered if he'd somehow suffered from memory loss that made him more likely to believe I would ever, for even a moment, fall for any of the lines he threw at me. We talked about music and men and a business trip that she had just taken to Detroit.

It was rather shocking for me to discover that though I'd made such a huge choice and commitment, the day-to-day, moment-to-moment activities still went on. Nothing had really changed.

"Excuse me," a twentysomething woman with a baby in her arms interrupted us kindly.

Had she noticed my glow? Was I actually glowing? I wouldn't have had difficulty believing it. I remembered that in *The Ten Commandments*, Charlton Heston had been glowing when he came down the mountain, carrying the tablets. Of course, his hair had also gone completely white at the same time, and that effect of being in God's presence was slightly less welcome.

"Yes?" I smiled at her, feeling what I can only describe as self-righteous humility, if that's a thing.

"Aren't you Raine de Bourgh?" she asked nervously, and just like that my glow faded.

"Um . . ."

"Oh!" She laughed. "I'm sorry. I know that's not your real name. I just wanted to say I love your books. Such a great escape when life gets to be too much." She rocked the baby, who was suddenly fussy, as if it detected a heretic in its midst.

"Um . . ."

That was all I could say.

"Well," the woman said, clearly being made to feel uncomfortable by my lack of conversational skills, "nice to meet you."

Piper barely made it until the woman walked

away before she burst into laughter. She had no doubt been holding it in the entire time.

"Sarah, had you forgotten that, despite your salvation, you are still one of the most famous romance authors on the planet at the moment, and that you will still be recognized for your kinky novels?"

The honest answer? "Sort of."

Piper laughed until she cried, for probably a solid three minutes, and then she went back to her coffee with a sigh.

I didn't see anything funny about any of it. While Piper had been laughing, I had been thinking about my life and my obligations. I'd already made commitments that wouldn't be easy to get out of, and people were counting on me. I was to sit down for an interview with Katie Couric in just a few days, and then it was off to London and Paris for a week of promotion. Not only that, I was on a deadline—though a loose one—with a new manuscript due to my publishers sometime the following year.

But suddenly I understood how Piper might have felt the night she stormed out of book club rather than read *Stollen Desire*. I was overwhelmingly ashamed of every word I had written.

" 'And we know that in all things God works for the good of those who love him, who have been called according to his purpose,' " she said, looking deep into my eyes with a smile still on her face.

Tears filled my eyes once again. "That was beautiful."

"Thank you." She giggled. "I wish I could take credit for it, but actually, the apostle Paul wrote that. Romans 8:28. God works for good in all things, Sarah."

I knew what she was trying to say, but I just had a difficult time believing it. Not because I didn't believe God was powerful enough, but because I couldn't see any good that could ever possibly come from *Stollen Desire*.

"How am I supposed to live a life for God when I am only known for . . ." I didn't even want to say the name of the book aloud anymore. "That?"

"Do you know what the apostle Paul was known for? I mean, prior to writing that verse, and the book of Romans, and most of the rest of the New Testament?"

I'd never seen a movie about him, so I shook my head no.

"He was a persecutor of Christians, Sarah. The Roman government paid him to find the Christians who were worshiping in secret, and he would bring them to the government to be punished, and usually killed. He was one of the biggest, most deadly enemies of the early church. And yet, 'We know that in all things God works for the good of those who love him, who have been called according to his purpose.' "

Okay, so I hadn't killed any Christians. That much was true, and it actually provided a small amount of comfort. But how many marriages were a little less secure because my books filled hearts with unrealistic romance and lust-filled imagery? How many women and men, in addition to my ex-husband, were willing to be unfaithful to their spouse or boyfriend or Kimberly because of debauchery presented by Raine de Bourgh? No, it wasn't fair to try to pass it off on a woman who didn't exist. The debauchery rested squarely on the shoulders of Sarah Hollenbeck.

"Look, Sarah. You didn't make them buy the books and you didn't make anyone read them. Yes, you put it out there, but you're only responsible for your sin. Don't hold yourself accountable for theirs as well. Deal with yours. Confess it to God, ask him to forgive you, and he will."

"Just like that?" I asked.

"Yes. Just like that."

I sighed. "You make it sound so simple."

"It *is* simple."

"See, I'm not sure I can agree with that, Piper. Next week I have to sit at a bookstore in London and read excerpts from a book I wish didn't exist. I have to sign hundreds of books for hundreds of people, and I'm just not sure that the booksellers will think my tear-stained apologies are good for business. How can you possibly say this is simple?"

"Oh no, sweetie." She laughed softly. "*That's* not simple. Absolutely not. There's going to be a whole lot to work out, probably. But you'll get there. *We'll* get there." She winked as she grabbed my hands. "But between you and God, it's simple. So focus on that. And then ask him the question you asked me."

I wiped away my tears. "What question was that?"

She smiled. "Now what?"

5.

Benjamin Sarah Delaney

Thankfully I was able to ease into my newly conflicted life somewhat gently. I had given Sydney a few days off, and I had no obligations until Monday, so I was able to put Raine aside and just be Sarah. At least for the weekend.

Piper invited me to go to church with her on Sunday, and I was excited by the prospect. And also terrified. All I knew of church was how to be a fake Catholic. At Mass, during my marriage to Patrick, I knew when to stand and when to kneel. I knew the readings. Most importantly, I knew which hands to shake, and I knew how important it was that Patrick and Sarah McDermott appeared happy, in love, and bound together by their devotion to God, family, and country.

It didn't matter if we'd been awake until 3:00 in the morning, fighting about the fact that he'd just gotten home and yet was about to take off on another two-week business trip. And it didn't matter if right before we had to leave for Mass I'd seen him quickly close his laptop when I walked into the room. And it didn't even matter if the night before, after he'd refused to make love to me, he'd told me, as he had for years, that soon the time would be right for us to start a family. None of that mattered. At church, we were still the McDermotts—a couple to be envied by all whom we encountered.

I think I called Piper ten times on Saturday, with different questions in preparation for Sunday. I bought a new outfit—classy casual, as Piper had described her church's style—and a new Bible. I think I owned a Bible already, but I had no idea where it was. I went to bed early so that I could get up and shower before meeting her for breakfast prior to the 10:00 a.m. service, but I didn't fall asleep for hours. I was like a child anticipating Christmas, except throw in a lot more stress and anxiety.

I was ready to learn more about God. That was what I was most excited about. It felt like the beginning of a new life, and I couldn't wait to dive in. But each time I pictured what it would be like, and my head was filled with the idea of songs and Scripture and fellowship with others who loved Jesus, my imagery was interrupted by the thought of someone coming up and asking, "Aren't you Raine de Bourgh?" Then, in my overactive imagination, there were disapproving stares from the pulpit and I was immediately excommunicated and thrown out the front doors of the church.

After a night full of dreams like that, and at least one featuring Father Horatio saying, "Nope!

God still doesn't believe in you!" I awoke with joy. The fear was gone. I got dressed and did my hair and makeup with confidence, certain that I was going to be an awesome Christian. I no longer worried about being confronted regarding the Raine thing. After all, if anyone had read the books, they wouldn't admit it at church, would they? I was safe.

After breakfast Piper and I drove to Mercy Point Church, which didn't look at all like I had expected it to. There wasn't a big steel cross, or any cross at all apart from a little one on the sign. And the imposing concrete steps I had dreamt of landing on when I got thrown out were replaced by a slight three-foot ramp. At least that wouldn't hurt my bottom as much.

My classy casual fit right in, and by the time we got in the building and had a seat in the auditorium, I felt very much in control of my nerves and the whole situation. People smiled at me and greeted me, and I was amazed to discover they were greeting *me*. Not Mrs. Patrick McDermott and not Raine de Bourgh. They didn't know me, but they were genuinely glad I was there.

I took a quick peek at my watch and saw that I had about ten minutes until the service was supposed to start, and I realized I should probably go to the restroom. The last thing I wanted to do was interrupt my first real worship experience because I had to pee. Piper offered to escort me, but, like I said, I was feeling confident. I got directions from her and with assurances that I would be back well before the service began, I was on my way.

I smiled at everyone I encountered, and they smiled back. I visited with a couple of women in the ladies' room, did my business, checked myself in the mirror, noting the huge, sincere smile that I couldn't wipe off my face, and then I barreled out of the restroom, excited to get my worship on.

Until I barreled right into someone.

"Oh my goodness. I'm so sorry," I said as I knelt down and picked up his Bible from the ground.

"Don't apologize. I ran into you. Sorry about that."

I stood up and handed his Bible to him, and then I stopped breathing. And I think he did too.

He was about 5'11" with dark, wavy hair and the deepest brown eyes I had ever seen. His long-sleeved henley did nothing to conceal his lean, muscular build, and all of the distance in the world wouldn't have been able to mask the amazing way he smelled. It was as if a mad scientist assigned with the mission of distracting me from my holy-minded endeavors had created this man just for me.

We were staring at each other, probably both

realizing how stupid we looked for just staring, and yet we couldn't formulate words, or breathe, and we certainly couldn't pull our eyes away. I had never been so instantly attracted to anyone in my life. I know it sounds insane, but right then, before either of us had muttered another word, I was picturing myself in his arms and imagining how his lips would feel on mine. And then I remembered that I was in church and that I had become a Christ-follower on Monday. So I told myself to get those thoughts out of my head. He was forbidden fruit, I lectured myself. Satan put that man there to distract me. Or maybe God put him there as a test. Maybe I had to walk away to prove my dedication to God.

But I couldn't walk away. I couldn't even look away. And then I thought maybe I wasn't supposed to.

"Are you okay?" he asked with legitimate concern as I struggled for breath. He put his hand on my arm and ushered me to a nearby bench. Needless to say, feeling his body touching mine didn't help with the breathing problem, no matter how innocent his touch.

I nodded, feeling like a fool, but also with a weird sense of clarity. I looked up at my handsome stranger, and for the first time in my entire life, nothing felt complicated.

On paper, that moment—what with my gasping for breath and my flushed cheeks, not to mention my inability to speak—should have been humiliating. And that's even with my above-average humiliation standard, having experienced such moments as Patrick and Bree acting like they were just in that room, half-dressed, looking for our Scrabble board. And yet there was nothing embarrassing about it. In fact, there was nothing in that moment that even made me think of myself at all. I could think only of this man.

I exhaled deeply. "I'm okay now. Sorry about that."

"Don't worry about it. You're sure you're okay?"

Looking into his eyes, I suspected I would never be less than okay ever again. "Yes. Thank you."

And then I chuckled a little bit, and he smiled. We had no words to say to each other that didn't seem insignificant and unnecessary.

Except perhaps our names. That seemed both significant and necessary.

"I'm Sarah," I said, putting my hand out to shake his.

"Sarah," he whispered, never breaking eye contact.

I smiled. "What a coincidence. Your name is Sarah too?"

He smiled and blushed, and my heart did somersaults. "Sorry, no. Sarah's just my middle name."

I laughed, but I almost hated to. I couldn't stand the thought that the sound of my laughter might interrupt anything he might say.

"Benjamin. Ben. That's my name. Ben Delaney."

"Benjamin Sarah Delaney. That's very pretty."

"Yeah, thanks." He had taken my hand to shake it, and he hadn't yet let go. I hoped he never did. "I always thought it was pretty butch, actually. Especially compared to my brothers Jeremy Marie and Jacob Diane."

I was in love. No doubt about it.

We talked for a few more seconds, continuing our slightly flirtatious banter, until the spell was broken by the sound of loud praise and worship music. Oh no. I had told Piper I would be back before the service started, and I was pretty sure I was now late. But if I left, would I ever see him again? What if he was on his way out, having only stopped in to ask directions? Okay, he was carrying a Bible, so that didn't seem incredibly likely. But what if we got separated by the crowd after church? What if, what if, what if?

"Hey, sorry. I need to run." I gestured in the direction of the sanctuary.

"Yeah, yeah." He let go of my hand and stood, looking very flustered all of a sudden, and I feared I had broken the spell. "Me too. Look, it was really great to meet you, Sarah."

"You too, Ben." I felt more confident than I

ever had in my entire life. "I really hope we get to see each other again."

He smiled and then leaned in and whispered, "I give you my word."

Dear Jesus, I prayed silently. *I hope that being really, really attracted to and frankly a little turned on by a man I just met at church isn't a sin—but just in case it is, please forgive me.*

We turned and went in opposite directions. I reentered the sanctuary and snuck into the aisle next to Piper.

"Good grief. What happened to you?" she whispered.

"Sorry." I grinned from ear to ear. "There was this guy God wanted me to meet."

"What?" She didn't have any idea what I was talking about, but she smiled in response to my giddiness.

I winked. "I'll tell you later."

"Please be seated," the worship leader instructed as we came to the end of the song, which I had missed almost in its entirety.

As I went to sit, I realized I'd lost track of my new Bible. I leaned down to look under my seat, and under Piper's. Meanwhile, the worship leader was talking. I wasn't really paying attention— not only was I searching for my Bible, I was also reciting "Sarah Delaney. Mr. and Mrs. Benjamin Delaney. Ben and Sarah Delaney" over and over in my mind.

I finally found my Bible under the row in front of us, and grabbed it and sat up just in time to hear, "The long wait is finally over, church. Many of you know how long we've been praying for a pastor, and how long we've been pursuing this pastor in particular! Well, it appears we finally wore him down, and we're just so honored and excited to welcome him to our family here at Mercy Point. Brother Benjamin, come on up here."

The congregation applauded warmly as the gorgeous man who had taken my breath away, just moments prior, made his way up to the pulpit. His eyes caught mine, which must have been the size of the forbidden fruit itself, and he responded with a sheepish grin and a slight shrug.

I was pretty sure I was going straight to hell.

6.

Let's Call Her Margaret

"To the best of my knowledge, Pastor Benjamin hasn't taken a vow of celibacy, Sarah."

As we ate lunch after church, I filled her in on all of the chaste and innocent, yet somehow steamy, details of my conversation with Ben, though according to her, there wasn't much to tell that she hadn't been able to figure out herself. I don't know what gave it away.

It may have been the way he seemed to involuntarily glance my way each time he said my name during his sermon. I mean, he wasn't just randomly saying my name from the pulpit. He preached on Abraham and Sarah that day. And each time his eyes met mine, I was shocked to discover I didn't want to look away. I should have been self-conscious, but I never was. I was only Ben-conscious.

Then again, maybe Piper took her clues from my doodles on the bulletin, which, depending on the moment, alternated between the practicing of what I hoped would be my future signature, and a badly drawn cartoon of Ben and me as Father Ralph and Meggie from *The Thorn Birds*, being cast into a fiery furnace.

The more likely culprits, however, were the events that took place right after the service ended. Ben ran down from the stage and made a beeline toward me, which obviously delighted me no end. But it was his first day as the new pastor, and he was swarmed by the congregation. I understood that, of course, no matter how annoyed I was. He grinned another sheepish grin at me and shrugged his shoulders again, and I smiled and shrugged back, ready to wait until the crowd cleared. But then one old lady said, "Your daughter was a delight in children's church today, Pastor Ben. You and your wife must be so proud!"

Apparently I had jumped the gun ever so slightly when I began doodling "Mrs. Delaney" on my bulletin. But how was I supposed to have known that I was just practicing another woman's signature?

I hurried out of there as quickly as I could, pulling Piper along with me. Of all the scenarios that could have ended with my being thrown out onto Mercy Point's front steps—or ramp, as the case may be—flirting with the married pastor on his first day wasn't one I had envisioned. It would, however, have been the most justifiable.

How had I gotten it so very wrong?

"Clearly there has been no vow of celibacy, Piper," I said with a sigh. "He's a dad, after all. But, although I'm new to this whole religion/

Christianity thing, I'm pretty sure adultery and/ or bigamy are not really recommended for most pastors." Or anyone.

"There has to be an explanation!"

She had been saying that for nearly an hour, all through lunch, and I wanted to believe that there was, but nothing made sense. I probably should have stuck around and at least given him a chance to explain, but I just couldn't stand the thought of that. Besides, what explanation could there have been?

"I wouldn't mind an explanation as to why he wasn't wearing a wedding ring." I sniffed and then sipped iced tea through my straw. "That's just setting a girl up to fail."

My fear was that he hadn't actually felt anything toward me like what I felt toward him from our brief encounter. I threw that theory out there, but Piper immediately knocked it down.

"A pastor doesn't walk in late to his first service at a new church so that he can sit on a bench with someone and not say anything," she argued. "He was clearly feeling something powerful as well." Powerful enough that he got as lost in me as I did in him.

"Or maybe he was just being kind, Piper. Maybe I was clearly out of place, and as the pastor he was trying to make me feel welcome."

"Out of place? What do you mean?" she asked. "At Mercy Point?"

"No." I sighed. "Just in general . . . trying to carry on an adult conversation."

"Listen, Sarah, at the risk of sounding repetitive, there just has to be an explanation."

"What makes you think that could sound repetitive?"

She ignored my jab and instead tried to convince me that the explanation could actually be quite simple. "Think, Sarah, think! You're a writer. Write this story. What is the simple explanation?"

"Maybe his wife is in an asylum," I began hesitantly, gaining steam as I went. "Maybe she's basically a vegetable, and just a thin veil of the woman he once fell in love with. His dedication to the beautiful young thing he married—"

"Sarah—" Piper interjected.

"Let's call her Margaret. His dedication to Margaret and their daughter, as well as his beliefs and his role in the church, has kept him from divorcing her. But every day is cold and lonely, and as sand falls through the hourglass of Margaret's life, Ben's heart is preparing him for the inevitable—to love once more."

Piper sipped her coffee and finished off her last bite of key lime pie as I spoke, and then set her fork down and smiled at me. "Okay, that one's on me. I forgot what types of stories you write."

"What?" I asked, bolstered by the ludicrous potential I was creating.

She laughed. "Sarah, in this scenario, are you hoping for Margaret to die or for him to divorce her?"

Well, huh. My walk with the Lord was new, but when she put it that way, it was pretty clear that I already knew the correct answer—not just as a Christ-follower. Also as, you know, a human.

"Neither?" I asked, though I hadn't intended to phrase it as a question.

"Very good." She winked. "No, I actually meant that maybe the simple explanation is that—"

"But what if Margaret is lifeless as it is, and Ben is miserably unhappy, and—"

"Sarah!" She placed her hand on mine with a laugh. "There's nothing you can say that will make me support your soap opera plot."

"Fine," I muttered as I pulled my hand from under hers and crossed my arms.

She leaned in and spoke discreetly. "But we haven't considered the possibility that just because he has a daughter doesn't necessarily mean he has a wife."

I sat up straight in my chair, willing to at least momentarily consider any scenario in which Ben was single. "I would love for that to be the case, but the lady said—"

She shrugged. "It's his first day. There's a lot we don't know about him yet. I mean, *I* wasn't on the hiring committee. Were you?"

"I was not."

"And that lady who talked to him about his daughter probably wasn't either. So there you go," she concluded, as if that truly were the conclusion. Mystery solved. The prosecution rests.

I really don't know how to explain it. I couldn't even explain it to myself, really. It didn't make sense that I was *this* upset, and yet I was. I didn't know how long Ben and I had been in the hallway together, but it couldn't have been more than three or four minutes. And then he preached for a while. Was that really enough time to have fallen in love with him? Was that really enough time for me to begin hoping for any far-fetched situation that would allow me to date him?

"How would that even work?" I asked Piper. "Dating a pastor, I mean. If he were single, which he's probably not. And actually interested in me."

She shrugged again. "Pretty much like any other relationship, I would think. Except you'd only go out to dinner at potlucks, of course."

I knew she was teasing me, but the idea that it would be just like any other relationship didn't seem right. He was a man of God, right? Surely there were different rules for that. Hadn't there been some sort of swearing-in ceremony during which Ben had been given a list of guidelines, and maybe his special clergy parking pass for hospital visits? Different rules had to apply. Granted, I didn't have much knowledge, or anything to compare it to. Father Horatio was single, but he was a priest who *had* taken a vow of celibacy. Apart from that, I knew nothing. Well, apart from movies. But *The Preacher's Wife* starring Whitney Houston didn't seem like the ultimate authority in this situation. Even to me.

"Can I ask you a question?" I asked Piper, knowing that I could. "This is going to sound stupid, and please don't judge me—"

She smiled and rolled her eyes as if to say, "Aren't we past that point?"

"So . . . Christians don't have sex outside of marriage, right?"

That felt like something I should have known, but I wanted to be sure. Even with my limited biblical knowledge, I knew about "Thou shalt not commit adultery." And the other one, about coveting thy neighbor's wife. It just seemed a tad unrealistic to me, despite the fact that my own sexual history wasn't grandiose. There were just a couple of guys that aren't even worth mentioning.

And then I met this irresistibly handsome guy from the wrong side of the tracks.

He maintained a solid C average, made me open my own door, and didn't have a dime to his name. The pain that fact caused my mother just made him more irresistible to me. Really, my mother's disapproval and his looks were the only things he had going for him for about the first three months we were dating. But one day he handed me a notebook, kissed me on the cheek, and walked away. I opened to the first page, and I fell in love. He was an artist. He drew beautiful sketches of flowers and animals and landscapes, and I'd had no idea.

About twenty pages in was a portrait of a beautiful girl. I mean, she was breathtaking. He'd captured hidden innocence in her eyes and obstinate determination in her chin. With just pencil he'd drawn hair so soft it begged to be touched, and a soul that begged to be loved.

"Sarah," the work was named.

From that moment on, Patrick and I were inseparable in every way. By the time Mr. McDermott made his first million two years later and McDermott Real Estate was rebranded McDermott & Son Inc., it was too late to walk away, no matter how much I would have preferred not to give my mother the satisfaction. I hated that she was so happy—her entire opinion of Patrick having shifted somewhere around the half-a-million-dollar mark—but I wanted to spend my life with him.

My romantic and sexual histories were completely intertwined, and I had nothing else to compare my own experiences to. Looking back on my past through salvation-colored glasses, I couldn't help but wonder if Patrick and I would have survived the two years of dating and three years of being engaged if we hadn't been sleeping together.

Might your marriage have survived if that had been the case? a still small voice from deep inside seemed to ask.

"Well," Piper began, "believing you shouldn't have sex outside of marriage and actually not having sex outside of marriage don't necessarily always go hand in hand. I can't speak for everyone, of course, but I believe that God makes it pretty clear that sex was created for marriage, and we're supposed to save it for marriage. But people make mistakes. People misinterpret. People give in to temptation."

She didn't tell me anything I didn't know, I suppose, but my goodness! I couldn't help but chuckle a bit.

"What's so funny?" Piper asked with a quizzical expression on her face.

"Nothing really. I'm just realizing for the first time that Maria had the right idea when she ran back to the abbey, rather than have to face Captain von Trapp. I get it now. I totally get it."

"Really?" She laughed as we signed our debit card receipts for lunch and stood to go. "You think it was all about her attraction to him? She was worried she wouldn't be able to keep her hands off of him?"

I stared at her as if it were obvious. "Um . . . it was Christopher Plummer."

82

"Yeah, okay. Good point."

And it was Ben Delaney.

"I'm okay with not having sex, Piper. Really I am. I mean, it's not like I've *been* having sex recently, and now I have to go cold turkey." It suddenly occurred to me to be grateful in a way I hadn't previously been that the few dates I had been on since my divorce had been with guys who were easy to resist. No, I hadn't known the Lord then, but at least I knew better than to be seduced by, *"Nice neighborhood you live in. I've always wanted to see the inside of one of these houses."* "But I think I always thought . . . you know . . . someday it'll happen—in the scope of being in love with someone. Someday I'd maybe even get married again."

"And why has that changed?" she asked.

Truthfully, I didn't know how to explain it. Even to myself. My thoughts had just run away with me, I guess. A few minutes in the presence of Ben Delaney had been enough to take away "someone" and "someday" and replace them with "him" and "now." In a matter of a couple hours I'd gone from not even thinking about having a love life, to imagining a future with Ben, to wondering how I would ever shake the memory of how I felt when he smiled at me.

I was a Christ-follower ever-so-slightly obsessed with my married pastor.

And the day had begun with such promise.

• • •

Raine de Bourgh's life resumed on Monday, and though I was determined to try and do the right things in my career and life moving forward, I honestly couldn't imagine how that was possibly going to work. I toyed with the idea of just calling it quits. I certainly wouldn't have hurt for money at that point.

And it wasn't like I had anyone else in my life to financially support.

Get it together, Sarah, I would have to lecture myself every time those thoughts entered my head. So what if I was destined to be alone forever, mourning the loss of the potential love of my life?

What? Occasionally I had to lecture myself to snap out of my previous lecture. How could I possibly think, for even a moment, that a man I'd just met was the love of my life? Patrick McDermott had been the love of my life, right? And just because he was too much of a treacherous, egocentric fool to see that, or to return my love with the power with which it was offered, that didn't make my former love for him any less real and eternal.

And then, almost without fail, when I would just about have myself convinced of that, I would see Ben's eyes and hear his laugh. And I'd think about the brief moment when I'd begun to believe that maybe Patrick wasn't the only guy I would ever love after all.

And then I would quickly remind myself that I was losing my mind.

I needed to write. That much I knew. I needed to once again escape to my literary world, where I was in control and men didn't cheat on their wives and women didn't fall in love with pastors who remained devoted to their wives, even though they could only see them during visitation hours at the asylum. But the only stories I knew how to write—or at least write well—were full of things that were no longer acceptable to me.

"What if you write a clean version of the Desire books?" Piper asked at Monday morning coffee after I expressed to her my moral dilemma.

I just stared at her, not understanding.

"You know . . . keep the story but take out the smut. The heart without the heat. The—"

"The book without 85 percent of the words?" I laughed. "It's a good thought, but it's just not realistic. If I took away the sex, my audience would quickly realize that these characters have no depth whatsoever. There is no substance. And no foundation for their relationship. If you take away the steamy stuff—"

"Now, wait a minute," Piper cut me off. "Who said you have to take away the steamy stuff?"

"I don't follow. I thought the steamy stuff was the bad stuff."

"The steamy stuff *is* the bad stuff," she said. "But it doesn't have to be."

I pinched the bridge of my nose, thoroughly confused. "Piper, honey, speak English."

She leaned in. "Okay, look, when Andrew and Angela were baking bread, or whatever they did—"

I laughed. "Alex and Annie."

"Whatever. Those scenes between the two of them where they're *just* baking together or whatever . . . a lot of people think those scenes are steamy by the way they're written, right?"

"Yes . . ."

"Okay. And what about when Ben leaned in and told you he'd make sure you saw each other again. Steamy?" She sat back in her chair to watch my reaction.

My reaction, of course, was to blush at a memory I'd been trying very hard not to think about and analyze every moment of the day. "No," I scoffed, my cheeks growing warmer. I crossed my arms as I put a lot of effort into playing it cool—and failed miserably. "Pastor," I muttered without purpose. "And, you know . . . Margaret."

"Sarah, seriously." She smiled. "I'm not talking about all of the potential life ramifications right now, and all of the reasons you can't be with Ben. I'm just talking about the moment. And I'm pretty sure if you really think about it, you'll realize that moment was steamier than anything you ever wrote for Albert and Agnes."

She lifted her coffee mug and got back to drinking, my stunned silence assuring her that her point had hit its target.

"I want to go in a different direction," I said to my agent on the phone later that day, after Piper had rushed off to work, leaving me to completely question pretty much every detail of my life.

"Sure, hon. What are you thinking? Want to go with more of an indie director for the film? I was thinking that might be best, actually. Somebody new and fresh."

Joe Welch is about twenty years older than I am, and when he signed me I was his only client. He'd worked for decades representing athletes—I called him my own personal Jerry Maguire—before realizing he hated sports. All sports. He dreaded draft day and March Madness, and if his client wasn't playing, he intentionally left the country during the Super Bowl each year, just so he didn't have to hear about it. He'd finally had enough and decided he was willing to leave the money and the celebrity clients in exchange for some peace and happiness. He retired but quickly realized how bored he was, so he turned to something he actually loved. He turned to books.

I signed with him because I liked him. He made me laugh and I made him slightly uncomfortable with my casual approach to business, something he certainly hadn't experienced with his athletes. And then, ultimately, we were making each other richer. The success of *Stollen Desire* and Raine de Bourgh made him a new brand of legend in the agent world, almost overnight. He'd taken on a few more clients since, but he could afford to be picky. First and foremost, he was loyal to me, and I to him.

I had a feeling that loyalty was about to be tested.

"No, Joe. I mean a really different direction. Away from the Desire books." I took a deep breath. "Speaking of that, how difficult would it be to get me out of this European thing?"

He laughed. "This European thing? You mean this huge promotional tour to celebrate the fact that *Stollen Desire* was last year's top-selling book in the UK and France? *That* European thing?"

I grimaced. "That's the one."

"Not a chance, Sarah. There's a parade, for goodness' sake!"

"They're throwing a parade for me?" I asked, a little bit flattered, but mostly horrified.

"No. But you're in it. Riding on a float or something."

"What's the worst that could happen? I mean, if I cancelled."

He sighed. "Well, first of all, you'd lose a ton

of money, not just on the trip but in future sales, I imagine."

"I'm okay on money, Joe—"

"And it wouldn't exactly be great for your reputation."

Ha! My reputation. Because my reputation was such a thing of dignity and virtue as it was?

"Sarah," he continued, "this is big, and you know it. Not only that, you *wanted* this. What's going on with you?"

And then I laughed, but nervously. It was time to test the waters of Christianity in Raine's world. I didn't figure it could possibly end well.

"I, um . . . I accepted Jesus as my Savior, Joe. I'm born again, I guess you would say. And, I know this sounds crazy, but—"

"Look, hon," he interrupted. "I don't care if you worship God or Buddha or the snail god—"

"Snail god?"

He was flustered. "You know, the thing in Hungary. Or is it Belgium?"

I couldn't help but smile. "I'm pretty sure that's not a thing."

He chuckled, just a bit, and then took a deep breath. "I know you're searching, Sarah. And if you think you've found something that you can believe in, then I'm happy for you. Really. And when you get back from Europe, we can sit down and look at what you've got coming up, and see if—"

"It's not just the promotional stuff, Joe. It's all of it. What if you just keep taking care of the business and everything for the Desire books, and I move on from them?"

There was a long pause before he finally spoke. "Well, sure, if you want to take a break." There was another long pause and then he added, "How long do you think this break might last?"

I was making it up as I went along. All I knew for sure was that my conscience would no longer allow me to be the world's favorite author of lust-fueled fantasies.

"I don't want a break, exactly. I was just thinking maybe I could try a completely different genre."

Due to my proven astronomic success, I had already been paid a ridiculous amount of money for a book I hadn't even conceived yet. There were no restrictions, no guidelines. It didn't have to be in the same genre as the other books, though the publishers may have assumed that would be the case. But my contract didn't state that it had to be. I just had to have a completed manuscript to them by the deadline. It seemed to me that there was unlimited potential.

"Sure, sure. You bet," Joe said, clearly already hating the idea and fearing the answer to the question he was preparing to ask. "So, um, what are you kicking around? What kind of book?"

I took a deep breath. "Well, actually, I was thinking Christian romance."

The five minutes of laughter that followed on the other end of the call gave me the impression that my agent wasn't completely gung ho about the idea.

I just sat there and let him laugh. After all, that was pretty much the reaction I had been expecting. When he finally regained his composure, I waited for him to speak, but he didn't. I don't know if it was the fact that I wasn't laughing that clued him in that I wasn't kidding, but he somehow got it all of a sudden.

"You have got to be kidding me!" he shouted. "There is no possible way for you to make a successful transition to Christian romance. You're just not the 'virginal schoolteacher on the plains of Oklahoma' type of author. Unless her first time with the renegade cowboy, after they're married, of course, involves chains and lots of leather." I didn't find him nearly as funny as he found himself, so he concluded resolutely, "I'm sorry, but it can't be done."

I thought all day about what he had said— not the part when he said it couldn't be done, but the virginal schoolteacher part. I was certain that Joe hadn't read a Christian romance in his entire life and therefore had no idea what he was talking about. But, perhaps not surprisingly, I realized that I hadn't either. I'd never read any

Christian fiction at all, in fact. That seemed like a good place to start.

I begrudgingly went on my European tour, comforted by two consolations that I knew to be true. First, I knew that this promotional tour would be my last for these books. Of course I wished the end was already in my rearview mirror, but at least it was just around the next corner. Secondly, the week away offered the consolation of being unavailable to go to church with Piper to face my forbidden crush.

I spent every free moment of the trip reading Christian romance on my Kindle. A lot of it was good. There were heroines who inspired me, and love stories that swept me away. But I couldn't quite see myself in those novels. I couldn't quite find a story that felt like me.

You know, the one in which the heroine becomes a Christian, turns away from her life of producing scandalous material for the masses, and then almost immediately falls in love with her married pastor. Where was *that* book?

The books I read didn't feel realistic. At least, they weren't *my* reality. Then again, my reality was messed up, so maybe I wasn't the best judge.

Still, I couldn't relate to how easy it was for the women in some of those books to avoid sex outside of marriage . . . simply because they knew they *should* avoid sex outside of marriage.

And some of them didn't even seem to face any temptation or know what it was like to feel a desire that they weren't sure they should be feeling. Was it really that easy? If so, I think a page had been left out of my Christianity initiation packet, because it didn't seem so cut and dried to me. Were those women also impervious to the power of Godiva chocolate and Manolo Blahnik pumps? Who *were* these superwomen? I'd made the decision to abstain from sex just days before I realized how difficult it might be to honor that commitment to God. Days!

While I knew with absolute certainty that Alex Stollen and Annie Simnel weren't to be our sexual role models, I was also pretty sure that there were women like me, searching for a love story, unable to relate to the idea of a life without desire and temptation.

There had to be some middle ground.

7.

What Nice Boys Do

"Exactly!" Piper concurred as we sat down at our favorite coffee place Saturday evening, the day after I got back to Chicago. "That's what I was saying. Why can't Christian romance be just a little bit sexy? You know . . . in appropriate ways."

"Yes!"

By the time I got around to throwing my idea past Piper, I was already convinced that I knew exactly what Christian women wanted to read—they just hadn't been able to put a finger on it. At the very least, I knew what I wanted to read, but from what I could tell, that book wasn't available. So I would have to write it.

"When we say we love *Bridget Jones's Diary*, or whatever, but we could just do without the language and sex, that's exactly what we mean! Just take out the bad language and the sex. We don't mean take away the humor or the attraction between the characters, and replace Hugh Grant and Colin Firth with, I don't know, Harvey Keitel and Billy Dee Williams."

I smiled. "Lando Calrissian kissing Bridget in the snow, after buying her the new diary at the

Cloud City boutique—that just doesn't do it for you, huh?"

She laughed. "Not really. But you know, that scene is a perfect example. 'Nice boys don't kiss like that' is this fantastic moment. Would it really have been any less sexy if Mark Darcy had just said, 'Oh yes they do,' and not thrown in the curse word? But no, it seems like it's either that or *Anne of Green Gables*."

"Hey!" I acted wounded, and it was somewhat genuine. "I love *Anne of Green Gables*!"

Piper's face contorted as she said, "Me too, actually. Bad example. But you know what I mean."

I did. I knew exactly what she meant. Now I just had to figure out a way to convince my agent, my publishers, and the entire literary world that I was the best one to tackle it.

The problem was this: I knew that a good "middle ground" Christian romance needed to be written, and I honestly thought I was the best person to write it. But I had no idea how to do it. I mean, what right did I have? I had been a Christian for only days. What did I know of what Christian women wanted?

My knowledge of the desires of Christian women could be summed up in two words: Ben Delaney.

I hadn't been able to stop thinking about him, and I felt guilty about that. I did. I couldn't explain it. Yes, I'd felt a sensual stirring when I met him, and I'd felt it every time I'd thought of him since, but it wasn't lust. I just couldn't escape the thought that what Ben and I shared that Sunday morning had made me feel many things—and none of them had felt forbidden.

I was obviously incorrect about that, no matter how I *felt,* and God was clearly teaching me a lesson or something. But the feeling was enough to inspire me to try to write a realistic Christian romance. I wanted to explore the temptations that Christian men and women experience while in pursuit of a Christ-honoring romantic relationship.

I think that a large percentage of the non-Christian world believes that sexless relationships prior to marriage are a myth. Well, they are a myth in relationships between attractive Christians, right? Can a handsome guy and a pretty girl really stop at kissing? Movies and television certainly don't portray that it's possible, do they? I don't know that most people think of it in those terms, it's just that I don't think most people really think of it at all. You meet someone, you date, and at some point you sleep together—that's the worldview. And that was my view, prior to my salvation.

Actually, that's not true. It's not as if there in the parking lot of the high school I asked Jesus to come into my heart and then suddenly felt my spiritual chastity belt lock, with the key magically being transported to my future husband. Once again, I didn't think about it. I was not at all aware that anything had changed in that regard until the moment I met Ben.

I've never been more attracted to a man in my entire life than I was to him, instantly. I really do mean never. Not Patrick, not Ryan Gosling, not Paolo, the beautiful Colombian waiter at my favorite restaurant. And that's saying something.

Patrick is an incredibly handsome guy. No doubt about that. I can't remember a time when I didn't think he was attractive—but there have definitely been varying degrees to which I have been attracted to him. If I had to pinpoint the moment when I realized I was no longer attracted to him at all, it would have to be a moment that occurred about a week before Breegate. I was feeling a renewed, and obviously short-lived, determination to add some spice back to our marriage. It was so clichéd and predictable. I'd bought a very sexy little designer black negligee, filled our bedroom with candles, scattered rose petals on the bed . . . the whole nine yards.

He walked in from work and there I was, looking like a million bucks if I do say so myself. I was ready to do anything that he wanted, and he had to have known it. I knew that our marriage was strained and I knew that he had been avoiding sex (with me, anyway), but he was still a warm-blooded American male, and I should have been irresistible.

"I noticed the credit card bill was higher than usual. Now I know where my money went, at least."

Strike one.

"Geez, Sarah. What if I'd brought somebody home from the office tonight and we'd walked in on you dressed like that?"

Strike two.

"I guess we can mess around a little, but I have an early morning meeting, so we need to make it quick."

Strike three, and you're out!

We did not mess around that night. In fact, we never messed around again. I'm pretty sure I still loved him—to some extent at least—but from that moment on, I didn't want him. Not sexually anyway. I wanted him to love me, but that was about it.

"So, do you want to grab coffee before church tomorrow?" Piper snapped me back to reality.

I laughed an empty laugh. "I think I need to find a different church."

"Oh, Sarah," she whined. "No. I want you to go with me!"

"And I want to go with you. But not there. I can't just act like . . ." I took a deep breath. "I've been talking to God about it, like you've been telling me to, and I'm praying so hard for God to take care of my attraction toward Ben, Piper. But I just can't go back there. I just feel like going will be like saying, 'Hey, God, please take away my desire for alcohol, and please give me all the wisdom I need to handle it while I walk into this bar and stare at a pitcher of beer for a while.' I'm trying to trust that God will take care of it for me, but I think I need to do my part."

Piper went all weird all of a sudden, adjusting her position and looking at me with huge saucer-sized eyes that were inexplicably full of humor and bewilderment. "I'm going to tell you one of my favorite passages of Scripture, Sarah," she began, and I leaned in, anxious to learn whatever I could. "First John 5:14–15. 'This is the confidence we have in approaching God: that if we ask anything according to his will, he hears us. And if we know that he hears us—whatever we ask—we know that we have what we asked of him.' "

"Exactly!" I said, sitting back in my chair, pretending to have a confidence that I didn't really possess. I didn't understand what the verses meant, or at least I didn't understand what they had to do with anything right then, but it sounded like I had gotten out of going back to Mercy Point, so I was fine with playing along.

"In other words"—she smiled a huge smile, which disturbed me a bit—"sometimes he gives us exactly what we ask for, but it turns out that we didn't really know what we were asking for in the first place. But he knows, and he knows what's best for us, and we can rest in the assuredness that, for instance, when we ask him to take care of something and we take certain steps to take care of what we asked him to take care of, and we don't really rely on him to take care of it—"

Hadn't I said "Exactly!" convincingly enough? I couldn't for the life of me figure out what she was rambling on about. I only knew that each word of explanation Piper threw out left me more and more confused.

"Piper!" I had to stop her. My brain was starting to hurt. "What are you talking about?"

She stood up abruptly, kissed me on the cheek, and whispered, "Pastor Benjamin just walked in and he's heading this way." Then she exited out the opposite door from where Ben had entered.

I believe that God has a sense of humor. But I didn't find anything very funny about my situation at that moment.

"Sarah, are you okay?"

Oh crap. Were my eyes actually closed? Yep. They were. I quickly considered my options to determine the best way out of the situation, but I decided there wasn't a best or even a less-than-mortifying way out of the situation. I ended up kind of squinting one eye open, and even still I couldn't filter out his effect on me. For one second I thought about bringing my hands up to my eyes and peeking through my fingers, like I was ten years old again, watching *Children of the Corn* at Mindy Corbin's sleepover.

"Oh, Ben, hi," I said, ever so awkwardly. "Or, um, I guess I should call you Father Ben. Father Benjamin. Wait, no, not Father. You're not Catholic. Neither am I! And any other use of the term 'Father' would just be . . ." I scrunched up my nose as I made it all worse by the second. "So, what? Reverend? Pastor? Brother? No, that's just as weird as Father . . ."

Oh dear Lord, please just let the giant, suspending CUP-A-JOE sign fall on me right now and put me out of my misery. But please don't hurt Ben. Or damage his beautiful face.

He smiled, I melted, and the CUP-A-JOE sign couldn't even do me the simple courtesy of falling on top of me and crushing me to death.

"Just Ben." He laughed, somewhat nervously.

There was such a different atmosphere between us than there had been in the hallway at church. It wasn't that the attraction we had felt toward each other was gone. It just didn't seem like we were comfortable with it any longer.

I certainly wasn't.

"Well, 'Just Ben.' " I smiled, desperate to hold on to my dignity. Somehow. "I'm glad you came over to say hi. I was just heading out, actually. Look at us," I said nervously while moving my eyes around in an attempt to look at absolutely anything besides *us*. "Wasting away a beautiful Saturday, drinking coffee all day." I scowled as I glanced out the window at the sun beginning to go down, though the sun had been hidden by gray, dreary clouds for most of the "beautiful" day anyway.

"Actually, I just got here."

"Oh, and you haven't ordered yet? You should probably go do that. Forgive me for holding you up."

"I ordered online. I think that's mine." He pointed behind me to the pick-up window.

"It's probably getting cold. I'll let you—"

My bottom got slightly off the chair before he sat down where Piper had been just moments ago, before she abandoned me in my hour of need. As he sat, he grabbed my hand, and I couldn't help but lower back into the chair. I wish I could claim I decided to sit back down because I knew I was strong enough to face him, but in reality my knees gave out the instant he touched me.

"Sarah, I think we should talk about this. I really don't want any awkwardness between us."

With all the might I could muster, I pulled my hand away from his. I wanted it to stay there. I wanted to touch him and never stop ever, ever again, but apart from the obvious moral implications I feared for my own soul, I was also worried for him. The new pastor did not need to be seen holding hands with a woman who was most assuredly not his wife. He seemed to flinch just a little as I pulled away, as if I had stung him.

I sighed, feeling as if I should apologize but then realizing that was preposterous. I felt so conflicted. Was he feeling the same way? *Lead me not into temptation,* I prayed, all the while unable to block out the vivid imagery of things that had not yet occurred. Things that could never occur.

"There isn't anything to talk about," I said with a forced smile on my face. "It was—"

"I should have told you," he blurted out. "I should have told you, right away, but if you lead with something like that, two minutes after you've met someone, how do you not look insane? I thought you were feeling what I was feeling, but what if you weren't? If I'm trying to play it cool and stay at least a little bit guarded, how can I possibly lead with that?"

So it was true. He was married. I hadn't allowed myself to truly believe otherwise, but the confirmation stung nonetheless.

My betraying heart leapt all the same at his words, knowing that he was indeed experiencing the same emotions I was. Had he also pictured our future together? Had he allowed it to get that far? No. Because he knew there could be no future together. Ben wasn't tied down by ignorance as I had been.

In the midst of the gratification that came from knowing he'd felt a connection, I became indignant with righteous anger. This man was supposed to be a man of God. This man had been chosen to lead the church to which my best friend belonged, and he had the moral character of, well . . . my ex-husband!

I couldn't help but wonder if any of Patrick's mistresses had ever felt this way. Had they thought they were in love with him? Had they been so overwhelmed by the emotion that they had to fight to maintain control? Had some of them been deceived by hope, even for a moment, that he was the man God had designed just for them?

I knew that my hope to maintain my dignity was lost. I didn't have any doubt that every single thing I was feeling was etched across my face for him to read, but I just couldn't help it. I felt betrayed by Ben.

"Oh, Sarah. I'm so sorry." It was obvious that he wanted to step in and do something, but he didn't know what to do. This was more complicated than the standard conversations with distraught members of his congregation, I was guessing. "I know that I should have told you. I do. I get that. But I also had no way of knowing that it would upset you this much. Truthfully, you could have just as easily not had a problem with it, right? But still, I should have told you."

Excuse me?

"Not had a problem with it? Are you kidding me?" I suddenly didn't have any difficulty at all allowing the righteous anger to win out. "What sane, self-respecting woman wouldn't have a problem with it, Ben? I mean . . . you're a pastor! You're *my* pastor." I didn't believe it was important at that moment to tell him that his first Sunday had been my first Sunday as well. "Of course it's going to affect me!"

He looked as perplexed as I felt all of a sudden—and, unbelievably, somewhat offended. Really? *He* was offended? "I'm sure there are plenty of women who would be fine with it," he said quietly.

Oh boy. Oh boy, oh boy, oh boy. I was fuming as I grabbed my purse and silently thanked God for making it so incredibly easy for me to walk out of there. "You're disgusting," I spat as I stood.

"Disgusting?" he repeated in shock, standing to face me.

"Yes, disgusting. You know what? Maybe you're right. Maybe there are women out there who wouldn't have a problem with it. Who would be *fine* with it. But I am not that type of woman, Ben. I'm divorced from a man who put me in situations where I was on the other side of this sort of thing, and my heart goes out to poor Margaret!"

I stormed out, propelled by my conscience and unresolved emotions from the past. I was feeling all sorts of girl-power confidence, like I'd stepped out of a Shania Twain song, but I was also so sad to see the dismantling of the image of Ben I'd hoped to carry with me forever. It was, apparently, an image I had created for myself.

"Who's Margaret?" I heard him shout from behind me.

I exhaled and rolled my eyes, in disbelief that I had actually spoken aloud my made-up name for Ben's wife.

"Or whatever your wife's name is," I said as I began walking to my car a little more quickly.

He picked up his pace to keep up with me. "Christa. Her name was Christa, but I really don't understand why your heart goes out to my dead wife."

I stopped in my tracks, huffing and puffing ever so slightly from walking so quickly. His dead wife. His dead wife?

"Then what in the world were you talking about?" I asked, turning around to face him—something I hadn't thought I would ever do again.

He ran the rest of the way to stand in front of me, and I couldn't help but observe that he wasn't breathing heavily at all. Knowing his wife was dead had apparently allowed me to spend a moment dwelling on his very nice physique once again. *Man! You're a disappointment,* I seemed to hear Shania grumble at me. He just stood there for a few seconds, not taking his eyes away from mine, and I could see the wheels turning.

Finally he broke the silence, and not in a way I had expected. He started laughing, and while I didn't understand what was so funny, I did love the sound.

"You thought I was married?" he asked.

"Well, I mean . . ."

"And you thought I was surprised you weren't okay with the idea of having an affair with a married pastor?" He was still laughing, and I felt my cheeks getting warm. I still didn't get the joke, but I had a feeling I was going to feel like an idiot once I heard the punch line. "Well, Sarah, under those circumstances, I just can't for the life of me imagine why you thought I was disgusting." The laugh transformed into a sly smile.

I wanted to ask for clarification, but I was too afraid to speak. There was just no telling how I would put my foot in my mouth next.

"The woman in my life is named Madeline, and she's five." He looked down, I think uncertain of what my reaction would be. "Christa died of breast cancer when Maddie was eleven months old. That's what I should have told you. I should have told you I have a daughter. But we'd just met, and there was no rational explanation for the way I was feeling. 'Hello, practical stranger who is making me feel things I haven't felt in four years.' " His eyes met mine once more, and I again lost the ability to breathe. He continued, but his voice was lower and the emotion behind every word he spoke threatened to overpower me. " 'Nice weather we're having, welcome to Mercy Point, and oh yeah, I have a daughter.' It just didn't seem like the time to bring it up. I was going to tell you about Maddie right after the service and invite you to go to lunch with us, but Mrs. Coughlin came up and talked to me and you ran away. I knew I'd blown it."

My heart ached. "Why in the world would you have thought I would run away because you have a child?"

"I don't know." He shrugged. "It makes sense to think that not everyone would want to date someone who—"

"You were thinking about dating me?" I asked, pretty much disregarding everything else he was saying. I chose instead to focus on the word that finally assured me that I hadn't imagined something which didn't exist. Yes, all of the words he'd said over the course of the minute or so prior had indicated the same thing, but finally there was a word that was unmistakable. There was no way I could have misinterpreted that one.

He smiled. "I told you, I was going to ask you to lunch."

"I would have liked to go to lunch with you. And Maddie. I'm sorry I didn't stick around." I laughed as I thought of how ludicrous my trains of thought had been for two weeks. "I'm sorry I didn't give you a chance to explain that you aren't actually a disgusting weasel."

"Well, I guess it was a relatively easy mistake to make. It makes sense that you assumed—"

"Oh no, I didn't assume," I protested. "The mistake was not mine, my friend. I mean, not entirely." He looked confused again until I opened my eyes wide and added with a sigh, "She said 'you and your wife' and you didn't correct her."

"Oh!"

"Yeah."

"Well, that would do it!" He laughed. "I guess I just didn't even notice that part. People don't really expect thirty-five-year-old widowers, so I get that a lot. Besides, by that point, I felt like you and I knew each other pretty well, I guess." He ran his hand through his hair and shuffled his feet. "Does that sound crazy? It does, doesn't it?"

"It would," I said with a smile, "if I hadn't been feeling exactly the same way."

We stood in silence, preparing ourselves for what we were embarking on, and having no idea what that was.

"So," he finally began nervously, "the fact that I have a kid doesn't bother you?"

Tears welled up in my eyes again as I thought

of the years I had spent so desperately wanting a child that I felt half of my heart was missing, off somewhere preparing itself for the day when that dream would come true.

"Why would it bother me?" I didn't think before I spoke my next words, but I honestly don't know if I would have changed them even if I had, there in the power of that moment. "If anything, it makes me love you even more."

I hit rewind in my brain and ran through that scene again to see if I had actually said what I had just said.

Ben has a kid? Good.

He was as into me as I was into him? Very good.

I don't have a problem with him having a kid? Very, very good.

Sarah is a crazy lady who just word-vomited all over everything?

Bad. So, so bad.

Before I could retract my way-too-early use of the word, or even breathe, his hand was in my hair and his lips were on mine. It was soft and tender and yet the most passionate kiss of my life. I also think it was every bit as unexpected to him as it was to me. He pulled away gently, somehow leaving me numb and feeling more than I ever had, equally.

It seemed to suddenly hit him and he took an additional step back. "I am really, really sorry about that," he stammered.

I couldn't help but smile. "Are you?"

He laughed. "No. But I feel like I should be."

We stood in comfortable silence, not sure what we should do next but also feeling no real urgency to figure it out.

"Are you coming to church tomorrow?" he eventually asked.

My fleeting thoughts of going to church anywhere other than Mercy Point were ancient history, so I nodded.

He smiled. "Okay. Good to know. I'll be delivering the sermon I was supposed to give that first week. Hebrews 11. I'm going to give it my all to not inadvertently switch to a sermon I wrote in seminary again, just because I can't get the name Sarah out of my mind. Although, Sarah is actually mentioned in Hebrews 11 too. So if I happen to glance your way, it's not my fault."

A few minutes later, we each went to our respective homes, but not before making plans for lunch after church the next day. We didn't kiss good-bye. Though we didn't say another word about our first kiss, I think we both knew we needed to be careful. Nevertheless, I couldn't help but think I had all the inspiration I needed for my Christian romance. After all, I'd just experienced firsthand the Christ-centered version of "Nice boys don't kiss like that." The truth is: yes. Yes they do.

No expletive required.

8.

Meggie, Hester, and Mary Matalin

"It's too *Thorn Birds*," Joe said when I ran my idea past him.

I was driving home from coffee, driving home from Ben, and I was on cloud nine. Though in many ways I was shocked by the evening's turn of events, there was also a big part of me that felt like finally things were going the way they were supposed to. And I don't just mean between Ben and me, though obviously that was a huge part of it all. It was bigger than that. My life. My entire life was in God's hands. I finally gave myself over to that, over to him, and look where it got me . . .

Don't get me wrong—I wasn't looking at Ben as any sort of reward or anything.

Okay, that was a complete lie. Yes, I was looking at him as a reward. I'm not now, of course, but then, less than three weeks into my salvation, I think I was. Maybe not a reward exactly. More like a door prize from God, welcoming me to his family. Yes, I realize how biblically messed up that was. Don't judge me.

Regardless, I just knew that there was a good

Christian romance to be found in my blossoming relationship with Ben, and I was determined to convince my agent of that.

"It's not at all *Thorn Birds*!" I argued, while making a mental note to make sure I had destroyed my Father Ralph and Meggie cartoon bulletin. "First of all, *The Thorn Birds* isn't exactly a Christian romance, is it?"

My Bluetooth went silent for a moment. "Isn't it?" Joe finally asked.

I laughed, certain he was joking, and then I realized he was dead serious. "Joe, have you read *The Thorn Birds*? Or at least seen the miniseries?"

"Oh, I've seen snippets. But I know it's about a priest and the woman he loves, and they have sex on the beach. Sounds pretty much like what you're talking about."

I was torn between wanting to laugh at his ignorance and just hanging up on him, but in the end I did neither. He had been a sports guy, after all. While women all over the world were falling in love with Father Ralph and Richard Chamberlain and feeling guilty about it, Joe Welch had been traveling the world with Jimmy Connors and John McEnroe. I knew I should let him slide, so I told him the story of *The Thorn Birds*. Three different times I said, "If you're bored, I can stop," and three different times he said, "No, go ahead."

I concluded just as I pulled into my driveway. "So Father Ralph told Meggie the story of the thorn bird and then he died in her arms."

I can't be sure, but I think he sniffed. "What is the story of the thorn bird?"

"I can't remember exactly, but basically it's a legend that there is this type of bird that spends its entire life searching for one particular type of tree or bush, or something. It won't rest until it finds it. Once it does, it lands on it, but the long, sharp thorns impale the bird in the chest. I think that's right. And then upon its death, right before it dies, the bird sings for the one and only time in its life, and it's the most beautiful song ever sung by any creature."

There was a long pause as I reflected on the beauty of the story and Joe took it in for the very first time.

"Hey, are you okay?" I asked comfortingly.

"That's the stupidest thing I've ever heard in my entire life! How stupid is that bird? At some point, through years of evolution and survival of the fittest and everything, wouldn't those birds have learned to avoid the thorns?"

"Good night, Joe."

"No, wait. Sorry. Okay, so maybe that's not the same as the story you want to tell. But if you write a story about a woman who falls in love with her pastor, you know there will be people who make comparisons."

"Sure," I agreed. "But since most people have either never heard of *The Thorn Birds* or actually have a clue what it's about . . ."

It was his turn to sigh. "Okay, let me think on it and we'll talk tomorrow."

"Maybe not tomorrow," I said, thrilled that my work was not coming first in my life.

"Oh, right. Church. And lunch with Father Ralph."

I laughed. "Good night, Joe."

"Night, Sarah." I was just about to hang up when I heard him say, "Hey, so, do you think *The Thorn Birds* is on Netflix or something?"

Oh boy. "Good night, Joe."

I was tempted to call Piper as soon as I got in. I wanted to tell her all about everything that had happened, before the feeling of Ben's lips faded from mine—but then again, I didn't know if that feeling would ever fade, so there wasn't really any rush. However, she had texted me about a dozen times, so I figured I should be nice and put her out of her misery.

But I was in such a good mood that I decided instead to playfully torture her, as any good friend would. "Heading to bed. Coffee in the a.m., before church. See you then," I texted, and then I turned off my phone with a laugh, clearly envisioning the frustration that was about to ensue.

I wasn't, however, actually heading to bed. I couldn't shut off my brain. I thought for one brief moment that I might call Ben, but I looked at the clock and realized it might be about the time a five-year-old would go to bed. Also, I didn't have his number.

"How did I not even get his number?" I wondered aloud to myself. I also hadn't given him mine, or any other way of contacting me, but I wasn't too worried about it. I knew the location of his pulpit.

The next morning when I got to the coffee house, Piper was already there, practically bouncing in her seat in anticipation. She scowled as I approached, trying to act as if she were mad at me for brushing her off with my text, but in the end she couldn't keep it up.

"So? Tell me. Did he talk to you? Was there a simple explanation? Tell me there was a simple explanation."

In light of the actual truth that had been discovered, I felt pretty guilty about the previous conversations.

"His wife is dead."

"Told you!" Piper squealed before immediately catching herself. "I mean, that's horrible, of course. But I just *knew* there was a good reason—I mean, not a *good* reason. That's a terribly sad reason. But I knew there had to be a simple reason. Not that I'm saying this is *simple,* of course . . ."

"No, no, I get it." I laughed—not at the circumstances, but at Piper. Then I went on to tell her the little bit that I knew about Christa and Maddie. And then I told her about the kiss.

"Seriously? Just like that, he kissed you?" she asked in shock, which I interpreted as scorn.

Oh no. Had I committed some sin of which I hadn't even been aware? Or had he? My mind was racing. Piper was the one who had said that Ben hadn't taken a vow of celibacy, but were there guidelines? Are Christians not allowed to kiss on the first date? Oh wait, we hadn't even had a first date yet. I was a Christian Hester Prynne!

"Wait! That's another one!" I spoke as if Piper had been reading my mind and following along with my entire train of thought, not to mention the previous evening's conversation with Joe. "Hester Prynne in *The Scarlet Letter*! Her affair was with a man of God too! What was the minister's name? Arthur something . . ."

"Another one?" she asked, as confused as she had every right to be. "What are you talking about?"

"I want to write a romance about a woman in a relationship with her pastor, but there is no example of that type of romance in which it isn't some illicit, scandalous thing. Is that how

117

it's really going to be?" I was going through the mental catalogue of every book I had ever read and every movie I had ever seen. "Am I making a huge mistake? Am I in way over my head?" I looked around to make sure no one would overhear and then I whispered, "Am I a modern-day Mary Matalin?"

"Sarah, calm down. Seriously, what are you talking about?" Piper looked amused, clearly not understanding the magnitude of the situation.

I took a deep breath, trying to calm down as she had instructed. "There is no telling of this story in all of history that ends with the man and woman together and still honoring God. At least not that I've read or seen. Meggie and Father Ralph are just one heartbreaking example. Hester Prynne slept with her pastor and had to wear an *A* until she died. By execution! And Mary Matalin had to go by herself to France after Jesus was crucified."

At the time I didn't notice, but looking back it is quite evident that my best friend was having to work very hard not to laugh in the face of my spiritual immaturity and lack of biblical knowledge and understanding.

"First of all, it's Mary Magdalene. Not Mary Matalin."

That didn't sound right. "Are you sure?"

She nodded her head. "Yes. Quite. Mary Matalin is the political lady, married to James Carville."

Oh. Yeah, I was pretty sure she was correct about that.

"Secondly," she continued, "please do not turn to Dan Brown or *The Da Vinci Code* as a scriptural authority. That stuff was made up. Jesus and Mary Magdalene weren't married, didn't have a child. The Bible doesn't give us any reason to believe there was any sort of romantic relationship at all, actually. She was a devoted disciple and a reformed prostitute."

"Hmm. Okay. If you say so," I said dismissively, still determined to check that out for myself later.

"And then let's examine *The Scarlet Letter*," she continued. "For one thing, Hester wasn't executed."

"Oh, really? I'm not sure if I ever actually finished that book . . ."

"And they were Puritans. They had a sexual affair, and Hester had a baby. And then her presumed-dead husband showed up. Personally, I can see lots of ways in which that differs from your situation with Ben. Maybe that's just me."

"You're making fun of me." I pouted, a bit hurt.

She laughed. "Of course I am! You change courses so quickly and I never know why! You were so happy about it all just a couple of minutes ago. What turned the worry back on?"

"You said, 'Seriously? Just like that, he kissed you?' and, yeah, just like that he kissed me. I just can't imagine what you must think of me. And him."

And then she released the laughter in full force. "Really, Sarah? You're so paranoid! I was just getting into it. It's like a romantic comedy or something. Frankly, it just sounded really sexy. I wasn't being judgmental or anything."

Oh.

"However," she continued, putting her index finger up as if that would help her make her point. "If it's that intense already, you probably do need to be careful."

Of that I was fully aware, but I wasn't worried. Maybe I should have been, but I wasn't. I thought about what it would have been like if I had met a man three weeks ago—if I wasn't a Christ-follower and he wasn't a professional Christ-follower. But if we'd had the same acute level of connection that Ben and I'd had? Yeah, I wouldn't have thought twice about kissing him. Well, that's not true. I would have thought about it twice and then continued to think about it until the next opportunity came to kiss him again.

An hour later we were walking into Mercy Point, and I felt like a teenage girl, desperate to lay eyes on her crush. I was on the lookout, anxiously awaiting the moment when I would next get a glimpse of his beautiful brown eyes. Finally I spotted them, but they had a different home from the one I had previously seen. The slightly tanned, five-o'clock-shadowed face I'd seen less than eighteen hours earlier had been replaced by flawless peaches-and-cream, perfectly cherubic cheeks, and the brown wavy hair had been replaced by golden curls. But the eyes were definitely the same.

I walked over to her where she stood, just inside the doorway to the children's church wing. She was holding a doll, brushing its hair.

"Madeline?" I said softly.

She looked at me, and I realized the over-whelming power of the Delaney charm must come from the eyes, for I instantly fell in love with her.

I smiled, squatting down to her height. "Hi. You must be Madeline Delaney. I've been wanting to meet you."

"Why did you want to meet me?" she asked with the voice of an angel.

"Well, just because everyone says you are a very special, wonderful girl. And when I heard that, I just knew you were someone I wanted to be friends with."

"This is Chrissy," she said, holding her doll out for me to meet her.

I shook the doll's hand. "It's very nice to meet you, Chrissy." I directed my attention back to Madeline. "Chrissy is a very good name for her. It suits her." I melted, and my heart broke for the little girl as I realized that Madeline had probably named Chrissy after the mother she didn't remember.

"What's your name?" she asked me.

"My name is Sarah."

"That's pretty. My name is Madeline, but everybody calls me Maddie. Do people call you anything else?"

I don't think I'd ever been called anything else in my life, apart from Raine de Bourgh, so I just said, "Nope. No one ever has. But if you're going to be my friend, you can call me whatever you want."

Her eyes got big and she smiled as she realized she had an opportunity to name another doll. She thought for just a moment and then she said, with authority, "I want to call you Applesauce."

Well, I hadn't seen that coming. "Applesauce? Okay," I said slowly. "If that's what you want . . ."

"I think Applesauce is the most beautiful name I've ever heard!" she exclaimed sincerely.

Dear Jesus, I prayed. *Thank you for bringing this precious girl and her father into my life.*

"Then Applesauce it is!" I giggled, so enamored by her.

"Applesauce," she said, "you should ask Miss Laura if you can come to lunch with us today. We're going to a restaurant!"

"Miss Laura?" Who was this Miss Laura, and why was she intruding upon my lunch?

"Miss Laura's coming, and Kaitlyn, and I think

my gram is coming. Please say you'll come, Applesauce! Please?"

"Well, um . . ."

"Maddie, it's time to get started. Come on in," a gorgeous twentysomething called to Maddie from further inside the room. *Please, Lord, don't let that Scarlett Johansson lookalike be Miss Laura.*

"You'd better go!" I smiled, grateful for the distraction so that I didn't have to commit to lunch with Ben, Maddie, my future mother-in-law, Scarlett Johansson, and Kaitlyn, whoever Kaitlyn was. "I need to get into church too."

"My daddy's the preacher," she said. And then she leaned in and whispered to me, "Try not to fall asleep while he's talking. He talks for a really long time sometimes, but that's what preachers are supposed to do."

My heart had never been as delighted as it was in the presence of that little girl. "Okay." I winked. "I'll do my best."

"Bye, Applesauce!"

I heard the music starting, so I hurried into the sanctuary, blushing as I walked past the bench where Ben and I had first talked. I quickly found Piper, who gave me a look as if to say, "Late again?" and joined her in the row. As soon as I got to the seat and turned around to face front, I saw him up on the stage singing along, not even trying to disguise the fact that he was looking right at me. I smiled and shrugged, as he had the first time we'd made eye contact from stage to congregation, and his smile widened. He then turned his attention to the worship song, and we both managed, miraculously, to stay focused on church for the rest of the service.

9.

Blame It on the Raine

When the service ended, I visited with Piper and a few others while Ben was once again swarmed by the entire congregation. Though I wasn't overly concerned, the Miss Laura mystery was still on my mind, and I couldn't help but notice that for every one man or elderly woman who stood around Ben, there were seven or eight pretty young things, giggling at every single thing he said.

"Look at that," I whispered to Piper, motioning with my chin in the direction of the swarm.

She laughed softly. "Yes, I wouldn't think that a young, gorgeous, widowed pastor would have too much difficulty finding a date." My natural insecurities rose to the surface for just a moment, but then Piper leaned over to me and put her head on my shoulder as she said, "And just think. With all of that in front of him, he wants you."

About thirty seconds later, he glanced my way. There were still at least ten women surrounding him, begging for his attention, but any bit of it they'd had was lost. He smiled at me, and I expected him to give a little shrug, like he usually would. Instead he politely excused himself and walked my way, never taking his eyes off of me.

"You okay there?" Piper chuckled quietly. I suppose I had involuntarily grabbed on to her for a bit of support in light of my recurring weak knees syndrome.

"Sorry," I whispered.

"Don't be. Have fun at lunch and call me after." I'm pretty sure she was smiling, based on the sound of her voice, but I didn't look away from Ben to be sure.

"No, stay. I want him to meet you," I pleaded.

"As if he'll even notice me," she snickered as he approached.

The way his eyes were locked in on mine, I couldn't deny her point was valid. "No, you have to stay." As much as I hated to, I stopped looking at him for just a moment so I could look at Piper instead. "It's important to me that you like him."

"I already like him. But what if he doesn't like me?" she teased. "Then you'll always have to be choosing between us, and Sunday mornings will be awkward, and—"

"Impossible! What's not to like?" I leaned closer to her and whispered, "You really do have to stay and meet him. You can't really tell how cute he is until you see him up close."

Her eyebrows and the corners of her mouth lifted simultaneously. "Well, in that case . . ." She winked at me before turning around to greet him, just as he reached us. "Hi," she said as she stuck out her hand to shake his.

"Oh, hi," he said. He smiled as he glanced quickly to me and then back to her. I think his senses were jarred just the tiniest bit. He had indeed been so focused on me I'm pretty sure he hadn't even realized Piper was there.

But I knew it wouldn't take long for him to discover, as I had long ago, that once Piper becomes a part of your life, you can't help but wonder how you ever survived without her.

"Ben, I want you to meet another of your many parishioners, and my best friend. This is Piper Lanier."

"Piper, it's great to meet you." He shook her hand. "Ben Delaney."

My heart swelled as I watched the two most important people in my life discuss Ben's sermon for a minute or so, and I marveled at how quickly they made each other laugh and how comfortable they both instantly were with each other. *Thank you, Lord, for Piper. She led me to you and she led me to him, but I have no doubt that you led me to her.* And then just when I thought everything was as perfect as it could possibly be, the moment was blissfully interrupted by the entrance of the one other person I already knew my life would be darker without.

"Daddy!" Maddie called out as she ran over to him.

He turned toward the sound of her voice with a smile and caught her in his arms as she flung herself into them. Before I even realized I needed it, Piper put her arms around me to provide some subtle backing. She knew, even before I did, the effect that seeing the two of them together would have on me.

"I want you to meet some friends of mine," Ben said to Maddie as he picked her up and turned around to face us again.

"Applesauce!" she squealed.

I laughed joyfully while Piper looked amused and Ben just looked confused. "Hi, Maddie." I winked at Ben. "We met earlier, before church, and I shall henceforth be known as Applesauce."

"Do I need to call you Applesauce too, or . . . ?"

"No, silly!" Maddie giggled. "Only I can call her Applesauce. You have to call her Sarah."

Ben pretended to be bummed. "Fine. If that's the way it has to be." He sighed dramatically, which elicited giggles from all three ladies in his presence. "Well, have you met Apple—I mean . . . Sarah's friend Piper?"

After introductions were complete, and Maddie had decided that Piper didn't need a nickname because Piper was the most perfect name ever, Maddie once again brought up the prospect of lunch with Scarlett Johansson. "Can Applesauce and Piper come to lunch with me and Gram and Miss Laura and Kaitlyn?"

Ben set her down so that she was standing on the chair next to where he stood. "Well, that would be very nice, I'm sure, but, you see, there's a problem."

Problem? What problem? Had the addition of his mother made him decide I shouldn't come along? Worse, had the addition of Miss Laura made him decide I shouldn't come along? I mean, I didn't want to eat lunch with all of those people, but I didn't want to not go because he didn't think I should!

"The thing is," he said, speaking to Maddie but looking at me, "I've already asked Sarah to have lunch with me." He turned back to her. "You can have lunch with her another day. Okay?"

Piper elbowed me in the ribs, which kind of hurt. Okay, so I had let my insecurities run away with me once more. And there was no need for it, I reminded myself. *God's got this, Sarah,* I thought to myself with joy and peace.

And it was a very good thing that I knew that and had given myself that little pep talk, because just a second later, Miss Laura came to collect Maddie, and she was indeed the ScarJo lookalike.

"Thanks, Laura," Ben said as he hugged Maddie good-bye. "I'll swing by and get her later this afternoon. I owe you one."

"Oh, it's my pleasure," Laura breathed. She even had that raspy, breathy thing going on like

Scarlett. "We always have a great time together, don't we, Maddie?"

I was just starting to think that maybe I had absolutely nothing to worry about, that Laura was just a family friend or maybe even a cousin or something, and then she said to Ben, just under her breath, "But if you think you owe me one, we can discuss that later."

Piper's elbow returned to my ribs, this time with a vengeance. "Ow!" I couldn't help but exclaim.

"Oh, sorry about that," she said halfheartedly and then turned her attention to Laura. "Hi, Laura. I'm Piper. Very nice to meet you. And this is Sarah."

"Piper." Laura smiled as she shook Piper's hand. And then the smile remained but the warmth faded as she turned to me and said, "Sarah. Of course. It's great to meet you."

I couldn't help but wonder if we, as women, had always possessed the instinctive skills for detecting cattiness in other women, or if the knowledge had been taught to us throughout our lives by the great masters of the trade, such as Joan Collins and Linda Evans on *Dynasty*. All I knew for sure was that if the ice in her eyes the first time we met was any indication, Miss Laura could have teased up her hair, thrown on some shoulder pads and big clip-on earrings, and taught the Carringtons a lesson or two.

"It's great to meet you too, Laura. I hope you ladies have a great time at lunch." I smiled at her in a hopefully genuine way.

If looks could kill, I'd have been sent tumbling down the staircase in my beaded Nolan Miller evening gown.

And then Laura and Maddie were gone, and Piper said good-bye before I could convince her to stay, and then Ben and I were alone. Well, we were surrounded by several dozen church members who were still hanging around, but we were alone.

"You ready?" he asked. "Do you like sushi?"

The man could not be more perfect. "I love sushi. Just please don't make fun of me for how much I eat. And my inability to master chopsticks."

We named the place and met there about ten minutes later. The restaurant was close to the church, so several people I recognized were there as well. As we walked in, they greeted Ben warmly and sized me up skeptically and then greeted me kindly. I think that was the first time the whole "dating the pastor" thing really hit me. I mean, I'd thought about it a lot, obviously, but always in the eternal ramifications sort of way. Now I was faced with the reality of being seen out and about with a man who a few hundred people at Mercy Point Church viewed as their spiritual shepherd.

"Is this weird for you?" I asked quietly as we took our seats at our table. "With all of these people from Mercy Point here?"

He looked around, as if he hadn't really noticed them, though he had acknowledged most of them by name. "No. Why? Is it weird for you?"

Every other first date I had ever been on in my entire life would have been a perfectly designed vehicle for dishonesty. I would have thought briefly about what my answer should be and then I would have nonchalantly replied, "No, of course not!" But there was no need to lie to Ben. I still knew very little about him, and he knew even less about me, but we weren't like any other couple on a first date. Perhaps we were having sushi, preparing to ask each other the unimportant things that couples on a first date ask, but I knew instinctively that even in that early stage, we were far beyond having to play those games that people play. I already knew I could be honest with him.

"Yeah." I sighed. "It is a little weird, actually. I mean, not bad weird, but . . . weird. Every person in that church, and probably in any church anywhere, thinks their pastor is slightly superhuman."

He laughed. "Oh, I don't think that's true. And in some cases, I know it's not." He leaned in and spoke conspiratorially. "For instance, Lenore Isaacs over there, by the fish tank. She thought her husband should have gotten my job. Never mind the fact that he never went to seminary, or college at all, I don't think. And I honestly don't think he's ever done any kind of public speaking. I assure you, I'm just a man like the rest of them, and most of them know it."

"That's true, I'm sure, but you have to know the standard is a bit higher for you, in their minds, than it is for their mechanic, or their plumber. They're going to want to know everything about any woman who you are seen with. They're going to want to unearth every piece of dirt they can find about me."

"Dirt, huh? Should I be hiring a private eye to investigate your secret double life?" He smiled and popped a bite of California roll into his mouth.

I laughed at the absurdity of what he was saying, and he laughed with me. Oh, how we laughed. Until, of course, I started choking on the little bit of seaweed that had been inhaled down my throat when my laughter turned to a panicked gasp.

Ben passed me my glass of water and asked me if I was okay as the choking transitioned to coughing, and my eyes watered in response to the temporary loss of air. Mortified, I sipped water slowly between hacks and raspy barks, and nodded that I was okay, buying myself as much time as possible.

Until that very moment, I had not given one single second of thought to the potential scandal that could result from the new pastor dating an author of very saucy romance novels. All of that thought about members of Mercy Point being curious about any woman the pastor decided to date, and I'd spent not one second thinking about my actual double life.

How could I not think about it, right? Yes indeed. How could I not? Well, I don't know! Maybe because I felt like it was all coming from God. Or maybe because I knew that one way or another, I was preparing to walk away from my life as Raine de Bourgh. The European engagements were finally in my rearview mirror, and I could no longer be associated with something so destructive, even if I had been its creator. I had no idea how I was going to do it exactly, but I was committed to walking away. I would no longer be the young postulant Maria, whom the nuns had referred to as a flibbertigibbet. I was going to be Maria von Trapp, and the nuns would be willing to remove a Nazi's carburetor in order to protect me.

Or maybe, just maybe, I hadn't thought of it because I was so caught up in how crazy I was about Ben, and so overwhelmed by the knowledge that he was pretty crazy about me too, that it was difficult to believe anything else mattered more than that.

Maybe it doesn't, I told myself as I finally began breathing normally again. I hadn't thought of the Desire books or Raine de Bourgh until after I had found out about Christa, and after Ben kissed me, and after I met Maddie. If I'd remembered before any of those things happened, I might have still been able to walk away. The shame and embarrassment, and the fear of judgment, may have allowed me to walk away.

But now? Not a chance.

"Ben," I began, scooting in just a little closer to him. "There's something I need to tell you."

10.

Really Crazy, Like, Certifiable

"You're Raine de Bourgh?" Ben asked for the third time. He'd yet to say anything else.

The first two times I had calmly nodded my head and confirmed that it was true. The third time, I started to feel a bit shaky. On *Days of Our Lives*, Roman Brady could come back to town after being dead for two years and everyone just accepted it—never mind that he was three inches taller and had a completely different face. No problem. *That* was easy to believe. But this? This was too much?

Perhaps it was the repetition that got to me, but I think it was more likely the emphasis. "You're Raine de Bourgh?" somehow didn't feel as bad as "*You're* Raine de Bourgh?"

"Look, Ben, I probably should have told you sooner, but it just didn't occur to me. Truly. I mean, it's kind of like you not telling me about Maddie right away. 'Hi, nice to meet you. By the way, I'm super-famous for writing sexy books.' It just isn't a conversation starter." I felt very proud of my defense for about half a second until I realized I was comparing the introduction of my sordid past to Ben's introduction of his angelic daughter.

I just couldn't take it any longer. "Please say something."

His eyes met mine for the first time since I had broken the news, and they were conveying emotions that I couldn't interpret. There seemed to be some sadness. Pain, maybe? I just couldn't tell. All I knew for sure was that nothing in those beautiful eyes said, "Everything's fine."

"I'm sorry, Sarah," he said quietly. "I really don't know what to say."

Tears ran down my cheeks, and I didn't even bother wiping them away. "I'll go."

I started to stand, but he put his hand on mine. "Don't go. Just . . ." He took a deep breath and rubbed his eyes, as if trying to shake off the stupor. "Sit. But . . . just give me a minute, okay?"

"Ben, I'm sorry that I—"

He squeezed my hand gently before releasing it. "Just give me a minute," he repeated, forcing a pained smile. "I'm just going to get some air, then I'll be back."

He stood and walked outside, and I was left alone with several sets of eyes on me. I could just imagine what they must be thinking. Who is this woman, why is she crying, and what has she done to our pastor?

I sat there for a few minutes that felt like hours,

and I tried to figure out how this could possibly end well. And if it wasn't going to end well, what had been the point of it in the first place? Had my amateur-hour Christianity led me astray? Had I seen something that wasn't there at all? Were Ben and I just attracted to each other and nothing more? As Piper had pointed out, he was not just a widower and a father. He was not just a pastor and leader of a congregation. He was a man, and I was a woman. Men and women fell for the wrong people all the time.

I couldn't keep sitting there, letting them all create stories about me in their minds. The more time that passed and Ben didn't come back in, the more certain I was that he wasn't coming back at all. At least not to stay. And then the horrible thought entered my mind that the longer I sat there, letting them all stare at me while making very little effort to pretend they weren't, the more of an opportunity they had to figure out who I was. They'd seen me somewhere, they probably knew. They probably figured they had gone to high school with me or that I had been a clerk at Neiman Marcus. But it was just a matter of time before they remembered seeing me in *People* magazine or on the side of a bus beside a blurb that said, "This woman is the devil, but I can't put this book down!"

Or something like that.

I flagged down our waiter and paid the bill, then

I grabbed my purse and rushed out, certain my cheeks would explode if any more blood rushed to them. I didn't see Ben when I stepped outside and I assumed he had left, though truthfully I knew he wouldn't leave without saying good-bye. I was still trying to convince myself that I had overestimated our connection and our feelings for each other, but in the pit of my stomach I still somehow knew Ben Delaney.

"Sarah?" he called out just as I opened my car door. "Please don't go."

I turned around, so broken by the thought of losing him already, and so shattered by the pleading tone of his voice. I could see through the pool of tears just enough to notice that he was on his cell phone, but he quickly finished up, very quietly, and walked over to where I stood.

"I'm sorry," he said as he approached.

I laughed bitterly through the pain. "Why are you sorry? I'm sorry. I'm sorry about everything. I should have told you. I'm really sorry about that, but mostly I'm just sorry that there is anything to tell. I wish I'd never written the stupid books. I really do."

He dug in his pockets to see if he had a tissue, but when he came up empty-handed, he wiped my tears away with his fingers.

"I'm not judging you, you know." He spoke so gently and carefully. "You know that, don't you? I don't care what you've done in your past.

I honestly don't. I have a past too." I arched my eyebrow, incredulous that there could be more secrets to be revealed. He correctly interpreted the eyebrow and smiled. "Don't worry. I don't think there are any more things in my past bigger than what we already know." The smile faded as he asked, "Is this the biggest one for you?"

I took the question very seriously and really thought through everything before answering, "I think that's safe to say."

"Good," he said as the smile returned.

There was a moment of silence, which I tried to decipher and couldn't. I wanted to believe that somehow things could work out between us. I wanted to believe that somehow we could keep moving forward and see what could be. But each second that we didn't communicate made it more and more difficult to believe, and if that was the case—if it just wasn't going to work out—I desperately wanted to let him off the hook. I already cared for him, and that meant that I needed for him to walk away from this as unscathed as possible, even if I didn't.

"Ben—" I began.

"That was Christa's mom I was on the phone with. It's funny. I never would have expected that when I need some honest advice, she would be the one I call, but that's totally the way it is." He leaned up against my car with his hands in his pockets.

I didn't understand why he was telling me that, but I couldn't help but find it interesting. "You have a pretty good relationship with her then?"

He nodded. "I do. My own mother is great, in her own way, but Christa's mom gets it, you know?"

I didn't really get it at all, and I wasn't really sure that I wanted to. After all, the honest advice he had called about was no doubt regarding what to do about me, now that my career had been revealed. And it didn't really take a lot of analytical thinking to surmise what a mother-in-law would say to a man considering moving on from his late wife. What mother in her right mind would believe her dead daughter should be replaced by someone of my ilk?

"I know that you're not judging me. I do. But we both know that won't stop every member of your congregation from judging me. As they should, probably. And it's not fair for me to put you in that position." I stood up straight with new resolve, determined to do the right thing for Ben. And isn't it cute how I thought I knew exactly what the right thing was? "We can totally tell anyone who asks that you took me out to lunch to stage an intervention or something."

"That's the first thing they teach us in seminary, actually. Interventions are most successful when they take place one-on-one, preferably in intimate little sushi restaurants."

"Don't make fun," I whispered sadly. I crossed my arms and matched his pose, leaning back against my car. It took too much effort to hold myself up.

He cleared his throat. "I'm sorry." I didn't respond, so he nudged me with his elbow. "I really am sorry. I didn't mean to make fun. You're just so . . ."

What? Pitiful? Depressing? Laughable?

"Adorable."

I scrunched up my nose at his word choice. Adorable evoked images of little girls and silliness.

"No, no. Maybe that's not the right word," he said in reaction to my expression, and I prepared myself for what I was certain would be a patronizing attempt to claw out of bubble gum and pigtails imagery. But he surprised me, as he usually did.

He stood up straight and faced me. "No, it is the right word. But not in the cute way, though you are unbelievably cute." He winked.

I just couldn't take it. "Ben, I should go." I wanted to stop leaning against my car, but he was too close in front of me. I knew that if I stood, I had no chance of not brushing against him, and I couldn't risk being rendered defenseless.

"Sarah, you are adorable. As in I adore you. Plain and simple. We've just met, and yet I am more comfortable with you than I have been with any woman since Christa died. You make me laugh and you make me think. You challenge me, and that was even before the Raine de Bourgh stuff. Now I'm really feeling challenged. And maybe I should walk away, for a million different reasons. I know that there will be some closed-minded people who will have a problem with it. I know that. And I'm supposed to lead the church, not cause problems within it."

I knew that he was audibly communicating his internal argument with himself, and I wanted to help him, somehow, but I didn't even know what was right for me, much less what was right for him.

But I couldn't help but whisper, "Then why don't you walk away?"

He looked me straight in the eye and said, "Because all I can think about is what I might miss. Isn't that interesting?" He smiled. "You just told me all of this stuff about your past and, admittedly, I don't know how to wrap my mind around some of it. But I also don't believe I have to wrap my mind around your past in order to focus on the present."

"But my past isn't going to go away that easily, Ben." I shook my head sadly. I looked away from him, too caught up in my own regret to accept the understanding he was offering.

"I'm sorry, Sarah, but you're wrong. Your past . . . it's already gone. And that doesn't mean you won't have to deal with things that were set in motion in the past, but the past is gone." He took a deep breath as he placed a finger under my chin and encouraged me to look up at him. When I was once again looking into his eyes, he said, "It doesn't seem like I'm getting through."

"It's not that. I know you're right. I know it's in the past. It's just that—"

" 'It's just that' nothing, Sarah. If you won't listen to the guy who's already pretty crazy about you, listen to your pastor." He smiled. "God doesn't look at you and see Raine de Bourgh, and neither do I. I look at you and see someone strong enough to have found a way to survive some rotten breaks—and not only survive but come out better on the other side. And I see someone who has no idea how smart she is, and funny, and breathtakingly beautiful."

I couldn't control the grin that crept onto my face as I said, "I'm not sure that's an appropriate thing for my pastor to say."

"Actually, that was the guy who's pretty crazy about you."

I laughed. "Oh good."

"I'm not willing to walk away, Sarah, so I hope you're okay with that. I'm just not willing to miss anything." After an intense few seconds of eye contact, he broke away and looked down at his feet. "Besides . . . and this is going to sound crazy . . ."

"What is?"

"No, I mean really crazy." He chuckled nervously, still looking down. "Like, certifiable."

I was pretty certain his crazy couldn't match mine, but I was intrigued. "Bring it."

"Okay." He looked around and then grabbed my hand. "Come over here." He walked me to a bench a few feet away. It felt a little more private and secluded, but even then I realized he was trying to create a more comfortable environment for us, not just escape the glances of his congregation walking to their cars now that they had finished their lunch.

We sat, and I tried to pull my hand away as Tom Isaacs, the man who apparently had wanted Ben's job, walked past us to his car and said, "Reverend," with a nod of his head.

"Have a good week, Tom," Ben said. "And Lenore, thanks for your help with the printer this morning."

Lenore just smiled and eyed me suspiciously. I smiled back, all the while trying to subtly pull my hand away from Ben's. And all the while, Ben wouldn't let go.

After the Isaacses drove away, I started laughing a slightly unhinged laugh. Maybe he *was* crazy. "That was bad, Ben. That was really, really bad. That woman will do all she can to cause trouble for you. You can see it in her eyes!"

"Sarah—"

"No, I'm serious. I've met women like that before. My ex-husband used to work with this horrible woman just like that, and—"

"You're divorced?" he interrupted, and I had a moment of panic, but then he cracked a smile. "I'm just kidding. You told me that. But now that I have your attention, you may recall that I was going to tell you something crazy. May I proceed?"

I cleared my throat, refusing to give him the satisfaction of acknowledging how unnerved I was for the brief second he'd had me convinced that I'd told him absolutely nothing. Instead I gestured for him to continue.

"Okay. So that first day we met, there in the hallway at the church, I had no reason to be going that way."

I simply stared at him, waiting for something "certifiable" to come along.

"Think about it," he continued with enthusiasm and awe. "I was going one way when I bumped into you, but when we both left to go to the service, I went the other way. That was the way I was supposed to be going. There was no reason at all for me to be going the way I was going when I ran into you." He shook his head. "Crazy."

"Are you . . . are you serious?" I asked, so underwhelmed that I didn't know how to react, but at least the crazy crown remained comfortably situated on my head.

"I told you it would sound crazy, and I wasn't going to tell you for a while because that seems pretty intense, but I think it's important that you know. I think you need to know how different and important this is to me. I've never had anything like that happen in my entire life, Sarah. Never."

I nodded my head, trying to appear impacted, but I didn't know why I was supposed to feel impacted. Finally I could stand it no longer. I held a straight face for as long as I could, but ultimately the absurdity of it all, combined with how cute he looked when he was being all earnest and reflective, made the laughter burst out of me in a very unflattering snort laugh.

"What are you talking about?" I asked, completely cracking up. "You've never gone the wrong way down a hallway before?"

He seemed momentarily bewildered by my question but then seemed to realize he'd left something out.

"I didn't go the wrong way, Sarah. I went your way. I had no reason to be walking down that hallway, and yet I *had* to walk down that hallway. I didn't know why. I just had to. And then there you were."

The expression on his face was so sweet and loving, and I probably should have worked harder to reciprocate, but I was still so baffled. I *was* able to eventually bury the laughter, which suddenly felt very inappropriate set against his sweetness.

"Oh. That's nice. Thank you." I didn't know what else to say.

"Umm . . . you're welcome?" He was suddenly as baffled as I was, and I realized I'd hurt his feelings.

"I'm sorry, Ben. It's just that I was expecting certifiable, and you gave me quirky." I began laughing as I realized why his declaration just wasn't having the impact he had anticipated. "You want to hear crazy? A few seconds after you felt an urge to head the wrong way in the hallway, as soon as I bumped into you, I was picturing us in . . ."

Oh no.

I coughed and cleared my throat and wished I had more seaweed to choke on, to buy myself a little time. I couldn't possibly allow myself to finish that sentence. At least not *that* way. I was picturing us in . . . what? In Cabo San Lucas, snorkeling? In matching sweaters? In a barbershop quartet? What crazy thing could I say that would somehow be less crazy than the crazy truth?

"I mean . . . okay . . . so . . ."

When would I learn? Wasn't it obvious that situations turned out better when I didn't speak?

The amused, intrigued grin on his face made it clear that no amount of clumsy backpedaling would be enough to get me away from telling the truth.

"You were picturing us in . . . what, exactly?"

Cabo did indeed sound lovely. Just me on the beach, relaxing waves crashing in the background, plenty of sand to bury my head in . . .

"Uh . . . love," I quickly mumbled. "But, you know, someday. Like, probably way in the future. I mean, not when we're old. Not that we wouldn't still be in love when we're old. If we ever were. I just mean—"

"In love, huh?" He grew more entertained by the second, as was evident by the twinkle in his eye.

I looked up briefly, hoping for a CUP-A-JOE sign to miraculously appear and finally finish me off, but I had only the sky to disappoint me this time. *You can make it work, God,* I prayed. *A meteor would be awesome right now.*

"Okay, here's the thing . . ." I began, with my eyes closed. I had hoped not being able to see his smirk would help with the embarrassment.

It did not.

"Yes. I pictured us in love. You know, with each other. I mean, obviously. It would be really weird if I just met you and started picturing us each in love with other people. Not that picturing us in love with each other *wasn't* weird." I squeezed my eyes closed even tighter,

149

all the while listening for meteor warning signs. Nothing? And I asked for so little . . .

"I swear I'm not crazy, Ben. Despite appearances. It was just . . . I don't know. A thought." I sighed. "With no thinking involved."

I wanted to keep my eyes closed forever— partially because I didn't want to see his reaction, but mostly because I thought I should allow him to retain his dignity as he ran away as quickly as possible.

"Sarah, will you please open your eyes?"

Okay, he was still there. That was a good sign. I opened my eyes slowly and was greeted with a smile.

"I get it now," he said softly. "I understand why you weren't too impressed with my story. But I also think maybe I didn't tell the story in the right way. Can I try again?"

I smiled and nodded my consent.

"I had to go down that hallway, though there was no reason at all that I should have. I just had to. My feet had a mind of their own, and that's all there was to it. And the really important thing that I forgot to add is that there has only been one other time that I can remember ever feeling so overwhelmingly compelled to do anything, and it was the very next time I saw you."

I tried to think about what he could possibly be referring to, but he didn't give me much time to think.

"I don't typically kiss women I've just met, Sarah. Actually, just to be clear, I've never kissed a woman I've just met. Except for you."

For a moment we got lost in each other. I noticed every single detail of him, and each one attracted me more than the last. The small lines at the corners of his mouth that were clear remnants from years of smiling and laughter, and their severe juxtaposition with the less noticeable but still unmistakable creases on his forehead. How many hours had that brow been furrowed in worry and sadness to result in creases that impactful? His thick eyelashes that would make any woman envious, and yet on him conveyed nothing but masculinity. And, more than anything else, I noticed the way he looked at me.

He took a deep breath and then exhaled a shaky one. "I don't know how to do this, Sarah. I want to do it. No, I will do it. But I don't know how." He let go of my hand for the first time since he had pulled me away from the car, and then he stood and started pacing. "It feels like we're already twenty steps ahead of where we are." He turned to face me but kept his distance, and I understood why. "But I don't know anything about your family. I don't know what foods you like, apart from sushi. I don't know where you went to college, or *if* you went to college."

I smiled. "DePaul. BA in Communication Studies."

"Good." He smiled back. "That's one thing we can check off the list."

"And you?"

"Oh. Bachelor's in Early Childhood Education from Vanderbilt, Master's in Theology from Yale Divinity School."

"Yikes."

"Yeah." He smiled sheepishly. "But the point is, this, whatever this is, just seems to go against the rules somewhat, and I just want to be very up front with you that I have no idea how to handle it."

I thought I understood what he meant. "That's okay. We'll figure it out."

"No, Sarah," he said, and then sat by me again. But still, he kept his distance. Then he looked around before very quietly saying, "I mean, I don't know if I can handle, um . . . my attraction to you. This is really awkward, and I'm sorry about that, but I think I have to be honest with you here. I need for you to know that I'm going to need some help from you and a lot of help from God. How do I say this?" He rubbed his eyes again.

"Hey," I whispered, and grabbed his hands from his face. I leaned in and kissed him softly on the cheek. "I get it. Thank you for telling me that. Really. And I know you're the theology expert and all . . . I mean, Yale Divinity School? Really?"

He laughed and shrugged.

"Nerd." I smiled. "So yeah. You're the expert. But here's what I think. I think we'll have to be careful, clearly. We'll have to be very aware of the positions we put ourselves in. But at the end of the day, if we ask God to help us, he will. Right?"

He grabbed a loose strand of my hair and played with it as he said, "You are very wise."

I chuckled as I stood and pulled him up with me. "Well, you may be the theology expert, but I literally wrote the book on sex. Between the two of us, I think we've got this covered."

11.

Wasabi-Stained Restraint

Since our Sunday lunch had been so rudely interrupted by, you know . . . reality, Ben and I decided our first date called for a do-over. So the next evening we went back to the sushi restaurant. As we ate, we laid down some ground rules, written on a napkin that I still have—wasabi stains and all.

1. We wouldn't allow ourselves to be completely alone together. Our dates would either be in public or with a chaperone; i.e., a double date, Piper, or Maddie.

2. We would only see each other outside of church and church functions three times a week: lunch on Sundays after church, one date night, and one Maddie date.

3. We would talk on the phone and/or email as often as we wanted in an attempt to get to know each other without the distraction of attraction.

4. Our relationship needed to be above reproach. We knew we would face a lot of scrutiny, especially once the members of Mercy Point figured out who I was, so we had to make sure we didn't give them any additional fuel for the fire.

5. Sex would not be happening, obviously. Hand-holding was fine. Hugs were fine. No kissing for a while, and then only within reason. More specifically, if we were okay with doing it in front of our chaperone, then it was okay.

6. We would trust God as to the timing of taking the next steps in our relationship.

7. No more surprises. No matter how small or insignificant details from our past seemed, we had to lay it all on the table.

In what I believe was an attempt to display our commitment to Rule #7, we talked about our marriages that day. I went first and made pretty quick business of it. There was nothing to keep from him, and he was welcome to all of the small and insignificant details, any time he wanted them. Ultimately I just couldn't think of any small and insignificant details of my marriage that weren't summed up beautifully by the large and extremely significant details of my divorce, so in my telling of the tale, I focused much more on the end than anything else. Specifically, I told Ben about Patrick's two most notable mistresses—Bree and his career. But while my marriage had been dark and depressing and mostly devoid of joy, Ben had gotten to experience the real thing.

Ben and Christa's marriage had certainly ended tragically, with the new mother being diagnosed with Stage 4 breast cancer on the day Maddie turned three months old, and losing her battle eight months later. But as Ben told the story of how they had been each other's first crush as children in Chicago, reconnected as college students passing through St. Louis, and went on to build a life together, ending up back in their hometown, I laughed much more than I cried. As did he. He'd had a good thing, and he knew it.

And yet I knew that he wasn't closed off to the idea that another good thing might come along.

I sat for a moment in grateful confidence that Ben was open to love again. Then a statement silently entered the discussion, and I knew it was something I needed to make sure I understood. I saw the statement written in my mind, as if written in a journal by an invisible hand.

He isn't open to love. He's open to you.

And suddenly my eyes were opened, and I saw his pain—still weighty though it had been four years. It wasn't about not being ready. He was ready for me. I had already understood that Ben was more mature than me—spiritually, emotionally—and that he would teach me and guide me. He would make me a better person. But that conversation was the first time I realized that Ben was broken too.

"You haven't dated since Christa died, have you?"

He looked up at me, I think mildly startled by words being spoken again, because he was so lost in his own thoughts.

He smiled and leaned back in his chair. "If by 'dated' you mean anything other than sitting at home playing games and watching movies with Maddie on Friday nights, then I suppose the answer would be no. Every time an opportunity came along, I always felt like I wasn't quite there yet. But I knew I would be the next time. Until the next time rolled around, that is." He sighed. "I don't know . . . I guess maybe it's extra difficult to get back out there when you never spent much time 'out there' to begin with."

Like mine, Ben's romantic history, prior to marriage, had been pretty limited. If Christa had been the bookends, there had only been one book in between. "The Bellamy girl," as Ben said his parents used to call her—his father because he couldn't ever remember her first name; his mother because the Bellamy family's wealth and prominence in Chicago at the time made her quite the catch. Ben dated her all through college and had been pretty close to proposing, until she cheated on him by kissing some guy in her study group. But he had been far from heartbroken. It was around that same time that Christa came back into his life.

He continued speaking, and it was as if he were asking a question he wasn't sure he wanted to know the answer to. "Have you dated? Since your divorce?"

I guess you could call it that. "Yeah. Quite a

bit, actually. I mean, not a ton. But some. Yeah."

He sighed. "For so long, I thought nothing would be as good as what I had with Christa. Everything would make me think of her. That didn't seem fair to any woman I could date, and honestly it didn't seem fair to me."

I didn't say anything, but he mistook my silence for hurt feelings.

"Oh, Sarah, I don't mean . . . I'm not saying that still applies. I hope you understand how different this is."

I did. Somehow I understood. "I know."

We were silent once more, but only because I didn't know what to say. I wanted to say something productive or beneficial for him, but we were outside my realm of expertise. If Christa had cheated on him, I could have proficiently comforted him all day long. But our marriages had nothing in common. He'd had an amazing wife and marriage. And he had an amazing daughter as proof of that love.

Ben handed me a tissue. I hadn't even realized the tears had begun. "What is it?"

"Nothing, really." I smiled sadly. I didn't mean to feel sad, but I couldn't help it. "I was just realizing why it was so easy—I mean, relatively—for me to leave Patrick. It wasn't even catching him cheating, though I have completely blamed the failure of the marriage on that."

Ben scoffed with a smidgen of barely restrained

anger toward Patrick that, I must admit, I found very sexy. "Of course you've blamed it on that. You deserved so much better than what that man did to you."

"You're right!" I laughed. "But being who I was then, knowing nothing else apart from the importance and magnitude of being Mrs. Patrick McDermott . . . I would have stayed with him forever. I was convinced I loved him, and I was convinced I could never do better. As terrible as it sounds—as terrible as it *is*—I really think I would have put up with the coldness and the other women and work coming first, and I'd have kept being a good little Catholic wife, if only he'd let me have a baby."

Ben, who had been leaning in holding my hand on the table, sat back in his chair as the weight of the statement hit him. "If he'd let you?"

I laughed again, this time more bitterly. "Well, I couldn't do it without him, could I?"

He was trying to understand, bless his heart, but for a man who had loved his wife and had wanted nothing more than to start a family with her, it was clearly a struggle. He leaned in again so he could be more discreet. "Are you saying he wouldn't make love to you?"

"I don't think Patrick had *made love* to me since we were newlyweds. But, yeah . . . we didn't have sex for the last . . ." I tried to think of the last time. Could that be right? "I guess for the last two years of our marriage." I looked up at Ben and grimaced, suddenly uncomfortable with the topic. "Sorry. Is this too much detail?"

"Rule #7. Go on."

"Okay," I resumed sheepishly after taking a moment to assess his reaction and make sure he was really okay with the conversation. "I begged him to try for a baby. Literally begged him. And he used it. 'After I finish this deal, maybe. I just need to make sure it all goes perfectly.' 'Of course, Patrick! What can I do? Play the perfect hostess? Organize a gala? Pack your bags so that you and your secretary can go to Cancun? You bet.' But there was always some reason that it wasn't the right time. Someday. Soon. After this, after that. After the divorce my mother tried to convince me that I could have held on to him if I'd gotten pregnant."

He sat up straight in his chair and made the "time out" gesture with his hands. "I'm sorry. What? Your mother said that?"

I smiled at his reaction. Sometimes I forgot what a piece of work my mother was, until I told other people stories about her. "That's my mother for you. Can't wait for you to meet her," I said sarcastically. "This is the same woman who told me my father had to leave the country because I asked him for too much."

"Why would that cause him to leave the country?"

"Well, technically he left the country to avoid being arrested on embezzlement charges. And I guess she was saying he only embezzled because I asked for too much." I smiled, having long ago become accustomed to my family's dysfunction.

"That's . . . I mean . . . I'm not quite sure what to say to that one," he said, completely dumbfounded.

"It's fine," I said dismissively and then added with a laugh, "But also not fine at all, of course. I think that my dad was the one guy she loved, even though she never really thought he was good enough. Go figure. So she dealt with it all in the best way she knew how."

Ben shook his head skeptically. "I'm not sure you should justify—"

"Oh no. I'm not justifying anything, I assure you. There's no excuse for how terribly she's treated me." Again I laughed. It was just my life. "But I think her feelings about my dad were why she was so incredibly awful about everything when I got divorced. I think she thought I was repeating her mistakes—letting go of this fantastic guy just because I asked for too much. But, of course, Patrick is not a fantastic guy."

"And I don't think that wanting to start a family was asking too much, Sarah."

"No," I agreed. "But for a little while I thought I had myself convinced that I hadn't really wanted a child all that much after all. That it was just my last ditch effort to try to make Patrick love me.

But that wasn't true at all. I didn't want a baby to try to hold on to Patrick—I tried to hold on to Patrick because I wanted a baby."

We sat in comfortable silence as we waited for the bill, and the silence continued as we paid and stood to go. I think we were both reflecting on what a heavy conversation it was for a first date, but I don't think either one of us believed it should have gone any other way. We walked outside and Ben escorted me to my car and opened the door for me. I don't think either one of us wanted it to end and we easily could have kept it going for hours longer. But we were both determined to follow the ground rules. And, though I wasn't sure if Ben had thought of it this way, I couldn't help but realize that on top of the already intense attraction we felt for each other, we had each just revealed that we hadn't had sex in years.

Those ground rules were going to be very important.

"Well, tell Maddie hi for me. I really do look forward to spending time with her."

His face lit up, as it seemed to each time he thought of his daughter. "I look forward to that too, Applesauce."

"Hey! You're not allowed to call me that!" I slapped him playfully on the arm.

"Oh, sorry." He laughed. "I'm going to go pick her up from Laura's now, and then—if you don't mind—I may call you this evening. Is that okay?"

I smiled. "I believe the rules state that you are supposed to call me as often as possible."

"You may regret those words, Ms. Hollenbeck."

I winked. "Try me."

I wanted to kiss him. It felt like I should kiss him. And he looked very much like he wanted to kiss me. That, strangely enough, is what gave me the strength to lean in and give him a hug. He held me tightly, but gently, and I immediately realized that we'd have to be careful with hugs as well. I pulled away and cleared my throat and felt how warm my cheeks had gotten.

"Bye," I whispered with a self-conscious laugh.

He sighed. "Bye." He crossed the street to his vehicle, and just before he got in, his cell phone rang. He pulled it from his pocket, glanced down at it, and then looked back at me with a conspiratorial grin. "Why, if it isn't 'the Bellamy girl.'" And then, with a wave, he got into the driver's seat as he said, "Hey, Laura. Yeah, I'm on my way now."

He drove away, but I stood frozen in place. Laura? Miss Laura? No . . . surely not. Could the Scarlett Johansson lookalike, whom I'd thought looked like she was in her midtwenties, actually be Ben's midthirties college girlfriend who had very nearly been his fiancée? Had the one his mother thought was such a good catch become the one his daughter loved?

Oh . . . not good. Not good at all.

12.

Feeling All the Feels

My mother used to tell me a story of a girl who was sickly and poor throughout her entire childhood. She had no one and nothing, except for the ability to sing beautiful songs. Night after night, day after day, she lay in her bed, shivering from the cold and nearly starving to death, singing with all her might. The song was her only friend and her only warmth. The song was the only thing in her life of value.

One day a local trader passed by and heard the song. "Who is that, singing with the voice of an angel?" he asked.

"Why, it's no one, sir," the townspeople said. "It is but only a sickly girl with a song in her heart."

"Lead me to her," he pleaded, but the townspeople refused, insisting she was not worth seeing.

Another day, a jester from the court of the king passed by and heard the song. "Who is that, singing with the voice of a majestic harp?" he asked.

"Why, it's no one, sir," the townspeople said. "It is but only a sickly girl with a song in her heart."

"Lead me to her," he begged, "and I will take her before the king." But the townspeople refused, insisting she was not worthy to set foot in the palace.

Still another day, the prince himself passed by and heard the song. "Who is that singing with the voice of my own heart's desire?" he asked.

"Why, it's no one, your majesty," the townspeople said. "It is but only a sickly girl with a song in her heart."

"Lead me to her," the prince commanded, "and I will take her as my wife."

The townspeople, of course, could not refuse the prince, but as they entered the girl's hut, the singing stopped.

"She's dead," the townspeople cried, somewhat thankfully. For they knew she was not fit to marry a prince.

The end.

I was always strangely, unexplainably touched by that story. My mother had told it to me at various pivotal moments throughout my childhood, and though I was never sure that I completely understood what she was trying to tell me, I knew there was a deep, hidden message that I would someday fully appreciate. I always found it somewhat maddening, actually. As a little girl, I believed that when I figured it out, I would finally be a woman. I know that sounds stupid, but if you had been there when my mom told me the story for the first time, you'd understand.

There weren't many wonderful, powerful moments between us, but the telling of that tale was something I treasured. I would ask her to tell me the secret. What did it really mean? And her reply, each and every time, was, "If I told you, it couldn't work its magic."

At coffee on Tuesday morning, I told it to Piper.

"That's really sad," she said. "Now, tell me about your date with Ben."

I was very ready and willing to tell her all about my date, and I had no doubt that her eagerness to hear all of the details was the only reason she'd insisted on early morning, pre-work coffee rather than lunch at a more humane hour, but I couldn't shake the nagging feeling that I was supposed to be learning something from the story, and I'd hoped she could help me. It was time for something to click.

"What do you think the moral of that story is, Piper? Seriously. I want to know."

She sighed, clearly disgruntled by my postponement of relaying the juicy details. "Oh, sheesh. I don't know! That your mother tells really depressing stories?"

I crossed my arms and continued to stare at her.

"Okay, let me think. I guess it's probably that sometimes we should sing through our problems?" She laughed, and I couldn't help but laugh with her. "Or no, I've got it. Other people decide what we are capable of when they . . . shouldn't? I don't know, Sarah!"

"That makes some sense, actually, but don't you think that's too easy? I mean, I had that much figured out by the time I was seven."

Just then my phone rang. I grabbed it from its position on the table and silenced it, with an apology to Piper before setting it back on the table, facedown.

"Aren't you going to answer that?" she asked eagerly.

"No, it's okay." I shrugged. "I thought I had it on vibrate—"

"But what if it's Ben?"

She really was very anxious to hear the latest on Ben, like an old lady at the hair salon sitting under the dryer for too long so she didn't miss any of the local gossip. Apparently the only thing that could make the information worth waiting for was the potential for more information.

"It's probably not Ben." I laughed, looking at my watch to remind myself of how ridiculously early it was.

"But it could be," she proclaimed as she grabbed my phone and hit the answer button as she handed it to me.

I stepped away with a laugh and a roll of my eyes. "Hello?"

"Morning, kid."

"Hi, Joe. What's up?" I sighed into my cell. I

hadn't expected it to be Ben, but I couldn't help but be disappointed that it wasn't.

"Dane is Ralph's son. Why didn't you tell me that Ralph and Meggie had a son together, Sarah?"

"What in the world are you . . . Oh." I smiled. "You finished *The Thorn Birds*, I take it?"

"Why didn't she tell him sooner? But at the same time, how stupid was Ralph that he never figured it out? How many times did people have to comment on the resemblance between them? Come on, man. Use your brain."

"Did you need something, Joe?"

"Oh yeah." He cleared his throat. "I think you should write your Christian romance."

I did a double take to the phone. "What? Are you serious?"

"Yep. Go for it. I've been giving it a lot of thought, and I really think that if you can crank it out pretty quickly, the publishers will be gung ho about anything you write. I'll find a way to convince them it's a brilliant move. You'll probably have to do tons of interviews about all your new salvation stuff when the time comes, so that readers understand what in the world is going on, but hey . . . all press is good press, I figure."

"Joe, you're the best! Seriously the best! I'm sorry about all of those horrible things I said about you."

He was silent for a moment. "What horrible things? I don't remember you ever saying any horrible things."

I smiled. "Well, no, I didn't say them to you, obviously."

"Hardy har har," he said, trying not to sound amused. "Now listen, kid. I've got some ground rules for you."

"Rules?"

"Well, not rules exactly. Just some guidelines. Some suggestions, you could say."

I didn't like where it was heading, but I also didn't think I could look a gift horse in the mouth at that particular moment.

"Okay, what are your suggestions?" I tightened my grip on the phone, very much unwilling to put up with any funny business, and I hoped that my voice conveyed that.

"Well, obviously, there's going to have to be some sex."

I was tempted to hang up on him, but I knew from past experience that he was relentless when it came to calling back. And that eventually just got annoying.

"Do we have to go through this again, Joe? It's a Christian romance. Let me clarify one more time: *Thorn Birds* is not a Christian romance. Please don't use that as your litmus test."

"Get 'em married then, Sarah. I mean, *Stollen Desire* could practically have been a Christian romance if Alex and Annie had been married, right?"

I couldn't help but laugh, and I laughed hard. "You're an idiotic man, Joe Welch, but you do entertain me. I'll give you that."

"Sarah, listen to me—"

"No, Joe. For once, you listen to me. Can you trust me that maybe, just maybe, I have my finger on the pulse of what women want to read more than you do? I mean, I did a pretty good job hitting the target last time, I would say. Can you just admit that I found a way to bring the innermost desires of women to the very public and, in retrospect, shameful forefront? I'm telling you, Joe. I can do it again. You have to trust me."

"So," he began skeptically, "the innermost desires of women involve less sex? You get them all in a frenzy, and then you want to return them to the monastery?"

I couldn't help but have such a warm affection for my clueless dork of an agent. "Monasteries are for monks, Joe. I think you mean convent."

"Ooh! There's a story for you! A woman mistakenly gets sent to a monastery, and she's there with all of those monks who . . . what? What vows have monks taken? Silence and celibacy, I would guess. Right?"

"Did you ever watch *Dr. Quinn, Medicine Woman*, Joe?"

He scoffed. "Please. I'm a little more masculine than that."

"Really, Father Ralph de Bricassart? You're going to go there, are you?"

He quietly cleared his throat once more. "You were saying?"

Dr. Quinn, Medicine Woman. Now that was when the entertainment industry knew how to market to women. The audience got to see nothing more than a few kisses, spread out over a couple of years, which somehow seemed borderline erotic. The eroticism stemmed from the built-up sexual tension, which was a direct result of the waiting. But the waiting wasn't preached to us. It was just a result of love and respect and a sense of propriety. And then, when the waiting finally came to an end on their wedding night . . . wow.

They were in the train, heading to their honeymoon, and Sully slowly, with excruciating deliberation, lowered each of the blinds on the windows—one by one. And then they shared a passionate kiss on the bed—still fully clothed— and the camera panned away, stopping on a lamp on the wall which was shaking from the motion of the train, matching the quivering action of wholesome women everywhere.

Fade to black. End of season.

"That was hot, Joe! Seriously." I had no idea if I was getting my point across or not, but he was being very quiet, which I knew from experience meant one of two things: he was listening and considering, or he had put me on hold, without telling me, to take another call.

I looked quickly over at Piper apologetically, though it was her fault I had taken the call, of course. Still, I felt bad that it was taking so long. She smiled and waved off my apology. I had no doubt that she still thought I was on the phone with Ben. I would hate to disappoint her when I returned to the table, but hopefully I could make up for it with news of the green light I had just received.

He exhaled, as frustrated with me as ever, but by virtue of the fact that he'd kept listening, I knew I had him. "You'll have that?" he asked, resigned to let me have my way. "Shaking lamps and a satisfying payoff for the reader?"

I silently mouthed an excited "Yes!" for no one's benefit but my own. "Oh, I'll have that, Joe. I'll have that in spades."

There was a brief pause before he said, "So apparently when you win an argument, you start talking like a 1920s gangster. Is that it?"

"Don't be such a bluenose, Joe. It's going to be a sockdolager. A real cat's meow, see."

"Just send me something as soon as you can," he said with a groan before hanging up.

I returned to the table, about to burst. "Guess what, guess what, guess what?" I trilled.

Piper looked about ready to burst herself. "Oh my goodness! Ben asked you to marry him!"

I stopped in my tracks and then started laughing. "There is so much wrong with that idea, Piper. We just met."

"I'm just saying, if you're going to keep me waiting this long, it better be something big . . ."

"You're the one who made me answer the call! Besides, if he proposed over the phone . . ." I didn't need to finish that sentence.

"Sarah, I was kidding!" She laughed. "So what then? Tell me, tell me!"

There was a moment of disappointment when she learned it wasn't even Ben on the phone at all, but as expected, she got over it pretty quickly when I told her my Christian romance idea had leapt over its first major hurdle. I was going to write it with or without Joe's blessing, of course, but knowing that I would retain my agent, and that Joe would have my back with the publishers, and that I could use my Raine de Bourgh notoriety for good instead of evil . . . that was pretty exciting. It was the open door that I felt God was preparing me for.

"Good call with Dr. Quinn." Piper nodded as she took a sip of her coffee. "I haven't thought about that show in years."

"Honestly, neither had I. It just came to me."

"Isn't it funny," she mused, "how we didn't need sex for that to be sexy? I mean, we never saw Jane Seymour's side boob—"

"And Joe Lando never so much as took off the traditional Native American wedding shirt Cloud Dancing had loaned to him! But there are lots of things like that. Think about your beloved Mr. Darcy." I smirked.

She raised her eyebrow and said nothing.

"We love men who are willing to wait for us and work for us. Mr. Darcy just went off and made himself a better person until Elizabeth was finally ready to love him."

"Ooh!" she exclaimed. "King Edward gave up the throne for Wallis Simpson. The more sacrifice the better, I say!"

We laughed and drank coffee, and I knew she was looking for a good opening to ask, once more, about Ben. I was grateful that she didn't ask right then. The segue was almost too obvious. Then again, maybe it wasn't to her, or anyone else. But it was to me. What would Ben have to sacrifice in order to be with me?

"I think there's a pretty decent chance he may be starting to fall in love with me, Piper."

"Ew, what?" She spit out a bit of coffee and then quickly grabbed a napkin to clean it up. "Isn't he kind of old?"

Oh good grief.

"Not Joe, you dork!" The segue had, in fact, only been obvious to me, it appeared. "Ben!"

"Ooh! Ben! Yes, that's much better." She

leaned in and spoke softly. "Did he tell you that already?"

Of course he hadn't, but I knew it wouldn't be long if the emotional intensity between us escalated as quickly as it had started. I'd had my embarrassing little slip about loving him, but mercifully we hadn't spoken of that since. I did sometimes wonder how those milestones would come along, since we'd already done so many things out of the traditional order during our short time together. I think, as schmaltzy as it sounds, "love at first sight" wasn't a far-off description from what we had felt. And we both knew it. So when would be the right time to say it?

"No, of course not. We're so new he hasn't even told me his birthday yet."

"Hope it's not today . . ."

"You know, that day Ben and I met . . . he felt something too." I blushed, no longer underwhelmed at all by his compulsion to walk down the hallway.

"Well, yes. That was made quite obvious by the little heart-shaped eye arrows he kept sending your way all through the service."

"No, I mean he felt that feeling of fate, or instinct, or whatever you want to call it."

My best friend was speechless for a moment, which I don't think I'd ever witnessed, apart from the one time I'd suggested we try drinking tea instead of coffee. She wanted to speak and ask questions, I could tell, but she just couldn't, so I answered the questions I knew were flowing through her mind.

"He told me he had no reason to be going that way down the hall right then, before the service when we bumped into each other. And"—I bit my lip, caught up once again in the magnitude of my attraction to Ben—"he said it was the same thing when he kissed me. He felt that he just . . . had to."

"So what can you possibly be afraid of? God doesn't trick us, Sarah. He doesn't set us up to fail."

"I guess." I sighed. And then my mind came to rest on the one thing I had tried not to think about, though of course it had found its way into every single thought I'd had for the last twelve hours or so. "You know Laura, the lady who took Maddie to lunch on Sunday?"

"Oh my gosh, you mean the one who looks like Rachel McAdams?"

For just a moment I tried to picture Rachel McAdams in order to make the comparison, but all I could see in my mind were scenes from *The Notebook*, and before too long, images of Rachel McAdams and Ryan Gosling making out in the rain gave way to images of Laura Bellamy and Ben Delaney.

I cleared my throat and tried to clear my mind of that Nicholas Sparks–infused torment. "Oh,

I don't know. I thought she looked more like Scarlett Johansson."

"Yes!" Piper exclaimed. "That's much better. She's pretty close to Rachel McAdams, but she's more voluptuous and sultry, like Scarlett."

Oh, that was helpful.

"Well, Ben very nearly got engaged to her back in college." I knew I was pouting, but I couldn't help it.

I knew that he'd thought he'd made it clear that "Miss Laura" and "the Bellamy girl" were one and the same. He was completely open with me, at least through his intent, so that wasn't what bothered me. What bothered me was that she was in his life at all. She was clearly not over him, she was clearly using Maddie to get closer to him, and it was clearly just a matter of time until they started making out in the rain.

But I knew Piper would set me straight and put it all in perspective for me. "I have nothing to worry about there, right?"

"I mean, realistically I don't think you need to be worried about Ben, but . . ." She spoke calmly, but her eyes betrayed her. "She flirted with him right in front of us. In church! It was bad enough, but knowing they were once that involved? Yeah. You should at least keep your eye on that situation, Sarah."

My eyed pooled with tears.

"Hey," Piper began as she scooted her chair

closer to me and wrapped her arms around me. "I just mean you need to watch her. Ben only has eyes for you. I promise you that. If I had to guess, I would say he is utterly oblivious to her flirting, and her perfume—which, I have to say, is probably the most exotic scent I've ever . . ." She trailed off as she looked over at my face, close to hers now, and caught my death stare. "Sorry."

"I just feel so out of my element. Why me? Why would God bless me with this man? And don't get me wrong. I mean, I am so glad it's me, but how can I possibly be the right woman for him? Considering everything in my past, and the fact that I'm a new Christian who barely knows Cain from Abel."

Piper laughed and, as was usually the case, I couldn't help but laugh with her. "That doesn't matter, Sarah. It really doesn't. Nothing says you have to memorize the Bible in order for your relationship to work out, or for your *life* to work out. Besides, Ben knows the Bible pretty well. At least I'd hope. I'd imagine he can help you learn all the Bible stories you'd ever want to know. Right?"

"Yale Divinity School." I smirked.

"Wow. Bible nerd."

I laughed. "That's what I said!"

"Okay. So he knows his stuff. Bible stories aside, let him know how you're feeling about some of these insecurities. And then pray through it together. That's really the only advice I have. This stuff doesn't happen every day, Sarah. God's not going to help you escape bondage and wander through the desert, only to abandon you as you search for the Promised Land."

I was still in Genesis in my Bible study, but I'd seen *The Ten Commandments*, so I was able to somewhat proficiently carry on with that conversation.

"But Moses didn't even get to go into the Promised Land, did he?"

Piper reached over and put her hand on mine. "No, he didn't. But that wasn't God's fault."

Well, no pressure there.

13.

Your Pot Holders Are No Good Here

"Go fish!" Maddie squealed with delight as I gave yet more evidence that I am the world's worst Go Fish player.

For an hour, through three games in a row, I had accused both the five-year-old repeat victor and her daddy of cheating, but we all knew that I was just really bad at the game. It doesn't seem like a game that you can really be good or bad at, does it? Alas, I was really bad. I tried so hard to pay attention and remember who was asking for which card, but almost without fail the card that I would be sure Maddie had just received from Ben was actually the card I had already asked for, and I would have to go fishing once more.

Her giggles made it a complete pleasure to lose, of course. And watching Ben's amazement, and the way he couldn't help but laugh each time the hilarity ensued, was nothing short of rapturous. It wasn't just his laughter—though I couldn't imagine ever getting enough of it. It was more the way he would look at me as I put all of my effort into keeping a straight face. His eyes said it all—like he'd been so sure that there would never again be such joy in his home.

It had been a month since sushi. Well, it had been a month since the first and second sushi. We'd had much sushi since then, but we considered that first sushi to be the real beginning. We'd managed to keep a very low profile, and there had been no fallout whatsoever to stem from the pastor dating Raine de Bourgh.

Yet.

I don't think many people knew that I *was* Raine de Bourgh, and I think even fewer people knew that we were dating, so that could be why, but I chose not to think of it that way for the sake of my own sanity. When they found out, it would be a catastrophe. When they found out, we'd have to go into hiding, like the von Trapp family. When they found out, Ben might decide I'm not worth the trouble.

No, I couldn't think about that. That was, however, my biggest fear. Actually, that's not true. That was my second biggest fear. My biggest fear was that he and I would fall too much in love with each other to walk away, even if that's what God wanted us to do. The very last thing I wanted was to come between Ben and God, but each time I let my worry overtake me on that subject, Piper insisted I wasn't giving either one of them enough credit. Touché.

Didn't it make sense that the only reason God had made Ben and me so undeniably certain that we were supposed to be together was because we would need that to hold on to when outside forces threatened to tear us apart? Something had to be on the horizon. However, even I, in all my fretful consternation, knew that I couldn't let all of that get to me. If I didn't find a way to control the anxiety, I knew that Ben and I would be history before you could say "Laura Bellamy."

In the weeks prior, I'd taken advantage of subtle opportunities to work Laura into the conversation and find out all I could, and what I discovered was mostly what I already knew. Ben considered her to be one of his closest friends, and he honestly and sincerely didn't recognize her attraction to him anymore. Actually, attraction isn't the right way to describe it. If a cheetah spent nearly twenty years hunting an antelope and had never given up the hunt even when it appeared a lion was going to swoop in and claim the antelope as its own, and it stood prepared to attack anything and everything that got between itself and its prey, would you say the cheetah was attracted to the antelope?

Apparently, Laura had never really come to terms with the end of her college relationship with Ben. Though it wasn't very Christian of me, I couldn't help but laugh a little whenever I thought of just how much more vexed she would have been if she'd known how close he had been to proposing to her. But it wouldn't have mattered, of course. Once Christa reentered his life, things never could have worked out with Laura—even if Laura *hadn't* kissed someone else. Ben was a one-woman man, and Christa quickly became that one woman.

Now I was that one woman. I knew that, and had complete faith in Ben's commitment to me. Unfortunately, I had just as much faith in Laura's tireless and persistent pursuit. She was good. I had to give her that. She had a way of making herself seem harmless, and she put forth the appearance of being nothing more than his oldest friend—someone with whom he shared so much history that they were really past the point of friendship. They were family.

Bull hockey.

She wanted him, and she would stop at nothing to get him.

"Applesauce, wake up!" Maddie giggled. "Give me all your threes."

I shook off thoughts of Laura, and everything else I considered a threat to my relationship with Ben, and looked down at my cards. Shoot. Not again.

"Aren't you supposed to ask?" I teased her. "You don't know that I have any threes, so you're supposed to say, 'Do you have any threes?' and then I can politely confirm or deny. This is, after all, a game of manners, Madeline."

Maddie looked at Ben and rolled her eyes

before looking back at me. He sat back in his chair, crossed his arms, and winked at me, prepared to enjoy the show Maddie and I were about to put on, as she beat me once again.

"But you do have threes. Doesn't she, Daddy?"

Just then the phone rang and Ben stood to go answer it, but not before saying, "Yep. She does. And two Jacks. And a nine, I think."

I laughed. He'd nailed it, and I was once again left to wonder how any self-respecting, successful adult could be as bad at Go Fish as I was.

"Traitor! Is anyone on my side?"

"No," Maddie said. "Now give me your threes." I cocked my eyebrow at her, which made her giggle as she said, "May I please have your threes, Applesauce?"

"Well, that's not a bad thing, is it, Tom?" Ben was saying on the phone, across the kitchen counter from us.

I looked over at him in order to perform a mental wellness check. In the past month I had witnessed some of the constant demands on a pastor leading a growing church. Ben had associate pastors under him, so he certainly didn't handle every call and every crisis, but he handled many of them. At any hour, day or night, he might receive a call that a church member was sick, or had died, or was in need of prayer.

He glanced up and saw me looking at him, so

he smiled a smile that let me know everything was okay. I smiled back at him and then turned my attention back to Maddie.

"Here you go, ma'am," I said, politely handing Maddie one three.

She took it and then stuck her little hand out again. "Both of them."

I pretended to be put out as I handed her the second three. I looked over at Ben, wanting to see his reaction as her giggles began once more, but he had turned his back to us. I could hear only emphatic whispers, and it was very obvious he was trying not to be heard.

Don't be paranoid, Sarah, I told myself. *It's probably just something Maddie shouldn't hear.* I told myself that but, as always, there was a little bit of fear that the moment when the other shoe would drop was quickly approaching.

A couple of minutes later, Ben forcefully hung up the phone. He didn't quite slam it down, but there was an unmistakable gravitas to it all. I turned back around, prepared to be a sounding board as he processed whatever bad or frustrating news he had just received, but all I saw was his bedroom door as it slammed.

I looked back to Maddie with a playful "Yikes!" expression. She didn't look fazed at all, and it suddenly dawned on me that there had probably been many times when the little girl had been her daddy's only sounding board.

"Should I go talk to him?" I leaned in and whispered, legitimately asking her advice.

"Probably not," she said, shaking her head as she put the cards away. "He comes out eventually."

An hour later, Maddie and I were on the couch, watching television. Well, I was watching television and she was asleep with her head on my lap. I was starting to get the impression Ben was never going to be ready to talk. I'd thought about leaving, but that didn't seem like the right thing to do. Having said that, it occurred to me that when Maddie was put to bed, he and I would potentially be alone together, and that didn't really seem like the right thing to do either. I decided I was safest right where I was.

At some point I dozed off too, I suppose. I was awakened by Ben's hand on my shoulder. Maddie was no longer on the couch with me, and the television was turned off. I took a quick look at the clock and saw that it was 10:00.

"Oh, sheesh. Sorry," I said, rubbing my eyes.

"Don't be," he said softly, sitting down beside me on the couch.

He looked tired. And worried. I knew I needed to get out of there before anyone saw my car parked in front of his house at that time of night, but something in the way his shoulders were sagging told me I couldn't go. Not yet.

"Everything okay?" I asked.

He took a deep breath. "That was Tom Isaacs on the phone earlier."

It had begun. I don't know how I knew, but I knew. I knew before he told me who'd been on the phone, and I probably knew even before he'd completed the phone call. I didn't say anything, I just held my breath and let him go at his own pace. And I prayed that it wasn't the end.

"Apparently Mercy Point's offering funds grew by leaps and bounds this week."

Okay. I was pretty sure that was my doing, though I certainly hadn't thought about how noticeable it would be. I allowed myself to breathe, not understanding what was causing Ben so much distress but feeling confident I hadn't done anything wrong.

"Of course they did." I smiled. "You preached on tithing. You woke some people up."

"Including you?" He turned to face me, and I was so saddened to see that all of the Go Fish joy had been wiped away, and I still didn't understand why.

"Well, yes," I said. "That was the first sermon I'd ever heard on tithing. And I've been reading the book of Numbers. Well, okay, I've been trying to read Numbers. I hope this isn't a sin, but I have to say, it's not the most interesting book of the Bible, is it?"

"Stop making light of everything, Sarah!" he

said, standing from the couch and walking to the picture window and looking outside, arms crossed. "Nothing about this is cute or funny. Absolutely nothing."

I was startled and I was hurt. And I could very plainly sense that I had in fact done something wrong. Or at least he thought I had. I still couldn't imagine what it was, but I felt my confidence shatter around me. I'd been so careful. How had I messed up and not even realized it?

"Ben," I said shakily, "I don't understand—"

"What'd you do?" He turned around and faced me again, but his arms were still crossed and he kept his distance. "Did you try to make up for years of not tithing? I mean, how could you not think about how much a check like that would stick out?"

I'd paid so much attention to Ben's tithing sermon, as I did all of his teaching. It wasn't about the money, it was about the faith. Right? God wanted us to give our first and our best to show that we trusted him to provide for us. Isn't that what he'd said? I had prayed as I wrote that check, and I had felt so good about giving my first and best. How had I managed to screw that up?

"Forgive me, Reverend," I sneered, having no doubt he would accurately decipher the disdain in my tone, "but I guess I wasn't thinking about what anyone would think. Why should I? I gave 10 percent, which the Bible presents as a guideline, and which my pastor also presented as a guideline. I prayed about it, and I gave. What concern is it of yours, or Tom Isaacs, or anyone else?"

"You're right. Of course you're right." The expression on his face made it difficult for me to believe he actually thought I was right. "But when you and I are trying not to ruffle feathers and trying to keep our relationship kind of inconspicuous, you had to have realized that there was no way of doing that if you were to write a check for 10 percent of your entire net worth! Retro-tithing really isn't a thing."

I was already so confused, and he wasn't helping. "What are you talking about? I just tithed my income. I didn't 'retro-tithe,' Ben!" I did air quotes as I said that in an attempt to demonstrate how ridiculous he was being.

His arms dropped, and he laughed an erratic laugh. "Good grief, Sarah! How much money do you make?"

If he'd asked at any other point in the month prior, I wouldn't have hesitated at all before telling him. For one thing, I was the author of some of the top-selling books of the past year or so, and my financial status was easy enough to find online or in *Forbes*. But more than that, we were still fervent believers in Rule #7. But at that moment, I wasn't too keen on the idea of giving him the satisfaction of getting an answer to anything he wanted to know.

"A lot," I said with a sniff.

"Well, yeah. I know that."

I didn't like his tone, and I really didn't like his attitude, but as the seconds passed and he kept staring at me, I also didn't like the idea of keeping anything from him.

"Okay, keep in mind that I've already been paid a whole bunch of money for a book I haven't even started writing yet. It's not like I make this much all the time or anything, so—"

"How much, Sarah?"

I sighed. "I've made about four and a half million."

He kept staring, mouth wide open. "Dollars?"

I looked at him and rolled my eyes. "No, pot holders. In my crochet class. Yes, dollars!"

I stood up and took a quick peek in the mirror and was horrified, but not surprised, to discover I'd been carrying on this conversation with mascara under my eyes, drool dried on my cheek, and the hair of a rooster before its morning coffee. Great. I walked to the door to grab my shoes and begged my eyes not to release the threatening tears.

"Where are you going?" he asked gently.

I knew I couldn't talk without crying, so I just muttered nonsense that sounded like *harumph, grunt, groan, growl* and pointed to the door. I got my shoes on and located my things and realized how unfortunate it was that I had chosen that day to break out my new Prada handbag.

I stormed to the door, hoping to make a dramatic exit, but he grabbed my hand as I passed. "Sarah, we can't storm out on each other."

Why not? Patrick had always stormed out on me when he was angry, or didn't want to deal with something, or just wanted to make it look like something was my fault. It felt like my turn to finally get to be the one to storm out. I had done nothing wrong, and yet I felt persecuted. Yes, persecuted!

"Why are you persecuting me?" I shouted passionately.

To his credit, he tried not to laugh. I saw him try. But he just couldn't help it. "Am I persecuting you? I didn't mean to."

For the first time ever, I didn't find his laughter sexy in the least. "Yes, actually, I think you are persecuting me. I make a lot of money. So what? And I wrote a tithe check to my church, and I still believe that was the right thing to do. What, is there some conflict of interest thing or something? Do you work on commission?"

He smiled and sat down on the arm of the couch. "No. I don't work on commission."

"Then I really can't see why my tithe, which really should just be between God and me, is of concern to anyone else. If I'm wrong about that, you're going to have to explain it to me." I lost the battle with my tears. "Because I just really don't understand."

He exhaled as he stood and pulled me to him. He held me and let me cry for a couple of minutes until we both knew I no longer wanted to storm out on him. Something in my mind had shifted, and all I could think about was how good he felt and smelled. And how disappointed I was in myself that I seemed to care less about standing up for my principles than I did his dedication to going to the gym every day. I still didn't understand what the problem was, but all of a sudden, I also didn't care. There was just enough rational thinking making its way through the fog that I knew I should pull away. I needed to go, or at least place some distance between us, but his breath in my hair and his hands on my back made it impossible.

We still hadn't kissed—not since the coffee house about a month ago—and I didn't know if I could stand to wait any longer. I knew that alone in his house, long after Maddie had gone to sleep, and very long after I should have gone home, was not the right time. And yet, in that moment, it felt like the perfect time.

Any little bit of resolve that I had to resist the power he had over me was lost when I heard how shallow his breathing had become, and I could have no doubt that he was facing the same internal struggle I was.

"Ben?" I whispered.

"What do you want me to do, Sarah?" he said quietly, with pleading in his voice. I was about to tell him that I wanted him to kiss me, but he wasn't through talking. "You're going to have to tell me what you want me to do, and I'll do it. If you want me to step away, I will. But it will be because that's what you want. I'm not feeling strong enough to want anything but you right now." He took a deep breath. "What do you want me to do?"

The power of the moment absorbed me. I never would have imagined that there could be something more powerful than the desire I felt for Ben in that moment, but the desire to not tarnish the love God was building between us was overpowering. It wasn't about a kiss, or even an evening of kisses. If I'd thought we'd have any chance of not letting our passion go any further than our lips, I would have begged him to kiss me and never stop. But it wouldn't have stopped there. I knew it, and he knew it. And he was asking me to be his strength.

I bit my lip and then mouthed a silent prayer of thanks and for assistance. "I want you . . ." It would have been so easy to stop there. "I want you to let me go home."

I felt every muscle in his body relax, and then

there was a shiver, just before he let go of me. "Thank you," he whispered, though I don't think it was really directed toward me.

I had to fight against every instinct I was feeling—to hug him, grab his hand, sit down and talk for hours—and just walk toward the door. "I'll call you tomorrow."

I opened the door after turning on the porch light and took one step out, but I stopped when he said, "They don't want your money, Sarah."

I couldn't turn and face him. I knew it wasn't coming from him, and I knew what a difficult position I had put him in. It all suddenly made sense. And it didn't matter that the money I had tithed was actually the advance on a book I intended to use for the Lord, because let's face it—the amount of the advance was a result of what had already been written, not what was to come. And it didn't matter that as of Sunday morning, I'd felt as welcome at Mercy Point as anyone else. It didn't even matter that I'd never even been given cause to suspect that anyone at Mercy Point, apart from Ben and Piper, even knew me as anyone other than Sarah Hollenbeck.

Someone had found out—probably *because* I had written that check. And now it was dirty money. They—whoever they were—didn't think the Lord would want them to accept money that had been earned the way I had earned it. Would they accept money made from gambling or prostitution? What about drug money? I don't know. But one thing was very clear. It wasn't okay for the pastor's girlfriend to tithe the royalties from her provocative books. As I'd suspected hours ago, the other shoe had dropped, and the fallout had in fact begun.

"Hey." I smiled, my back still turned, too humiliated to face him. "That's good. That check probably would have bounced anyway." I couldn't even come up with a good joke to defuse the tension.

Instantly he was behind me with his arms wrapped around me and his lips by my ear. "I'm so sorry. I didn't know what to say—to Tom or to you—and I'm just so furious. I don't know what God wants me to do, and I don't know if I'll be strong enough to do it. I don't want to face those people again. Not because I'm embarrassed or ashamed, because I'm not. And I am so proud of you and where you are now, and that just makes me even more disgusted with them. You're living by faith, and following God's path, and searching for his will for your life while they're just busy judging you. And I'm so sorry that I can't just walk away from Mercy Point, but God's telling me to stay. And, I'll be honest, I'm not real happy with him about that right now." He took a breath but kept holding on to me. "Please tell me you're still going to be by my side. Please."

The floodgates opened and I turned around and

wrapped my arms around his neck and cried into his shoulder.

"We're done with low-key. Do you understand me?" he whispered. "I am not ashamed of you, and I refuse to act like I am, or in any way give the impression that I am. To them or to you. There are bigger things in our lives than trying to please everybody. Some people are just Pharisees, Sarah. That's all there is to it. They can think what they want to think, and they can fire me if they want." He pulled away enough to look at me and smile. "Besides, I think you could support us for a while if necessary."

I laughed a very unsexy laugh through my tears, which made him laugh too. He released me just long enough to step back inside and grab a tissue from the kitchen counter, then he wiped away my tears.

"I love you," he told me for the very first time as he finished the job, and then he kissed the top of my head. "I love you like crazy, and Maddie loves you like crazy. Even if you are shockingly bad at Go Fish." He smiled at me as I laughed. "And I'm sorry that some people at Mercy Point are apparently set on not loving you, but I assure you, it's their loss. And someday they'll realize that."

Suddenly I really didn't care if the Pharisees of Mercy Point ever loved me or not.

14.

Seven Minutes at 350 Degrees

There are certain words that feel to your soul like that first shower after you've been in the woods camping for four days. That's how I felt about Ben's declaration of love.

I had been so worried about that—even more than I had realized. Like I already said, I knew he was falling in love with me fast, but when would the timing be right to say it out loud? I didn't want him to feel pressured to say it or feel any uncomfortable expectations from me about those words.

But Ben's "I love you" was perfect. Just perfect.

In my opinion, just as exciting and fear-inducing as the words "I love you" are the words "I want you to meet my mother." Or, worse yet, "My mother wants to meet you." At least with "I want you to meet my mother" there is a feeling that your guy is proud of you and your relationship, and he's serious enough about you to take you home to meet the first woman he loved. "My mother wants to meet you," on the other hand, is a mixed bag of Oedipal chaos. He's been talking to her about you—that's the first thing you know. But after that? You know nothing. Maybe it's his low-pressure way of saying he really cares about you and can't wait to take that next step with you. Then again, it could mean he's not really sure about your relationship at all, and he wants to get his mommy's two cents to see if he should even continue on with you.

Thankfully, Ben told me, "I want you to meet my mother." And then he tagged on with a smile, "And my dad. But there's a very good chance he'll just watch football the whole time. Don't take it personally."

I hadn't had to deal with meeting mothers all that often. The last time I'd met the mother of a boyfriend, I was a teenager being introduced to my future mother-in-law, Lucy McDermott, at the senior awards banquet. Lucy was fine. I didn't even have to call her Mrs. McDermott. We were never close, but looking back, I do think there was always a sort of solidarity or sisterhood between us. We'd both had the grave misfortune of falling for McDermott men, and though she loved her husband and practically deified her son, I think she understood better than anyone the burden of being a McDermott wife.

I was dreading meeting Ben's mom. Absolutely dreading it. I was confident about our relationship, and I knew that her two cents, or any other amount of intrusion, wouldn't shake his love for me. But considering who I was to much of the outside world, I felt as if there was some additional stress piled on top of the already scary meeting of my boyfriend's mother. At the very least, I worried it might not be pleasant.

Of course, it didn't exactly help my anxiety subside to learn from Ben that Joanna Delaney viewed Laura Bellamy as the daughter she'd never had. She'd wanted Ben to marry Laura, of course, but she did love Christa as well. Christa was no Laura, but she was the next best thing in Joanna's mind.

I felt no doubt that I wouldn't make it into the top ten.

After Ben and Laura broke up, and once she finally accepted the fact that they would not be getting back together, Joanna tried to get her other sons to succumb to Laura's limitless charms. Laura and Jeremy, the oldest, went out a few times, but her resistance to give up on Ben stood in the way. As did her unplanned pregnancy, which Jeremy had nothing to do with.

That would do it, wouldn't it?

Ben seemed hesitant to tell me about that, but that really didn't alarm me. His friendship with Laura worried me, but his reluctance to tell me about the scandal that surrounded her daughter Kaitlyn's conception and birth was, I was certain, just a means of protecting his friend. He was not only her ex-boyfriend and her long-time chum, after all. He was also her pastor. I could respect that.

But that didn't mean I liked it.

"Obviously you don't have to tell me anything that you're not supposed to tell me. Because of pastor/sinner confidentiality or whatever." I grinned as he rolled his eyes with a laugh. "But you can honestly say that if I needed to know something about your history with Laura that I don't already know, you would tell me, right?"

Joanna had invited us over for dinner. It was the first Saturday evening after the tithe call, and therefore it was the last evening before Ben and I would have to walk into Mercy Point, prepared to face a throng of faces that we no longer felt confident belonged to friends. We didn't know who was out to get us—apart from Tom and Lenore Isaacs—and who wasn't, so we'd been trying to brace ourselves for whatever came.

"Of course," he said as he pulled onto the street on which he'd grown up.

"Of course, like 'there's nothing to tell but if there was I'd tell you'? Or of course, as in 'there's nothing you need to know, and I'm better off keeping it all hidden'?"

"Of course, as in 'you're a crazy lady who scares me just a little bit sometimes.'" He laughed.

It was good to see him laugh. The past week,

since the Monday evening phone call, had been a tough one. He'd spent a lot of time in prayer, as had I, though I knew we were praying for different things. He wanted to leave Mercy Point. I think he'd known that was his preference from the moment he hung up the phone and stormed into his bedroom. He'd spent the hours until he'd come out and found me asleep on the couch praying that God would just let him know it was time to move on. But God had other plans, apparently.

Ben wasn't afraid of a fight. That much I knew. He welcomed the fight, but he feared he wouldn't be able to adequately minister to his congregation while he was embroiled in a moral war with them, and that was certainly a valid concern. But he couldn't back down. He couldn't allow anyone's closed-minded, judgmental attitudes to dictate the terms of our relationship or my relationship with God. Ben and I were fully aware of who the judge in our lives was, and it certainly wasn't Tom Isaacs.

So while he prayed for a peaceful, but satisfactory, way out of the fight, I just prayed for him.

I wasn't thrilled with the idea of meeting his mother the Saturday evening before our first Sunday back after the offending phone call, but I was hoping that maybe before the end of the evening we would have another ally at Mercy

Point. Of course, hoping and having any actual optimism that something will occur are different things entirely. I'd been at Mercy Point for about a month and a half, and Joanna had been there since the Nixon administration, I believe. And yet we'd never met. Piper and I sat in the same row each week, just one section over and two rows behind where Joanna sat with Laura—except for the Sundays when Laura was in children's church convincing Maddie she should be her new mommy—and yet I could never even catch Joanna's eye. Catching Laura's eye, however, was much easier. All I had to do was breathe near Ben.

I expressed my concerns about Joanna ignoring me to Ben as we approached his parents' house, but he was quick to assure me that was no reason to assume his mother didn't approve of me.

"She ignores me at church too," he stated matter-of-factly.

I was certain he was just trying to make me feel better, but then I thought about it. Ben was almost always by my side at church, or at least within eyeshot. And I'd never seen him talking with Joanna.

"Well," I scoffed. "She ignores you because you're with me."

He chuckled. "No. She ignores me because she doesn't want the rest of the congregation to think that she pulled some strings to get her son hired as the pastor."

"But you grew up there, right? Don't most people know she's your mother?"

"Oh, absolutely. But I think she figures if she just appears indifferent to it all and doesn't draw attention to it, no one will undermine my position. Of course I've never understood what strings she thinks she has access to, but I'm not going to tell her that. It's better to let her think she has strings she doesn't have than to have her shout, 'That's my Benji!' every time I step up to the pulpit, like she used to when I stepped up to bat playing ball in high school."

I laughed and relaxed, feeling more confident that I wasn't dealing with Joanna already disapproving of me, after all. I was just dealing with a quirky mother. I knew a thing or two about quirky mothers. That I could handle.

"Hmm, wonder why *she's* here . . ." Ben muttered as we pulled into the driveway.

I glanced up just in time to see Laura getting out of her car, carrying a casserole dish. She smiled too happily and waved too enthusiastically when she saw us.

And I—too successfully—fought the temptation to grab the wheel from Ben, throw the transmission into reverse, and squeal away like we were being chased by the bad guys in an action film.

"I thought she was watching Maddie," I said with a pout, and then I quickly realized I was pouting and summoned the strength of every muscle in my face to try and act like I didn't want to cross my arms and go to the corner, stomping my feet and throwing a temper tantrum each time I saw my boyfriend's gorgeous ex.

"Well, no. Kaitlyn is, technically. She said Laura wouldn't be home tonight, but she didn't mention she'd be here. Oh well," he said as he put the car in park, and he meant it. Oh well. He didn't even think twice about it.

I loved him, but he was an oblivious man.

"I'm not really sure this is a good idea."

He took off his seat belt and then reached for and grabbed my hand. "Oh, come on. She's going to love you."

"Who is? Your mother or Laura?"

He smiled a small smile. "Well, both! But I meant my mother. I'm not even thinking about Laura."

Don't get me wrong: I was comforted knowing that was true. I believed him completely. But I knew that Laura's presence meant I'd just lost all of Joanna's attention from the get-go, and that seemed like an unfair curveball when trying to make a good first impression.

Ben reached for the door handle, ready to step out, but I grabbed him just before he could open it. I worried I didn't have time to make him understand. Laura was standing at the door to the house waiting for us, watching every move.

"Hey, before we go in, I just want you to understand where I'm coming from here. I know that you couldn't care less about Laura as anything other than a friend, and I know that you love me. But I also know that your mother could register the two of you at Tiffany's and it wouldn't faze you, because you really don't *see* it. But I see it. The odds were stacked against me with your mother to begin with anyway because I'm not Christa—but Christa's not here, and suddenly Laura is. Do you understand what I'm saying?"

Laura, apparently, had gotten tired of waiting at the door for us, but instead of going inside as I *really* wished she had done, she started walking toward us.

"Sarah, you have nothing to worry about."

"I know that. I'm not worried. It's just that—"

"Look, I am just so excited to finally introduce you and show you off a little." He looked up and waved to Laura and smiled at her oh-so-adorable, sexy pouty-lipped impatience, and then held up his finger to indicate we would be just a second. "But if you're uncomfortable—"

"I am uncomfortable. Yes. Very uncomfortable. But I'm not asking to leave or anything. I guess I just want you to realize *why* I'm so—"

"Come on, you two!" Laura opened Ben's door

from the outside. "My deviled eggs are going to get warm!"

"You brought deviled eggs? You know that's not fair." He got out of the car, and with a sigh I decided I should too. "Sarah, Laura's deviled eggs are to die for. She puts some secret ingredient in . . ."

"I'll never tell!" Laura laughed, and then she flipped her hair over her shoulder and turned around to head into the house.

Ben stopped and glanced at me with a smile on his face and then put his hand out for mine, and I was completely thrown off guard by the expression on his face. It was a sweet mixture of innocence and ignorance. I smiled at him, my trepidation subsiding as I reminded myself that this was not like any other relationship. I could march into the Delaney home with the full confidence and backing of the man I loved.

Laura Bellamy and her rapturous deviled eggs didn't deserve any further consideration.

"As long as I have that secret in the palm of my hand," Laura said with a smile, "I figure I'll have Ben there as well." With that, she threw open the door and walked in without knocking. "Joanna, we're here!" she trilled.

Why? Why did she have to say something like that just when I had rallied enough poise to pretend I was okay? I couldn't help but notice the practiced sway of her hips as they sashayed into a home that I was about to enter for the first time, but which she seemed to consider her own. And then there was that southern belle lilt to her voice. She was from Chicago, just like the rest of us, but her voice evoked thoughts of drinking sweet tea while you sat on the porch swing, fanning yourself and watching fireflies. Worst of all, there was the way she looked at Ben. The more I observed her, the more I realized she didn't even have the decency to look at him as something she hoped to attain. It was so much worse than that. She looked at him as something she already possessed.

"Ready?" Ben smiled at me one more time, ready to usher me into the great unknown.

"Not just yet," I whispered to him, there in the open door of his parents' house, and then I locked my fingers in his hair and pulled him to me.

He didn't resist, not that I gave him an opportunity. I hadn't set out to manipulate—but I'm only human. I suspected Laura was going to do all she could to steal Ben's attention away from me that evening—what with her hips and her deviled eggs and that raspy ScarJo laugh. I just wanted to make sure he remembered who he loved.

There was a brief moment of shock, that's for sure, but within seconds his lips and mine were entangled in a passionate dance a month and a half in the making. I guess he threw down the bag of dinner rolls we had brought? I don't really know—I just know that all of a sudden his hands were on my waist, pulling me even closer.

I'd never experienced anything like it. In all honesty, I don't think even Alex and Annie had ever experienced anything like it. To be simultaneously so attracted to someone and so respectful of them—I'd never imagined a kiss could be so all-encompassing. I lost all sense of time and space and location.

Especially location.

"Ahem." Ben's dad, Nate, subtly cleared his throat as he bent down and picked up the dinner rolls from the porch. "I'll take these in to your mother." He turned around and walked back in the house, shutting the door behind him.

I was momentarily mortified as I struggled to catch my breath and make sure no one else was watching. Ben blushed and laughed an embarrassed laugh as he called out, "Thanks, Dad."

"Oh my gosh," I muttered into my hands as I buried my face in them. "Ben, I'm so sorry."

"Don't be." He pulled my hands from my face and intertwined our fingers as he lowered them to either side of my body, and then released them as he wrapped his arms around my waist. "I'm not."

"Oh, really?" I responded through my nervous laughter.

"Well, I mean I didn't *love* the part when my dad caught us, but I thought the rest of it was pretty great, actually."

While I nervously glanced around, surveying the neighborhood—specifically the Delaneys' door—he never took his eyes off of me. Ben's body was still molded against mine as he kissed me softly and gently on the lips, over and over. He was relentless, and only when I finally stopped caring if anyone was watching did he say, with a giant grin on his face, "I suppose we should probably head in there now. Don't you think?"

I laughed, still trying to catch my breath. "Honestly?"

The grin faded just a bit, but not in an unhappy way. "Yeah," he breathed. "Honestly."

"Honestly, I'd love to take a rain check on dinner with your family at this point, but I guess that's probably not a good idea." And it *definitely* wouldn't have been a good idea to kiss Ben again right then, no matter how much I wanted to. No matter how much my lips were already missing his . . . I cleared my throat and forced myself to focus less on the gorgeous man with his arms around me and more on the gorgeous man's parents and ex-girlfriend, just on the other side of the door. "And our dinner rolls are already in there, so . . ."

"I guess we did kind of throw away our best

shot at a subtle departure. Or a subtle entrance, for that matter."

He dropped his arms from my waist and found my hands again. He kissed my lips one more time—so gently—and then held one of my hands tightly as he reached for the doorknob with his other hand. I took a deep breath, feeling more confident than ever in my love for Ben, and his for me. Nothing was more important than that— not a Southern-belle-by-way-of-Chicago who had her sights set on the man I loved, and not a mother who had always preferred "the Bellamy girl." Not even being caught kissing on the front porch like a couple of teenagers. With Ben by my side, I could face it all.

So why weren't we moving?

I looked down at his hand still resting on the knob. "Is it locked, or—"

"What are we waiting on, Sarah?" he asked quietly, not looking at me.

"I was waiting for you." I shrugged. "I'm ready, so . . ."

"No, I mean . . ." he began as he turned to face me once again, but once our eyes met, it was as if he lost the ability to speak. At least I think that's why he stopped talking. I was busy losing the ability to breathe.

His eyes were full of love and unspoken words.

He was about to kiss me again—he wanted to as much as I wanted him to—but I stopped him. I shifted uncomfortably, convinced that everything he said—with his words and his eyes—referred to the sparks and intensity we were both feeling.

"We've got to do this right, Ben. We've got to." I was so uncomfortable with sex talk that I thought I might just pass out from embarrassment if I had to say too much. And yes, I know that must sound ridiculous. But Alex and Annie's sex life is entirely different from mine, and Patrick and I had certainly never communicated openly—about sex or anything else. But I knew I could say anything to Ben and never be judged or laughed at. "I want to make love to you—so much," I whispered as he lifted his hands to my face and gently caressed my blushing cheeks. "That—what just happened—that was the most unbelievably sexy, fantastic, perfect thing I have ever experienced. And knowing that is just a small, tiny, minuscule glimpse of what's to come . . . that's paralyzing to think about, Ben. I don't want us to set ourselves up to regret even one moment of it. I want us to be able to look back on it for the rest of our lives as the most erotic, but also somehow the most pure, experience of our lives."

He took a deep breath. "Okay, well, I have to be honest. That didn't help get the heart rate back to normal." He smiled and I blushed again. "But, surprisingly, that wasn't what I meant. I mean, why am I wasting a single moment just dating you, acting like we're just going to see where it goes, when all I want is to start looking toward forever with you? We both know that we want to spend the rest of our lives together. We may still have lots to figure out in life, but we know where this is headed, Sarah. God's made it perfectly clear, I think. I'm so in love with you I can't see straight. I can't imagine any aspect of my life without you in it, and I don't want to. Ever. So what are we waiting on?"

My mind was telling me to slow things down. It was telling me that it might not be the best idea to have such a serious conversation on the front porch of his parents' house with Laura and her secret-ingredient deviled eggs inside. And it was telling me that the dinner rolls we brought only needed to be warmed at 350 degrees for seven minutes, so we didn't have much time left. But the world was swirling around me, and everything was Ben. I knew what he was saying and I tried to argue with him, at least in my head. I tried to plan out a valid argument, but nothing was sticking. Of course it seemed too soon to talk about forever, but why? It was too soon according to common practices and what others would think was acceptable. And you could say we still didn't know each other well enough yet, but I didn't care about that one. Also his mother wouldn't approve, but he didn't seem to care about that. But then I finally landed on an argument that I thought could stick.

"Ben, I love you. You know that," I stated matter-of-factly.

He smiled another resistance-melting smile. "Do I? Or, do you, I guess I should say?"

After saying it so prematurely, I'd been very careful not to let it slip again. As a result, I guess I'd been holding on to it a little too tightly. "I do. So freaking much!" I shouted through ecstatic giggles.

He laughed and picked me up and swung me around and kissed me and then said, with his lips two inches from mine, "Marry me, Sarah."

Oh boy, he was difficult to resist, not that I wanted to resist anyway. I prepared to throw my one argument out there, knowing I should say it just in case it was credible.

"What if we're rushing into marriage just because we desperately want to have sex?" Apparently I wasn't as self-conscious as I had been a few short minutes prior.

His eyes locked with mine, and the pleased and mischievous expression on his face told me he was confident he was about to win against my weak, halfhearted argument.

"First Corinthians 7:8–9: 'Now to the unmarried and the widows I say: It is good for them to stay unmarried, as I do. But if they cannot control themselves, they should marry, for it is better to marry than to burn with passion.'"

Joy filled every part of me. I knew he didn't want to marry me because he was burning with passion, but it was nice to know he was feeling that way just the same.

"Bible nerd." I smiled.

He returned my smile, and then he grabbed my left hand, which wouldn't be deprived much longer, and got down on one knee. My smile widened and the tears fell. And then the door opened.

"Hey, Ben, I really think you should get in here. Your mother—" His dad cleared his throat awkwardly, with none of the composure he had surprisingly possessed during his last interruption. "Oh shoot. Sorry, son."

I couldn't help but giggle as Ben winked at me and then called out behind him, over his shoulder, "Yeah, thanks, Dad. Maybe give us just another minute?"

"Of course. Sure thing. Sure thing," he said, but he didn't move.

I couldn't stop giggling as I faced my future father-in-law, whom I'd still technically not met.

"Is he still there?" Ben whispered through clenched teeth.

I nodded, touched by the devotion and love in his dad's eyes.

"Umm, Dad—"

I looked down at Ben, kneeling before me, and placed my hand on his cheek and winked before looking back at Nate. Ben wasn't seeing what I was seeing, and from what he'd told me about life growing up with Nate as his loving but stoic father, it was possible he'd never seen what I was seeing.

"I love your son, Nate." I smiled as tears pooled in my eyes. "More than I've ever loved anyone. And I cannot wait to be a part of your family. I'm pretty sure we're about to take a step in that direction." I laughed through the joyous tears. "So maybe if you don't mind giving us just a few more minutes . . ."

Nate cleared his throat awkwardly again. "Yes, ma'am."

I returned my attention to Ben as the screen door opened and closed.

Ben seemed to be at a loss for words for a brief moment before taking a deep breath and finally opening his mouth to speak again.

"Hang on," I whispered before glancing up at the door, where Nate still stood on the other side of the screen. He was silently, but wildly, gesturing.

"Joanna," he finally called out in a voice I'm sure he thought was quiet. "Jo! Come here."

Ben groaned, twisting his neck to look back at the door. "Oh, you've got to be kidding me."

I couldn't help but laugh. I mean, what else was there to do?

"What is it?" we heard Joanna say as she

approached the door. "Are Ben and Sarah ever coming in or—oh my goodness! Is he . . . ? Are they . . . ?"

"Yes," Nate said. "Now be quiet so he can get on with it."

Ben looked back to me in disbelief. "Are they really just standing there?"

"They are." I sighed. "But if it's any consolation, your dad's just kind of peeking through the door from the side."

"Oh yeah, that's much better." He smirked. "Hey, guys, um . . ."

"He just met her! He's really doing this *now?*" Joanna asked Nate, with no subtlety whatsoever. "Should I turn off the oven? The apple pie only has about two more minutes, and I don't want it to burn."

"Be quiet, Jo," Nate said in what he seemed to think was a whisper, endearing himself to me even more.

"Did he introduce you?" she whispered to her annoyed husband, and I erupted into giggles once more. "Shouldn't we at least officially meet her before—"

Ben groaned and then called over his shoulder, "Mom, Dad, this is Sarah. Sarah, these are my parents. Now, if it's okay with everyone, I have a question I'd really like to ask her."

"It's very nice to meet you both." I laughed, and then I looked back at Ben and all of the humor was gone, replaced by determination and absolute resolve.

"This somehow doesn't seem as romantic as it did when I started," he whispered.

"Oh, don't be silly, Ben. This was *never* romantic. But if you still want to ask the question, you have about two minutes until the apple pie is done."

He chuckled as he put my hand to his lips and kissed it. "Sarah Hollenbeck, I am mesmerized by you. Absolutely enchanted. And I could make a speech, and I could tell you all the reasons I'm sure about us," he said, so softly. Though his parents were clearly determined to watch closely, the quiet, gentle nature of Ben's voice made it clear he spoke only to me. "But I think we both know no words will ever be enough. And I'll never get enough of you. And you make me want to sing, and I'm a horrible singer." The happiness burst out of me as delighted laughter. "I don't know why it is, but every time I leave you, I'm singing for hours. It's like there is just so much joy inside of me that it has to break free somehow. Much to Maddie's chagrin, it breaks free in song." He smiled and looked quickly over his shoulder. "Is my mother having spasms, trying not to miss anything?"

I sniffed as I chuckled. "Yeah. Pretty much."

He sighed. "I guess I should get on with it."

"If not for their sake then for mine!" I laughed.

And once again the humor was gone as his eyes communicated everything that didn't need to be said. "Sarah, will you marry me?"

I couldn't stand another moment not being in his arms, so I knelt on the porch with him and only had time to whisper "yes" before his lips were on mine once more.

Joanna blew her nose into a tissue and said "That's our Benji" to Nate, her concerns seemingly forgotten for the moment. She opened the screen door and seemed poised to come over to congratulate us, or at least formally meet me face-to-face, until the oven timer buzzed from inside the house and she ran off shouting, "My pie!"

Nate returned to his standard stoicism and muttered, "Congratulations, you two. Now can we please eat?" before turning around and leaving us alone—finally.

But we weren't alone for very long.

"What in the world is all the racket? Did I miss something?"

Oh, Laura. I had managed to forget all about her. What a joyous few minutes that had been.

I cleared my throat and pulled away from Ben just a touch as Laura appeared in the doorway. Despite the fact that I didn't care for the woman and felt absolutely no loyalty to her, I wanted to think of the best way to break the news to her. I wanted to be delicate and sensitive and—

"Sarah just agreed to marry me!" Ben blurted out, as blissfully ignorant as ever that she had believed he would someday be hers.

"Oh!" she cried out, making a sound that sounded vaguely like air being released from a balloon. "Well, isn't that . . . I'm just so . . ." She tried to get out words that would support the passive-aggressive smile on her face, but when words failed her, she settled on more balloon noises.

I know it's not very Christian of me, and I assure you I have asked for forgiveness and made my peace with God, but the sight of Laura walking past us to her car in a flurry of excuses and balloon noises filled me with so much merriment that I nearly overflowed.

15.

Lurking in a Dark ~~Corner~~ Alley

I walked into the coffee house the next morning, before church, and was greeted by the sight of Piper trying to get my attention, holding up two cups of coffee. I knew what that meant: she'd gotten there early and ordered for both of us so we didn't have to waste a single moment of our time together with a little thing like ordering and paying.

"Thanks." I smiled at her as I took my cup from her hand and sat down.

"How was it? Tell me everything," she ordered before I had even taken a sip.

I'd spent a lot of time that morning looking forward to telling Piper everything—but also feeling uncharacteristically nervous about it. After all, as far as Piper was concerned, "every-thing" went no further than dinner with my boyfriend's parents.

"It was nice. Joanna made a pot roast. It was delicious. And the woman's mashed potatoes are quite possibly the creamiest I have ever tasted in my life. I think she uses buttermilk in them."

She raised her eyebrow and stared at me, unamused. I'd answered her question, but not with a single detail she cared about. She didn't have to clarify. I knew what she was really asking.

"And Nate and Joanna are lovely, for the record," I added. "It was a little awkward at first, but by the time we left, I think we all felt pretty comfortable."

She exhaled. "Oh good. So they approve of the match?"

I grinned as I set down my cup. "Yes. In fact, they aren't even requiring my entire dowry, as long as my father's village sends them a few goats."

"You know what I mean!"

Of course I knew exactly what she meant, and looking back over the evening, as I had nonstop every waking moment since the evening ended, I was surprised and delighted that none of what I had worried about had even been an issue. Of course there had been some things I hadn't been counting on . . .

"Laura was there," I stated calmly.

The statement was not received with equal calm.

"What?" Piper fumed as she set her coffee down on the table a little more forcefully than she intended, sending overflow drops to the table. She quickly grabbed a napkin and started cleaning up the spill, but she didn't take her eyes off of me.

"It was fine. Really," I stated emphatically in response to the disbelief in her eyes. "She didn't even stay around very long. She left before dinner. And it was probably a good thing that she was there. It kind of pushed me into saying some things to Ben that probably needed to be said."

She leaned in with a look that indicated she thought the conversation was finally getting good. "What things?"

"Oh, you know . . . I told him I felt a little uncomfortable because of how oblivious he is to Laura's feelings for him. And I told him I felt like I had to work extra hard, because his mother loved Christa and she loves Laura, and she doesn't know me."

"Good." Piper nodded. "I'm glad you were up front with him about that."

"Oh, and I told him I love him."

She looked decidedly underwhelmed.

"For the first time, Piper. I told him I love him for the first time. I mean, the first time on purpose."

"But he told you he loves you almost a week ago," she replied. "You didn't tell him then?"

"No," I scoffed, as if I'd put even a second of intentional thought into not telling him. "I wasn't going to tell him just because he told me."

"No, you would tell him because you *do* love him." She laughed. "But I must admit . . . I'm impressed. Whatever the reason, I'm impressed by your restraint. How very un–Sarah Hollenbeckish of you!"

"Hey!" I threw a napkin at her and pretended to be offended, even as I realized she wasn't going to be impressed by my restraint for long. "I also kissed him," I muttered into my coffee as I lifted the cup to my lips.

"Really? How was it? Sorry. Wrong first question. How did that . . . ? How did he . . . ? Why did you . . . ? Never mind. That was the right first question."

"It was . . ." How could I ever put it into words? I wasn't sure I could. I set my cup on the table and raised my hands to my warm cheeks as I shook my head and smiled.

"That good?" she asked, eyebrows raised.

"That good. And then we were getting ready to walk into his parents' house and—"

"Hang on." She raised her hand. "Where were you?"

"On the porch." I smiled, a little embarrassed. "His dad walked out on us, and Ben had dropped the bag of dinner rolls on the porch, so Nate just picked them up and took them in . . . it was horrifying." I took one more sip of coffee and then followed it up with a deep breath before blurting out, "And then we were getting ready to walk in and Ben asked me to marry him."

It was the first time I'd had the opportunity to speak the words aloud, and I marveled at the way they felt on my tongue and sounded to my ears. And then my eyes distracted me from my marveling as they observed that Piper wasn't smiling or squealing or jumping up and down or doing any of the other things best friends always do in movies when someone gets engaged.

"Did you hear me?"

Finally a smile broke out on her face, but it was more restrained than I had anticipated. "I did. I guess I'm just a little surprised."

"Not half as surprised as I was, I bet." I winked, and then my smile faded. "You don't look happy about this."

"No! I am!" She reached across the table and grabbed my hands. "Of course I am. You know I am. Sorry. I'm just . . ." She sighed and scrunched up her face. "I don't know, Sarah. I know you'll have plenty of people talking about how fast this is happening, and you'll have plenty of people asking if it's too soon. You know I'm not those people. But—"

"But you're thinking about how fast this is happening, and you're wondering if it's too soon."

"Of course I am." She smiled. "You know how I feel about you and how I feel about Ben. And you definitely know how I feel about you and Ben." She sighed again and held my hands more tightly. "You're happy about this?"

Tears sprung to my eyes, and I laughed as

I swiped them away. "Of course I am! But I'm not clueless here, you know? I know it's fast. But I also know that Patrick and I waited an 'acceptable' amount of time before we got engaged, and then our marriage was a disaster. And I know that Ben and Christa knew each other a lifetime before they decided to spend their lives together, and now Ben understands better than most of us how precious every moment is." I pulled my hands away from Piper's and grabbed a napkin to wipe my eyes, and then I scooted my chair closer to hers. "I am madly in love with him. But I'm not taking this lightly, I promise you. Neither of us are."

"I'm really not those people, you know." She smiled. "In a few months I would have been dropping Ben little hints and 'accidentally' giving him directions to jewelry stores when he's supposed to meet us for lunch. Stuff like that."

"I know." I giggled as I threw my arms around her shoulders.

She hugged me back and then said softly, "I'm happy for you, Sarah. I really am. Yes, it's fast, but I see how happy he makes you, and how good you are for each other. In fact, he may be the one guy in this whole world who I think is good enough for my best friend. So don't ever think that I have any concerns about the *who*. Only the *when*. I just . . . I just want you to be careful, okay? You went from one accidental 'I love you' and one somewhat accidental kiss in a month and a half to . . . this. And when things start moving quickly, it's easier for everything to move quickly. So just be careful. Okay?"

I nodded with a loving smile, and then we stood to go.

We drove to church separately, as we had begun to do since my Sunday afternoon plans always included lunch with Ben and Maddie, and I made use of the silence in the car to consider everything Piper had just said—and, with memories of the evening before flooding my senses, admit to myself that she was absolutely right.

Ben and I were going to have to be very careful.

Let's face it: as wonderful as it was that Nate, Joanna, and I ultimately hit it off, and as much as my heart was threatening to burst from the joy of Ben's proposal, the kissing had been the really good part of the evening. I hadn't been able to stop thinking about it. There in front of his parents' house, our love had grown deeper, as had our faith in God. After all, there was no earthly way we ever should have been able to walk away and go to our respective homes that night. It wasn't easy. As he drove me home from his parents' house that evening, we'd caused traffic issues at stoplights all over the Greater Chicagoland area, and got honked at repeatedly.

When we got to my house, I couldn't even

allow him to walk me to the door. Ever the gentleman, he had walked me to my door every single time he had taken me home so far, but that particular evening I knew we wouldn't have been able to stop until we had gone much farther than the doorway. So instead he kissed me good night in the vehicle.

About the time the windows of his CR-V began to steam up the tiniest bit, I pulled away and mumbled "Rule number five" as I gasped for air and opened the car door.

"Yeah," he mumbled back as he gripped the steering wheel tightly and lowered his forehead to rest on it. "Which one is five again?"

I had already begun to step out of the vehicle, determined to walk away before I forgot that I was supposed to. "Kissing only within reason. Nothing we wouldn't do in front of a chaperone."

"Oh yeah," he said as he rolled down his window to get some air. "Chaperone. Forgot we were supposed to have a chaperone."

Not being completely alone together had been rule number one and had obviously been treated with all the seriousness of that law in Michigan that says a woman can't cut her own hair without her husband's permission, or the one in South Dakota that makes it illegal to sleep in a cheese factory.

For better or for worse that night, in an attempt to make sure, once and for all, that he wasn't giving one iota of consideration to Laura and her deviled eggs, I had taken a sledgehammer to a metaphorical flood levee that had very meticulously and gingerly been holding back our passion for each other.

Oops.

Yes. We would have to be very, very careful.

After that evening, Ben and I couldn't even look at each other without breathing heavily—so it was somewhat inconvenient, to say the least, that the next time we saw each other was at church the next morning. I was just sure the entire congregation was reading our thoughts. I was also fairly convinced that the apostle Paul had been talking to the Corinthians about Ben and me when he wrote all of that "better to marry than to burn with passion" stuff.

So I sat there in church that Sunday, Piper by my side, Laura nowhere in sight, and I contemplated how desperately Ben and I needed to change our normal after-church sushi routine for that week only. It was very evident that the best thing to do after church was hop on a quick flight to Vegas, get married by Elvis, and book a honeymoon suite at a place that also offered a sushi buffet. And then, by next Sunday, we would once again be normal adults capable of restraint.

I knew that he was feeling it just as strongly as I was. I knew because he never looked at me from the pulpit. Not once. I saw him go to a great deal of effort to avoid looking at me, in fact. Instead, he presented his sermon on Daniel while glancing at random people, and occasionally his mother. And each time his eyes landed on Joanna, whom he usually avoided as resolutely as he avoided me that day, she couldn't help but let her maternal emotions get the better of her. All of the effort she had put into not drawing attention to herself as the pastor's mother had been for naught.

After the service, as he made his way through the crowd and approached Piper and me, she whispered, "Do I need to stay with you this afternoon to make sure you two can control yourselves?" I didn't respond right away, which caused her to laugh and say, "For goodness' sake, Sarah! Are you actually considering whether or not that's necessary?"

I wasn't, in fact. I had been distracted by Ben being stopped, about thirty feet from me, by Tom Isaacs. He leaned in and softly said something to Ben, and then they shook hands. Tom walked away and Ben just stood there for a moment, facing away from me.

I'd put the tithing controversy pretty much out of my mind at this point. Everything but the joy and happiness we were experiencing had faded away, but suddenly the dark cloud was back. Sure, it hadn't looked too terrible, whatever had just transpired, but I couldn't imagine any possible scenario in which everything was okay, as if nothing had ever happened.

Ben stood there for another moment, and I started to worry—not about the situation, but about him.

"Is he okay?" Piper asked, sensing my sudden mood shift and following the direction of my eyes to their target.

"I don't know," I muttered, and then I walked over to him. I didn't say a word when I got to where he stood, and I didn't touch him. I just wanted him to know I was there.

He was clearly deep in thought as I approached, but when I stopped right in front of him, he seemed to shake something off, and then he looked up at me with a smile. It wasn't a completely genuine smile, though. Something was still very much on his mind.

"Hey, I didn't know you were here," he joked, and his smile became a more sincere Ben Delaney smile. "In fact, I think I did all I could to avoid knowing you were here. You look beautiful. Where should we go for lunch? I think Maddie's in the mood for pizza, but I'm always hesitant to eat pizza in the Sunday best. Sauce stains and all. There's always sushi, of course. Do you want to meet us somewhere or go together?"

It was the first time I had seen him dance the dance of avoidance, and I was amazed by how bad he was at it.

"What did Tom say?" I asked quietly.

"Hmm?" He acted like he hadn't heard me, but I knew he had.

"Ben, you do know that you're freaking me out *more* by avoiding telling me, right?"

He exhaled and his shoulders sagged, then he pulled me aside, a little bit away from traffic. "He apologized for the call the other day and said he hadn't had any idea you and I were together. Then he shook my hand, said 'Enjoyed the sermon,' and walked away."

I stared at him in confusion. "Are you serious?"

"Yeah." He frowned.

"Ben, that's great! I mean, seriously, it's amazing. Like, almost—" I froze.

"Too good to be true?" He completed my thought, but with a very different tone from the one with which I had begun the thought. "What does not knowing we're together have to do with it? And how does he suddenly know?"

Those were very good questions.

In the end, we didn't go anywhere for lunch, for the first Sunday since the first sushi, because I wanted to go home and write. At least that was what I said, and there was certainly truth to it. I did end up writing, and what I wrote was good, but I also just needed some time to think. Right then, at that particular time in our relationship, I had a difficult time thinking when I was with Ben.

Ben was initially somewhat concerned when I skipped out on lunch, but I think there was a small amount of relief there as well, and I wasn't offended by that. Rule number two, the rule in which we committed to only seeing each other three times a week, had also been abandoned long ago. And though neither of us was sorry about that, and I knew that we would happily spend every moment of every day together without complaint if we could, it felt like the appropriate time to take a breather.

I say that it felt like the appropriate time, but of course it also felt like the worst possible time, and that was probably the greatest evidence that the slight step back was absolutely necessary. We couldn't get enough of each other, and while God's rules were still the top priority, our own rules, so carefully considered and thought out, seemed like naïve ancient history.

So I went home and I thought and I wrote, and I threw all of my worry and concern, and also all of my passion, into new characters who, just like Ben and me, were struggling to stay focused on God under less than conducive circumstances.

"I can't believe I'm saying it, kid," Joe said almost three weeks later when I answered the phone, "but this is good stuff."

Something in me had been unlocked. It seemed as though being engaged agreed with the author in me. The *real* author in me. I appreciated Joe's words, but truthfully he hadn't told me anything I didn't already know. It was good stuff. I had started working on the manuscript as soon as I'd gotten home that sushi-free Sunday, and I hadn't stopped long enough to look back since.

"So, you really like it so far?"

"I do," he said. "I can't believe how much I do. I feel emasculated by how much I do, actually."

Those words were rich coming from the man who now had "Theme from *The Thorn Birds*" as his ringtone.

"Well, I can't tell you how much that means to me, Joe. Do you think the publishers will go for it? I mean *really* go for it?"

"About that. I just got off the phone with Kent, and he's crazy about the snippet you sent him a couple weeks ago. He's in. I think he finally saw the marketing potential. You know, if we really push this thing as your 'come to Jesus moment.' Literally!" He laughed.

Joe didn't understand my newfound dedication to Christ, I knew, but he was never disrespectful about it. Well, at least not intentionally. It was all coming together so much better than I ever could have anticipated, and I knew I had Joe to thank for that. On the surface he could act like it was all about selling books and making money, but I knew he cared about me. And what I desired with every fiber of my being was to be able to turn this book into a positive influence on the lives of women, relationships, and marriages. In other words, I was making a literary U-turn.

"But they're a little antsy, kid," he continued. "It's certainly not a safe and traditional move. I'm thinking we need to move fast and not give them a chance to back out."

"Back out?" I asked. "I mean, technically my contract doesn't say what kind of book I have to write. Right?"

"Right. But that doesn't mean they won't edit it to within an inch of its life. Right now, they're pretty fired up about it. That's the way we want it, Sarah. We want them to believe in this project as much as you do. So how much longer do you think you need? To finish this thing up?"

It was shocking to me just how quickly I had gotten as far as I had. *Stollen Desire* had been written quickly, but let's face it: it had also been crap. On the other hand, I was so pleased with the new work. I was proud of so many aspects of where it seemed to be heading, but most of all I was proud of how romantic and sexy it was without ever being inappropriate. I knew I would have a legion of people saying I wasn't capable of writing anything but smut, and until very recently, I may have been chief among them.

But it was going extremely well, and I knew that God deserved all of the praise and glory for that. So how much longer did I need? I guess that depended on whether or not I could keep up my current pace.

I suppose it also depended, in no small part, on whether or not my fiancé and I began speaking to each other again.

"I'm not quite sure how much time I need, Joe. Let me give that some thought, and we'll talk again tomorrow."

As I thought about Joe's question and tried to calculate how much more time I would need, I took into consideration how much I had written in the three weeks since I'd begun. Over the course of those three weeks, I had settled into the writing sweet spot that all authors cherish. Not always, but sometimes, you enjoy a creative burst during which you can't type quickly enough. It's almost as if the story is already written and simply waiting for you to get it down on the page. The more I wrote, the more I wanted to write. Those periods don't always come along, so when they do, you can't do anything other than enjoy every single moment of it and try to keep up.

I considered the enhanced creativity a blessing, but it hadn't been the easiest thing to try and get Ben to see it that way. The initial step back he had welcomed, I think. He was worried about what Tom wasn't saying much more than he had worried about anything that had been said or done, and he needed some time to think it through and sort it out. So we took Sunday off. I think he expected that to be the extent of the break.

"I miss you," he'd said on the phone on the Friday morning after the Sunday we skipped sushi. It was only the third time we had spoken that week, and we hadn't seen each other at all.

"I miss you too," I replied honestly into my Bluetooth, but I didn't stop typing.

My assistant, Sydney, was there, on orders from Joe, doing her best to facilitate the creative process. What that meant, usually, was making sure I wasn't disturbed and making sure I ate and went to the bathroom once in a while. When you're going through one of those creative periods, it's shockingly easy to forget stuff like that. She'd been hired on as my assistant shortly after book one in the Desire trilogy hit the *New York Times* bestseller list, so she'd been by my side through most of the insanity. She knew her job and she did it well, but of course this time around she had to contend with something she hadn't prior.

"I didn't think Sydney was even going to let me talk to you," Ben said with a laugh. I think he thought it was a funny thought that couldn't possibly be true, but it was absolutely true. I'd only gotten her to finally give me the phone by promising her that I would make sure he didn't call back for the rest of the day.

"About that . . ." I began hesitantly, succumbing

to the glower being directed toward me by Sydney. "She's just doing her job. I mean, I know the rules don't apply to you, but—"

"What's that mean?"

"It means the rules don't apply to you."

I gestured to Sydney that I needed some water, so she ran off to get it for me. I should have been happy to have a moment alone to talk to Ben, but honestly I don't think I was even paying enough attention to him to think about it.

"Well, it just sounded a little sarcastic. Like I think I'm above the rules or something."

I laughed, still not really realizing what a bad mood he was in. "You are above the rules, so it doesn't matter if you think you are or not."

He sighed. "So then what is Sydney's job exactly? Keeping me from distracting you?"

I laughed again, still oblivious and searching thesaurus.com for a word I liked better than *countenance*. "Pretty much."

She walked back in and handed me my water, and also looked very irritated that I was still on the phone. I silently thanked her and apologized at the same time. "Hey, I should probably get back to it. Can I call you tonight?"

"Sure. Sorry to have bothered you."

Okay. I caught that one.

"Hey," I said, softening my tone and forcing myself to stop typing. "You're not bothering me."

Sydney rolled her eyes, implying that he was

bothering her, whether I was okay with it or not. I stood from my desk and walked over to her and gently pushed her out of the room, with her protesting all the way, and shut the door behind her.

Finally I was focused on Ben. At least I was mostly focused on Ben. I still had lines running through my head that I was terrified I would lose if I didn't get them recorded soon, but I quickly asked God to help me remember everything worth keeping, and then I plopped down on the couch to find out what was bothering my uncharacteristically moody fiancé.

"I'm sorry if I made it sound like you were bothering me," I said sincerely. "You could never bother me."

I felt him thaw out some in response to my warmer tone. "No, it's fine. I know you're busy."

"What's going on? Talk to me."

"Why are you pulling away, Sarah?" he asked directly.

Seriously? "Ben, I'm not pulling away. I've just got to keep the flow going while I can. Writer's block could be waiting for me in a dark alley somewhere." Ah! "Dark alley"—that was the better version of "dark corner" I had been looking for. I ran to my laptop and found the passage and made the substitution.

"Are you sure? Because if you ask me, it seems

like you're using that as an excuse to stay away from me."

"What?" I scoffed. "Why would I want to stay away from you?"

I was thinking that through, trying to figure out how he could have possibly drawn that ridiculous conclusion, when I realized he was right. He was absolutely right.

"Oh my goodness, Ben. You're right. I hadn't realized! But why? Hold on. Let me pray about it. Okay. Got it. Apparently, despite the mind-blowing happiness that I feel due to my love for you, and my belief that you genuinely love me as well, I am still harboring some feelings of unworthiness that lead me to subconsciously be certain that once you realize what kind of person I really am, you'll run away faster than you can say 'deviled eggs.' What's more, I really don't know if I can control my desire for you, and sometimes I get so caught up in you that I almost forget that I *should* control it. And then of course God tells me, 'You aren't in control. I am.' And that's awesome, but once in a while I don't want him to be in control. I don't want to give it over. I just want to give in and somehow find a way to not feel guilty about it the next morning. But I know that's not possible, so truthfully it's easier to just put some space between us and think good Christian thoughts about this new couple I'm writing about, and funnel all of the desire I feel for you into them. It's easier, and it's safer."

That's probably what I should have said, because that was the truth. Ben would have understood that. He would have made sure that I understood that he loved me as much as I loved him, and he wanted me as much as I wanted him. Perhaps then we would have set some new ground rules, a date for the wedding, and started counting the days until we could finally be together in every way.

But my return to the laptop had pulled my focus away from him once again. Everything I should have said to Ben? That was good stuff for my heroine to say.

"Look, Sarah, if you're having any second thoughts, that's really something we should talk about."

My fingers froze on the keyboard.

Second thoughts? Had he just brought up second thoughts? Why? Was *he* having second thoughts?

"Well, you know, if you want to . . . I mean, I don't want you to feel any pressure . . . But if you did already feel pressured . . . There's certainly no obligation . . ." I couldn't do it. I couldn't complete any of the sentences. I took a deep breath and swallowed down my tears and blurted out, probably a bit more harshly than I meant to, "It's not too late to back out if you don't want to marry me."

His mood was back. "Thanks. It's good to know I have your permission to make my own decisions."

"There's no need to be a jerk, Ben." I was shocked that he was talking to me the way he was. I didn't know what was going on with him, but I was suddenly a whole lot less interested in finding out.

"I'm sorry, but it was just a stupid thing to say, Sarah. Of course I don't want to back out. Why would you say something like that?"

I threw my hands up in the air. "Well, I don't know!" I shouted. "You're the one who brought it up!"

"I brought up you having second thoughts, and you still haven't said that you're not."

"What, because I'm more likely to have second thoughts than you are? Why is that? What are you trying to say, Ben?"

He growled under his breath before saying, "I'm not trying to say anything. I'm saying it. You're clearly pulling away, and I think I have the right to know why. It's okay if we have some regret about the way things happened, but shutting yourself off isn't going to make it go away."

I'm sorry . . . regret? Second thoughts and regrets are very different things. Second thoughts involve decisions, but regrets involve actions.

"Oh," I said.

I heard him take a deep breath, and I could almost hear him counting to ten in his head. While he worked hard to calm himself down, I reverted to the ways of my first marriage and did all I could to stay mad. He may have taken my subdued "Oh" as an indication that he had broken through, but I wasn't done fighting yet.

"Laura took off on Saturday night, Sarah. She hasn't been home since."

Okay, that broke through. At least for a moment.

"Kaitlyn has been staying with Laura's mom," he continued. "Apparently she's called to check in a couple of times, and she said she just wanted to get out of town for a while, but I'm getting sort of worried. I'm not sure, but I can't help but wonder if you were right about her. Do you think this has something to do with our engagement? Maybe she does have some leftover feelings for me."

I love men, and I love that man in particular, but men can be idiots.

"Of course she does, Ben. She's in love with you. It's as plain as day to everyone but you. Every move she makes and everything she says is about making you love her! How can you not see that?"

I felt like right then, in that particular moment, a battle was being waged for my soul. On my left shoulder was a little white angel in a broomstick skirt and a peasant top—in my imagination bearing a strong resemblance to Roma Downey. That little angel was telling me to be supportive and understanding, and to put aside all of my petty jealousies and insecurities. On my right shoulder was a demon in a sexy red dress and stilettos, looking a lot like early Stevie Nicks, but with fewer layers and less eye makeup. Stevie was asking me why Ben cared so much, and even planting the idea in my mind that Laura was just staying away in a last-ditch effort to win him.

"Don't miss an opportunity to shine God's love," Roma said in her Irish accent.

Stevie just sang "Edge of Seventeen," but it was somehow very effective.

"I don't know," Ben said, sounding concerned enough to simultaneously make me love him even more and frustrate me. "I just can't stop thinking that if that's true, and she does think she wants to be with me, it probably wasn't the best thing for it all to happen right there, where she could walk out on everything."

I should have felt guilty, and maybe I did just a little bit, but Stevie was winning me over with her incessant chorus of white-winged doves singing *Ooo, ooo, ooo.*

"It's been, what . . . fifteen years since you two broke up? You shouldn't have to worry about what she'll think or what she might walk in on. Besides, what was she doing there that evening anyway? It was completely inappropriate for her to be there, if you ask me."

Ooo, ooo, ooo.

"I tried to make you realize how uncomfortable I was," I continued, "but you didn't even seem to care. She comes on to you right in front of me, all the time. How do you think that makes me feel?"

Ooo, ooo, ooo.

"If she can't handle the fact that you've moved on with your life, maybe it's best if she's gone. It sure doesn't break my heart to think of a Laura-free life."

Ooo, ooo, ooo.

Roma and Stevie disappeared in a puff of smoke and glitter as Ben said, "You don't really mean that."

Unfortunately for him, I did.

"Laura's a big girl, and if she's finally gotten it into her head that she needs to move on from you, then good! I say we leave her alone and let her get that figured out."

Sydney peeked her head back around the door and held up my home phone while she pointed to it and mouthed "Kent." I nodded and motioned for her to come in.

"Look, Ben, can we please talk about this later? My editor is on the other line, and I'm supposed to be getting a few chapters of the new book to him today, and I just don't—"

"Sure," he said—not coldly, but certainly not warmly. "I'm sorry to have bothered you."

I sighed. "Like I said, you could never—hello? Ben, are you there?" I pushed the Bluetooth further into my ear, certain the click I had just heard was just the symptom of a bad connection.

"Sarah." Sydney pushed the phone toward me.

I pulled my link to Ben out of my ear and instead focused on Kent, and writing, and all of the other things I hadn't managed to mess up in a matter of minutes.

On Friday morning, I called Joe back, as promised.

"Hey, kid, so what do you think? How long do you need to get this thing finished up?"

It had been two weeks since Stevie had twirled and twirled her way to victory. It had been two weeks since I'd retreated into my former self, not caring who I hurt in the process.

It had been two weeks since I had spoken to Ben.

I swallowed the lump in my throat and gave Joe the answer I knew he wanted. "I should have plenty of time to write. I'll have it finished up pretty quickly for you."

"Great! I know the team will be thrilled. You're going to revolutionize the Christian market, kiddo. Who knows?" He laughed. "You might even fix a few of those marriages torn apart by *Stollen Desire!*"

Ooo, baby, *ooo, ooo.*

16.

Number 7,483

"You and Ben really need to get this worked out so that I can throw you an engagement party," Piper said over coffee at my house.

It was Saturday evening, the day after I promised Joe lightning-speed productivity in completing what we both hoped would be my fourth bestseller. Sadly, the writer's block that I had so feared was lurking down a dark alley—not a corner, heaven forbid—had jumped out, flashed its knife, and stolen my wallet.

"That was a horrible metaphor," Piper uttered honestly and sympathetically when I'd spoken the thought aloud.

See? Writer's block.

"Engagement party? Ha! I don't even know if we're still engaged."

I don't know if it was the pressure of Joe's statement about undoing the damage I had done or the pressure he was placing on me to get it done quickly, but something had stolen every ounce of creativity and passion that had been propelling me forward. I'd hung up the phone the day before, returned to my laptop, and then . . . nothing. I had a problem with that. A big problem. When my sadness and fear and depression, not to mention love and desire, weren't able to be expressed vicariously through the lives of my fictional characters, they were left to churn within me once again, and I didn't handle that well.

"Of course you're still engaged, dummy!" Piper smiled, but I couldn't return the smile. "Has either one of you told the other that the engagement is off?"

"We haven't told each other anything!"

"Well, then, there you go. It's not off unless someone says it's off." She reached over and placed her hand on mine as I started crying for the 7,482nd time in the forty-five minutes she had been there. "This isn't some insignificant relationship that just suddenly ends. You know that, he knows that. And most importantly, I know that. Therefore, we're going to plan your engagement party, you and I. Do you have a pen and paper?"

She stood up and started looking around my kitchen, lifting things up from the counter to look under them.

"Piper, that's ridiculous. We are not going to plan a party right now."

Her search continued, undeterred. "You're a writer, woman! How do you not have any paper?"

I couldn't help but giggle a little as she looked under everything, including the refrigerator.

"I don't use a quill pen and parchment, you know."

Finally she found a pad of sticky notes and a pencil, and decided that would be good enough for the moment. It was easy to see her determination to plan a party as what it really was, and I appreciated it. I didn't, however, believe it was going to do any good. She wanted to cheer me up, obviously, but she also wanted to help me through my writer's block by getting me focused on the potential of things to come.

My fictional characters had followed, largely, the path that Ben and I had been on. Things began in a blaze of glory, only to settle into a God-given and God-driven passion. And then, for two weeks, I had written through their darkness as a way of dealing with my own. They had their own version of the tithing controversy, and their own personal Tom Isaacs. They also had a Laura. But through it all, there could be no doubt that eventually it would all work out. Eventually the world would no longer be able to stand in the way of something so powerful it had rendered defenseless the barriers built by two people so previously beaten and battered by what love had done to their hearts. This was not a book that called into question whether or not our lovebirds would end up together. Of course they would. From the opening line, through all of the ups and downs, there could never be any doubt that there would be a happily ever after.

But what sort of people would they become before they reached the finish line? Some scars would be healed, sure, but some new injuries were just as certain. It was all about the journey, not the inevitable outcome. But you see, I had already written most of the journey. For two weeks, I had written the journey. It was time for them to come out on the other side and face their glorious future together, and I didn't know how to do that. There was no point of reference, and I feared that perhaps I had been a fool to assume that I knew how the love story would end.

"Originally I was thinking an open house sort of thing, but would you rather have a nice sit-down dinner for a select few?"

My lip quivered as I tried to hold it in.

"I like that idea," Piper continued. "What do you think? Just twenty people or so? Oh wait, Ben has a pretty big family, doesn't he? What, two brothers? Do they have kids? Should we even allow kids or do you want it to be more formal than that? Oh, wait. That was stupid. I forgot about Maddie." She laughed as she erased "Adults Only?"

She looked up with a smile, which quickly faded as she saw my despair reach a new, unparalleled depth. "Oh, honey." She set the pencil down, scooted her chair next to mine, and wrapped her arms around me. She held me and let me sob. The first 7,482 times I had cried, it had been relatively manageable, but I had been holding back. For two weeks I had been holding back.

Number 7,483 was one for the ages.

"I just can't believe he hasn't even called," Piper said as I cried. "It may not be fair, but I can't help but hold him to a higher standard. As my best friend's fiancé it's despicable, but as my pastor? Unforgivable." I wailed further and buried my tear-covered face in her shoulder. "Actually, it's the other way around," she said softly as she rested her head on mine.

Once I finally gathered enough composure to sit up, I thought it only right that I clear Ben's name in one regard. "It's not that he hasn't called," I said with a sniff.

"What, sweetie?" Piper leaned in to try and decipher whatever words were attempting to make their way through the treacherous peaks and valleys of the land of despair and heartbreak.

"It's not that he hasn't called," I repeated a little more audibly. "He's left me a million messages." My exasperated eye roll quickly turned back into a trembling pout.

Piper cleared her throat, clearly trying to understand. "I'm sorry, he's called you?" I nodded my head. "Multiple times?" More nodding. "And yet you haven't spoken to him in two weeks, why?"

Wasn't it obvious? "I don't know what to say!"

Piper stood up in a frenzy, accidentally knocking her chair over as she did. She began to pick it up but realized she could make her point more dramatically if she left it right where it was.

"Sarah Hollenbeck, I don't even know what to say right now I'm so frustrated with you!"

I didn't understand what was happening. Just a moment prior my best friend had been my greatest comforter and a shoulder to cry on. All of a sudden, I found her to be just a tad bit terrifying.

"What did I say? What did I just say about this not being some insignificant relationship? This isn't junior high, Sarah. This man loves you and has invited you into his life and his daughter's life. He has put aside the ever-so-slightly tawdry fact that you are known worldwide as the woman who put sex in the kitchen in the forefront of culture and has been prepared to proudly defend you at the church where he is the pastor." She was storming all around my kitchen, arms flailing and guns ablaze. "And in case that's not enough, please don't forget about Maddie. She is his link to Christa and the symbol of the love they shared. He has raised that little girl without a mommy, and he's done an amazing job. He has protected her and loved her and shielded her from all the pain that he knows all too well exists in abundance in this world, and yet from day one he has shared her with you."

I sniffed again. "Not day one," I protested weakly, feeling my defense slip away.

"Only because you ran away!" she shouted. "Good grief, Sarah! Call him." I shook my head. "Call him!" She picked up the phone and handed it to me. "Call him now."

I took the phone, but I didn't dial. "I don't know what to say, Piper! I've never—"

"What?" she interrupted me, not unkindly, but very emphatically. "Never had to be an adult? Never been with a man who cares enough to listen to what you have to say? Never had someone love you enough to not give up on you? Well, you've got it now. He's not going to stop trying, and he's not going to stop calling. But why are you making him prove that?"

7,484.

"I love you. You know that, right?" Piper sighed as she knelt down next to me. I cried, and though she did it silently, I knew she was praying. "All you have to do is agree to stay in the fight, Sarah." She lifted her head and looked up at me from her position on my kitchen floor. "You don't have to have the answers. You don't even have to know what to say to him. Just stay in the fight and let him love you."

I knew she was talking about Ben, but I couldn't help but think that she also meant God. I mean, it's Piper, so I'm sure she did. Why was I making it so difficult? Why did I always make it so difficult?

I think that sometimes I forgot that I'd only been a Christ-follower for a matter of months at that point. Literally falling into your future husband, who happens to be the pastor, on your very first Sunday after salvation can tend to elevate your faith pretty quickly. My relationship with God was very similar to my relationship with Ben in many ways, when you really think about it. For both of them I had fallen fast and I had fallen hard. And with both of them, the beginning was easy. Everything was exciting and awe-inspiring, and it was easy to forget my past life and everything that I'd been desperate to escape. But then what?

"The Spirit you received does not make you slaves, so that you live in fear again; rather, the Spirit you received brought about your adoption to sonship. And by him we cry, 'Abba, Father.'"

Piper recited those words from Romans 8 to me, and I couldn't help but laugh when she explained to me that "Abba" was Aramaic for "Father" and that the apostle Paul hadn't actually been in the mood for a little "Dancing Queen."

"You don't know that he wasn't." I smiled. "You don't know that he and Timothy, or Barnabas, didn't occasionally release a little tension among the Corinthians by belting out 'Super Trouper.'"

She laughed as she stood and walked to the front door and slipped on her shoes.

"Where are you going?" I was feeling better, but I wasn't sure I was feeling better enough for her to leave.

"You have a phone call to make." She winked.

I looked at the clock—9:34. "I really shouldn't. Maddie's already in bed, and he's probably putting the finishing touches on his sermon . . ."

I trailed off in response to the glare on her face, which once again scared me.

"Okay," I whispered.

She ran over to me and gave me a hug. "Just let him know you're still in the fight. That's all you need to do."

I held on to her for dear life, once again so grateful for her. "And what if I'm too late?"

She pulled away enough to look at me. "Not a chance," she said, very seriously. She walked to the door again, and as she picked up her purse, she called out, "I'm picking you up for church in the morning. Be ready."

I scowled. "Now, that seems a little premature, Piper."

"Actually, it seems a little past due, Sarah. Besides," she said sternly as she crossed her arms, "do you go to church to worship Jesus, or do you go to worship Ben Delaney?"

Ouch.

I smiled sheepishly. "Coffee first?"

"Of course! Now, make that phone call. If for no other reason than church will be much less awkward tomorrow if you've already broken the ice."

"Oh! You manipulative little—" I laughed as I looked around for something to throw at her.

"Love you!" she shouted with a giggle as she shut the door behind her.

I waited until I heard her pull away before I picked up the phone. *Dear Lord, I don't have a clue what I'm doing. Help me.* I tried to remember Romans 8:15 and recite it in my head as I dialed, knowing that the part about not living in fear would be helpful, but I just couldn't get rid of mental images of Paul in platform shoes and spandex.

"Sarah."

That was how he answered the phone. He didn't say "hello" and he didn't put a question mark after my name. It was said with relief.

"Hi, Ben," I said softly.

I still had no idea what to say, but there could be no doubt that just hearing him say my name had presented a certain peace. *Where do I begin?* I prayed.

"I'm glad, I mean, thank you for . . . it's good to hear your voice," he said, sounding as awkward as I felt.

"There once was a girl who was sickly and poor throughout her entire childhood," I stammered, not having a clue why these words were coming out of my mouth. "She had no one and nothing, except for the ability to sing beautiful songs. Night after night, day after day, she lay in her bed, shivering from the cold and nearly starving to death, singing with all her might. The song was her only friend and her only warmth. The song was the only thing in her life of value . . ."

I told him the fable, word for word. I don't know why, but it was what I felt led to do.

" 'She's dead,' the townspeople cried, somewhat thankfully. For they knew she was not fit to marry a prince."

I was in tears as I concluded, wondering why I had told him that, and why I had let the stupid thing nag at me for thirty years. I felt like an idiot and was trying to figure out something I could say that would somehow make the fable somewhat relevant, but he spoke first.

"Why'd you stop?" he asked gently.

I grabbed a tissue and softly blew my nose. "That's the end."

"No, it's not."

I thought back through the entire story, making sure I had covered it all. Sickly girl? Check. Beautiful song? Check. Trader, jester, prince? Check, check, check. Death? Yep. I'd covered it all.

"Yes, it is," I insisted. "My mother told it to me

countless times when I was a little girl. I know it as well as I know my name."

"Well," he said with a sigh, "my mother used to tell it to me too, and I hate to break it to you, but your mother left off the ending. She wasn't really dead."

He might as well have told me that King Tut wasn't really dead.

"I'm sorry, what? What do you mean she wasn't really dead? You can't just say it like that!" I exclaimed. "You have to tell me the story!"

I heard him chuckle just a bit. "Okay, let me see if I can remember. What was your last line again?"

" 'She's dead,' the townspeople cried, somewhat thankfully. For they knew she was not fit to marry a prince."

"Oh yeah, okay. First of all, it's not that she wasn't fit to marry a prince. She wasn't fit enough. As in, she wouldn't have survived the excitement. Anyway, after the prince had left to return to the palace, the townspeople went to their homes and changed into their mourning clothes . . . Sorry, I don't tell it as well as you do."

"No, no." I shook my head even though he couldn't see it over the phone. "Go on. Please." I was in disbelief and could hardly stand the anticipation as I waited to find out how it actually ended.

"Okay, so they changed into their mourning

clothes and cried out in despair. They'd all spent so long protecting her. That's why they refused to let people see her. They were protecting her, but suddenly she was gone. But they went into her hut, or whatever, and she wasn't dead at all. She was sitting there healthy and smiling. I think that was it."

What? "Okay, that sucks," I exclaimed, extremely disappointed. "That's even worse than my ending."

Ben laughed, and in spite of everything and the two weeks of darkness that were still very much in the forefront of my mind, I felt my breath catch in my throat.

"No, it's not. Okay, I probably didn't tell it right, but don't you see? She sang because that was all she had. The song was her only friend, she thought, but it wasn't really. She didn't have to sing anymore. The townspeople were willing to sacrifice their happiness in order to protect her, so they were her friends."

Thirty years. For thirty years I had tried to put together a jigsaw puzzle, and I had unknowingly been missing the corner pieces. Finally I had all of the pieces, and they didn't fit.

"No, they weren't! They weren't willing to sacrifice their happiness. They were willing to sacrifice *her* happiness!"

Ben was silent for a few seconds. "Yeah, you have a point."

"At least in my version they're just awful people. But if they're supposed to be her *friends?* That's so much worse."

"You're right. I must have told something wrong. Really wrong."

"I kind of hope so." I laughed.

"So, um . . . why are we talking about this?" I started laughing harder, and he chuckled as he continued, "Don't get me wrong, you can call to ask me the time if you want. I'm just curious."

I thought for a moment before realizing I didn't have a good answer. Which just made me laugh even more. "I have no idea!"

"Well, the time is now 9:43 p.m., Central Standard Time," he replied. Then he took a deep breath and softly added, "Any other random things we should discuss?"

It didn't feel normal, and we were both supremely aware of the discussion we needed to have, but at least the ice was broken. *Thank you, Jesus. Even if that was the only purpose of that stupid fable, thank you.*

"Are you mad at me?" I asked, the simplicity of the question not at all doing justice to the complexity of the situation.

"Mad at you? No. Not exactly. More frustrated with you, I guess. Confused. Hurt. And, yeah, okay, maybe there has been some anger mixed in here and there."

I knew I deserved all of that.

"Look, Ben—"

"I love you," he whispered.

I grabbed my tissue as the relief flooded my soul and the tears flooded my face. "I love you too. And I just need to say—"

"I love you," he said again.

Wow, he knew how to make an apology difficult. "I love you too, but listen—"

"I love you," he said once more, and the third time I heard the smile in his voice.

I got it. I understood. He wasn't shutting me out, and he wasn't saying we didn't have things we needed to discuss. He wasn't acting like everything was fixed and that neither of us had apologies to make. We did, and we would. But he was telling me that he loved me, and nothing mattered more than that. All I'd had to do was show him I was still in the fight.

His confidence in our relationship, and in me, was staggering. There was no question and there was no doubt. When I asked him—trying to keep it light but also desperately needing to know the answer—if we were still engaged, he said only, "Unless you've gotten a better offer."

I laughed, confirmed that I had not, and continued on with the conversation. It wasn't until we were about to hang up the phone that he addressed it with a tad more seriousness.

"You didn't really think our engagement would

be off, did you?" he asked, by then sounding so sleepy and groggy, and a tad hoarse.

Once again Roma and Stevie were present on my shoulders, but this time Stevie's delightfully expressionless twirling was no match for Roma's "Don't tell him what you think best protects you. The best protection is the truth."

"I really didn't know." I sighed. "Honestly—oh gosh, please hear me out on this—I think there was a part of me that hoped so."

He was completely alert once more upon hearing that. "Okay. Ready to hear you out."

I went on to explain my insecurities regarding, well . . . everything! I explained that the idea of failing at another relationship was almost easier to reconcile in my mind than the constant pressure I felt when trying to hold it all together. Most importantly, I explained that to me he represented all things good and godly. That's not to say that I thought he was perfect. I thought he was better than other men, but I was never under any delusion that Ben Delaney was anything other than a man. It wasn't what he was, it was what he represented.

On the other hand, my insecurities, temptations, and shortcomings were all represented by my failed first marriage. Yes, Patrick was a loser with the moral integrity of a prairie dog, but there had always been a part of me that believed a better woman might have changed him.

"This isn't about me wishing I could have made things work out with Patrick. You know that, right?" I said five minutes into my ranting. Once I'd decided to really display all of the crazy, out in the open for Ben to see, there was no stopping me.

"Of course I know that," he said. "Okay, I hate to do this . . ."

I looked at the clock once more. "Oh, yikes. I'm so sorry. You need to get to bed."

He laughed and said, "Are you serious? You are finally opening up to me. You are finally telling me the things I don't think you've even wanted to tell yourself. How in the world can you think I would be like, 'Hey, gotta run,' at a moment like this?" He paused, I think waiting for an answer, but I didn't want to give him one.

Ultimately, I didn't need to.

He sighed. "Because that's what Patrick would do. Okay, listen to me. What I was going to say was 'I hate to do this, but I'm going to go into pastor mode for a minute,' and then I was going to talk about how difficult divorce is, especially for Christ-followers. But there's something more important that I think I need to make you understand. Sarah, I'm not Patrick."

"Ben, I know that—"

"I know you know that. But now it's time for you to *know* that. And you need to know why. I have three things he never had, and it's these

263

three things that ensure I will never be like him."

I couldn't help it as my mind ran away with me, trying to predict which three he was referring to. In my mind, Ben had a million things Patrick didn't have.

"Number one, I have a relationship with Christ," he began. "And that relationship shapes who I am and what I value and who I try to be. I struggle, and I have moments of extreme weakness." He lowered his voice as he said, "Talking to you in the middle of the night, wishing you were lying here next to me instead of on the other end of a phone call, brings those weaknesses to light, believe me. But that relationship is the most important in my life, and it's not based on some stupid, self-centered desire to look holy. It's based on the complete understanding and acceptance that I will never even be worthy, much less holy, and yet the God of the universe knows my name. So that's number one.

"Number two, I have Maddie. I'm sorry that you experienced the pain of being denied motherhood, but truthfully I have thanked God every day that you don't have to share a child with that man, and I think it's time that you start looking at it that way too. God has a plan. A perfect, bigger, and better than anything we can ever imagine sort of plan."

Ah, the baby topic. Of all the topics I could ever

discuss, nothing was more gut-wrenching and devastating than that. Ben and I hadn't discussed any of that since the very first time, over sushi. Until that moment, there on the phone, I think it had been the one thing he kept off the table because he didn't want to hurt me. It wasn't that we couldn't discuss it, but what good would it do? For him, I felt the same way about discussing Christa's death. Apparently this conversation was one in which everything—everything—was on the table. I figured I had probably heard it all—every pep talk that was meant to be encouraging but was actually just patronizing. I grabbed a tissue, bracing myself for whatever he would say next, but I couldn't have possibly been prepared.

"I know it's selfish of me, but if you'd had kids with him, he'd be in your life. Our lives. And I don't think that could have possibly been good for you, or us, or any poor little McDermotts who had to have him as a father. I know we'd have made it work, and those kids would have been blessings just like Maddie, but I just . . . gosh, Sarah, I don't how to say it except to just say it. Once we're married, I intend to knock you up absolutely every chance I get."

"Well, it's the first time anyone's ever given me *this* pep talk," I said with a laugh.

He chuckled. "I hope so." He took a deep breath. "I consider it my God-given gift to be able to be the one you raise a family with. I know what that love is like—that love for your child that is unlike any other—and you and I are going to share that. So, there you go. That's number two."

I didn't know if I could handle more, but I still asked, "And number three?"

"Well, that one should be obvious. Number three, I have you."

I didn't really know where he was going with number three, but I was intrigued. "Well, so did he. For a time."

"No, he didn't. Not really. He was a placeholder. God gave him a chance, and he blew it. I'm the one who gets to really know you and understand all of the miraculous things about you." He exhaled and I somehow knew that it was his turn to brace himself. "I couldn't have loved Christa any more than I did, Sarah. I loved that woman with everything I was and everything I had, and I still thank God every day for letting me share that time with her. When she died, I thought that was it. My heart was done. But God had a plan—a perfect, bigger, and better than anything I ever could have imagined sort of plan. The love I'd known and the love you'd been denied . . . they were God's preparation for this. Right now. You and me. This is the plan."

When Piper showed up early the next morning to pick me up, I was a new person. I wasn't even just back to my old self. I was new. Ben and I finally hung up the phone at 2:15 a.m. after I had promised to make paper airplanes out of my bulletin and throw them at him if he started to drift away while delivering his sermon.

As I got Piper all caught up in the car and over coffee, I marveled at how God had worked throughout my entire conversation with Ben.

"Wow" was all Piper said as I concluded my rehash of all of the highlights of the conversation. Her cheek was resting on her hand and she was staring at me as if she were a little girl listening to a fairy tale.

I finished off my coffee and then smiled and said, "I know."

As we walked out to her car and climbed in, her phone rang. She quickly said, "By the way, if you die, I have dibs on him," and then answered her phone as I laughed and buckled my seat belt.

"Oh, hey Ben," she said.

"Hey! You don't get him until I die!" I said, not even trying to keep my voice down, certain she was faking the phone call.

"Oh my goodness, are you serious?" she asked as she quickly fastened her seat belt and then pulled out of the parking lot in a chorus of squealing tires, revving motor, and gravel kicking out behind us. "Yeah, she's with me. Tell me what to do."

17.

That Bellamy Girl

I turned to her, suddenly panicked. "What's wrong? Is he okay?" And why had he called her instead of me?

She used her hand to gesture for me to be quiet so she could hear, so I leaned in, trying to hear what he was saying. I couldn't hear a thing.

"Okay. Yeah. You bet. Do you need me to get Maddie or . . . Okay. Yeah, I'll stay with her." She looked at me, and I knew she'd been given the assignment of being my guardian, though I didn't know why.

At that point, though, I was actually okay. She was on the phone with Ben, Maddie was clearly fine if Piper was offering to pick her up, and Piper was with me. The three most important people in my life were safe, so nothing else could hurt me. Or so I thought.

"Yeah, call when you can. Do you want to talk to her?" She looked away from me. "Sure. Okay. Call when you can."

She hung up the phone but didn't say a word to me.

"What's happening?" I asked, trying to remain calm. When she didn't answer me, the calm went away pretty immediately. "Piper, tell me what's happening."

She pulled out on the expressway, very noticeably headed in the opposite direction of Mercy Point. "It's not any big deal, really," she said, looking in her rearview mirror. "Apparently there are some reporters and news crews at Mercy Point."

Well, that wasn't nearly as bad as anything that had been running through my head. "Oh. Why? And why are we not going . . ."

Oh.

"Are you telling me there are reporters and news crews at Mercy Point because of me?"

"He didn't really tell me much."

That didn't make any sense. I mean, it made some sense. Chicago was a town in which I could manage to live a relatively normal life, and nine times out of ten when I went to dinner or the grocery store, I wouldn't encounter anything more than autograph-seekers and people wanting a selfie with me. I'd been able to establish safe places—my house, Ben's, Piper's, the coffee house—where no one seemed to care. I'd thought Mercy Point was a safe place as well, and I felt bad knowing that services may have been disrupted by news crews showing up.

"What's the story, though, Piper?"

She swerved in and out of traffic pretty dramatically, but that didn't cause any additional panic. Riding in a car with Piper Lanier at the wheel was always a pretty exciting adventure. What *did* cause additional panic was the way she was ignoring my question.

"Did someone leak something to the press?" I pushed. "I suppose if someone found out Raine de Bourgh is engaged to a pastor, that could be of some interest." But enough interest to merit reporters and news crews? Maybe. That was the type of story that I knew was bound to come to light eventually, but when it did, I guess I'd thought there'd be one reporter who sat through a service and then cornered Ben and me on our way out, and then the coverage would grow from there. "No," I argued with myself. "Why now? That doesn't make sense. *Is* it about me, Piper?"

Still, she said nothing.

"Talk to me!" I groaned in frustration. "This obviously has something to do with me. You don't have to tell me what it is—I guess I'll find out soon enough—but you do have to tell me why we're driving away. Whatever it is, I need to go be with Ben. So why aren't we going to Mercy Point?"

"Because Ben didn't want you to be there," she stated matter-of-factly.

I thought of the passion and love that had been evident in his voice when he told me we were done with low-key. He said he refused to give the impression he was ashamed of me. So how could I possibly drive far away from Mercy Point and allow him to face this—whatever this was—alone? He wanted to keep me away to protect me, but we needed to face it together.

"Turn around," I demanded.

She didn't even act as if she had heard me.

"Seriously, Piper. Turn around. What's the worst anyone can say? I've become a Christian and fallen in love with a fellow Christ-follower? I'm prepared to handle that backlash. I welcome that!" I said emphatically. "There's nothing I want more than for people to know that. Please turn around."

She pulled off at an exit headed downtown, and I was satisfied that she had listened to my impassioned plea. But rather than turn around, she just pulled off on the side of the road and stopped the car.

"You need to think about him, Sarah. He doesn't want you there. I don't know all the details of what's actually going on, but he doesn't want you there. Not right now, okay?"

Was he ashamed of me after all?

Piper's phone rang again, and she gently pushed me away as I tried to get to it first. "Hi, Ben," she said, shooting me a dirty look as I tried to grab the phone from her hands. "Yeah, hang on." She held the phone out, and I took it as quickly as I could.

"Hey," I said, not knowing where else to begin.

"Hey," he said in a tone I didn't recognize from him. He wasn't trying to comfort me, and he clearly wasn't feeling too comforted himself. "Sorry, I don't know why I called Piper's phone again. I meant to call yours."

He sounded so flustered, and that made me feel horrible. I needed to be there with him. "No problem. Listen, I want Piper to take me to the church. I mean, this is all my fault. You shouldn't have to deal with it alone."

"This isn't your fault, Sarah. Nothing about this is your fault."

I couldn't help but think everyone was taking it all way too seriously. No, I didn't typically have to deal with reporters and paparazzi following me everywhere I went, but I was pretty famous. Whatever story they had, or thought they had— we'd sort it all out.

"This is just part of the reality of my life, Ben. I'm sorry it's happening at church. I mean, that seems like it should be off-limits, as far as class and taste go, but I guess it's something I should have considered. Let me just get there and let them get a picture or whatever they're going for, and then we can proceed as normal."

He laughed cynically and said, "Normal doesn't exist anymore. She saw to that."

She? What in the world was he talking about? "Ben—"

"Look, we need to talk, but not like this. Can you meet me somewhere in half an hour?"

"Of course, but you'll be in the middle of your sermon." I looked at my watch. "Won't you? You didn't have to cancel, did you?"

It was as if he hadn't heard anything I said. He just gave me an address, told me he loved me, and then asked to speak to Piper again. As he talked to her, she snatched the address, written on the back of a receipt, out of my hand, glanced in her side mirror, and got back on the road. When she hung up, she put her phone in her pocket and then asked for my phone.

"Why do you want my phone?" I asked as I pulled it out of my purse and handed it to her. "What did he say?"

She jammed my phone into her pocket, alongside hers, and then said, "He asked me to make sure you didn't check out any headlines on your phone."

What in the world was happening?

Twenty-five minutes later we pulled into a middle-class neighborhood I'd never known existed and then up to a house I'd never seen before. There was, however, a familiar CR-V in the driveway. Piper put her car into park and jumped out and ran over to the passenger side door, and pulled me into a tight embrace as soon as I stepped out.

"Piper, you're scaring me," I said. I tried to say

it lightly, but I hadn't succeeded. My voice was trembling.

Just then I saw Ben open the front door. Piper caught his eye, and then she looked back to me.

"You love Ben and he loves you," she said, tears in her eyes. "That's what matters. Do you understand me? And it's not fair. It's not fair to either of you, but it's really not fair to you. I know you, Sarah. Your instinct is going to be to doubt yourself and be convinced that you aren't worthy, but you are. You are. I know it, and I promise you that man over there knows it. So when your crazy insecurities start to rise to the top, you rest in the peace and glory of our Lord, and you trust in the love Ben has for you. Trust in who you know Ben to be. God has big plans for you—that much is clear. So whatever this is, it will not destroy you if you don't let it. And if you don't think you're strong enough to handle it, well, that's what Ben and I are for. All you have to do is let God know you're still in the fight."

I was terrified but also somehow at peace. I nodded once, not able to imagine anything that could possibly be worthy of all of this hoopla, but ready to face it as long as Ben and Piper were by my side.

So it didn't really help that Piper suddenly wasn't by my side and instead was back in her car, pulling out of the driveway.

"Come on in," Ben called from the door, stretching out his hand.

I was saddened by the expression on his face as I took his hand and walked into this strange home with him. He offered to get me some coffee, which I could smell brewing, and I accepted. He went into the kitchen, and I was grateful for a moment to take in my surroundings. It was almost as if I were in a parallel dimension. It was clear that no one else was in the house, or anywhere in the vicinity, so Ben had clearly let himself in. I watched him as he maneuvered around the kitchen, as comfortably as if he were in his own home, popping popcorn for Maddie and me.

I looked around the living room where I stood, surrounded by elegant furniture without the trappings of pomposity. A beautiful Tiffany lamp in the corner sat on an end table that was covered with coloring books and crayons, presenting in one perfect image the feel of the whole room. I walked to a bookshelf that held a few books but which served primarily as an exhibit of family photos.

One face—one of my favorite faces in the world—appeared more than any other, and I smiled as I looked at a photographic history of Madeline Delaney's first five years. I was especially touched by one I recognized imme-diately as one I had taken. In it, Ben and Maddie fed the ducks. Well, that's how it had begun anyway. What the photo showed was when it all fell apart disastrously and Maddie was left in fits of laughter as Ben ran away from a very large goose who seemed to think Ben had been a little too stingy with his breadcrumbs. I ran my fingers over the top of the frame, the sound of her high-pitched laughter still ringing in my ears and warming my heart four weeks later.

And then I saw the picture that made it perfectly clear whose home I was in. Ben was in blue hospital scrubs, leaning over the bed of a beautiful blonde woman. They both looked exhausted, but their faces shone bright with the love they couldn't contain, for each other and the tiny pink baby with a scrunched-up face asleep in the woman's arms.

"Hi, Christa," I whispered.

She was everywhere, in photos all over the shelves and on the walls of the home that undoubtedly belonged to Christa's parents. There were photos of her as a child and in high school. In one, she and a gangly boy with brown hair and very familiar eyes sat together on a Ferris wheel, laughing, clearly unaware that they were being watched. Others showed the same boy and girl with their wedding party, in front of a Sold sign, next to a sonogram machine. In one, they stood on a beach in front of a setting sun, laughing together in spite of the dark circles under their eyes and the scarf on her head.

"Thank you for loving him so much, Christa," I whispered. "Thank you for being a woman worthy of his love. Thank you for Maddie." I wiped away one tear that fell. "Thank you for preparing him to love me."

"Here you go," Ben said as he walked out of the kitchen with my coffee. I turned around, and he saw my expression, but I don't think he knew quite how to read it.

"She was gorgeous, Ben. Just . . . gorgeous."

He set the coffee down on an end table and walked over and looked at the pictures with me. "Yeah," he said.

As his eyes moved from one frame to the next, I noticed that he seemed to be taking it all in as if for the first time. I hadn't thought about it before, but I suddenly realized that despite spending almost as much time in Ben's house as I had my own over the past couple of months, I had never seen Christa before that day.

"Why don't you have any pictures of her up at your house?"

"I do. They're just mostly in Maddie's bedroom. Except for my copy of this one. It's hanging up in my room." He pointed to the one taken immediately after Maddie's birth. He sighed. "I don't know. At first I didn't hang anything on the walls at all, because I couldn't imagine staying in Chicago for long. Too many memories, you know? We'd been in Connecticut from the time I started at Yale, up until she found out she was sick and wanted to come back to be close to her folks. And then it all went so fast, and I just couldn't imagine staying. I guess at a certain point it just seemed like it would belabor the grief to hang up memories I was trying not to be consumed by."

"Well"—I swallowed down the lump in my throat—"if it's okay with you, I'd really like to put some of these photos in our home after we get married. She's part of your story, so she's part of our story." I thought of everything that had been said by Piper and Ben over the fourteen or so hours prior, and I knew I was ready for whatever was coming our way. I glanced again at the photo that had instantly become my favorite—the one on the Ferris wheel. "Even then, God was preparing your heart to love me."

He pulled me to him, and as I rested my head on his chest, listening to the heart that I knew beat in time with mine, I silently prayed, *Whatever it is, Lord, help me to be his strength.*

"Let's sit," he said quietly, guiding me to the couch.

He opened his mouth to start talking, but I stopped him. "Ben, before you say whatever you're about to say, I just . . ." I felt like I needed to say something to assure him of my love, but I had no idea what it should be. So I kissed him, gently, and then pulled away and grabbed his hands. "I love you," I said.

He smiled. "I love you too." The smile faded. "Okay, so here's the situation—"

"I love you."

He rolled his eyes. "Are you using my own Jedi mind trick against me?"

"Sorry." I winked. "Go ahead."

I was terrified and yet I was at peace. I'd never felt anything like it.

"Laura's back," he said.

"Oh good," I said, somewhat sincerely.

"Yeah, well . . . that's a matter of opinion, I suppose." He stood up and started pacing, running his hand through his hair.

"Just say it, Ben. It's okay."

He stood staring out the window for a few seconds, and then he slammed the palm of his hand up against the wall. I walked up behind him, wrapped my arms around his waist, and rested my head on his back.

"She called the reporters. At least I think it was her. When I got to church this morning, there were dozens of them." He turned around to face me. "I thought they were for you—"

"They weren't?"

"Yes and no." He laughed bitterly. "She used your name to get them there, certainly. And they did seem very interested in the fact that you go to church there and, honestly, that you go to church at all. And of course our relationship was getting quite the buzz. If she had just stopped there . . ."

I couldn't imagine what it could possibly be. If they weren't there for me, but I was obviously somehow connected . . . Dozens of reporters? And a big enough story to merit my phone being taken away? I took a deep breath, having a very bad feeling about it all. And Piper knew. Whatever it was, he had told her on the phone, so she had known. She had known when she said, "Trust in who you know Ben to be." The story wasn't about me at all.

The story was about Ben.

I took one more deep breath, imagining the worst, certain that the truth wouldn't be that bad. "Do you want to get married?"

He looked at me funny. "Of course I do. That was kind of what I meant by 'Will you marry me?' actually."

I shook my head, not sure, just like with the fable, why I was saying anything I was saying, but knowing I meant every word of it. "No, I mean right now."

Bless his heart. I think back on it now and I can't help but laugh. He was so confused. "Umm . . . like, right now?" He looked around the living room, probably searching for a clue as to what the heck I was talking about.

"Listen to me," I said, and then I pulled him back to the couch and forced him to sit. When he did, I sat next to him, my knees beneath me so that I was his height and we were eye-to-eye. I held his face in my hands, forcing him to look at me and listen. "What I'm saying is I would marry you, right now. I know that you're about to tell me something that you're afraid is going to shatter us. I can read it in your eyes. But nothing is going to shatter us. I would marry you right now, and whatever you're about to tell me would be an afterthought. Got it?"

He cleared his throat. "I have never been so intimidated by someone and yet so attracted to them at the same time. You're kind of scary when you're take-charge like this." He added, "I'm not complaining, mind you."

I smiled, but I didn't move. I hadn't gotten the answer I needed yet. "Do you hear what I'm telling you? There is nothing you can say that will shatter us. Got it?"

"Got it," he said quietly.

And then he finally let me in. "Laura announced to, from what I could tell, every single major news outlet, that Raine de Bourgh's pastor boyfriend had fathered a child out of wedlock with one of his parishioners."

I said nothing. It was ridiculous, of course, but I got up from the couch and stood by the window for a moment, letting it sink in. I wanted to make sure I understood.

"Sarah, are you okay?" he asked, keeping his distance as he awaited my reaction.

I was fine. I was so fine that I broke his statement down and analyzed it in my mind, convinced I was missing something.

Raine de Bourgh. Okay, that was me.

My pastor boyfriend was Ben, of course.

The whole child/parishioner thing was a little blurry, but still I didn't see why anyone was taking it as seriously as they were.

I couldn't help but smile. "I know it's none of their business, but I really think you should tell them you haven't even had sex in a few years." I started laughing. "While we're at it, let's make sure they know I haven't either! That one might blow their minds."

Ben wasn't laughing. Or smiling. "The thing is, she didn't give details to the press—just the generic claim that I'd had a child with a member of the church. I'm guessing she figured she could do more immediate damage by being vague, and she was probably right. But she got a little more specific with the church board. She claims it goes back more than a few years, Sarah." He moved a little closer, in retrospect clearly trying to break it to me gently. He hadn't yet gotten to the part that he feared would cause my unraveling. "The child is fourteen now."

Of course I suddenly understood perfectly, and I have to admit I was slightly less fine, but I didn't unravel.

"Does this out-of-wedlock child happen to be Maddie's regular babysitter when you and I go out?"

He rushed in and grabbed my hands, I think still expecting a meltdown. "Kaitlyn is not my daughter, Sarah. She's not."

Trust in who you know Ben to be.

"Of course she's not," I said, relief overtaking every inch of me. "Of course she's not."

He grabbed me and pulled me to him and held on for dear life. I felt the release of tension in his shoulders and down his back. Had he really been worried I wouldn't believe him? How could I not? The thought was just ridiculous to me.

"Okay," he said, exhaling and finally allowing himself to smile. "Okay. So, now I guess we just figure out the next step."

"Next step? Why is there a next step? It's not even worth acknowledging, is it?" I took another sip of coffee, feeling unbelievably calm, apart from my increased dislike of Laura. "What a psycho! What could she possibly hope to accomplish? Okay, here's what we do. We call a press conference or something and you tell the world there is no truth to any of it, she's a family friend, blah, blah, blah. I mean, whatever you want to say. It's all over and done before the end of the day. We'll just want to make sure you have all of the facts laid out. What were you doing fourteen years ago? Or, what, fifteen, I guess? Were you with Christa yet?"

The smile faded from his face as he realized I wasn't as caught up as he had thought I was. "Fifteen years ago I was dating Laura."

"Oh. Right. Oh." The room started spinning. "She couldn't be yours, right? I mean, it's impossible. Right? When is Kaitlyn's birthday?" I began to panic. For just a moment, I began to panic. "Is . . . I mean . . . how sure . . ."

Okay, Lord. I'm in the fight. I love him and I'm not going anywhere. But . . .

He wasn't talking. Why wasn't he talking? "Why aren't you saying anything, Ben? I need you to say something. I need you to tell me that you were on a mission trip to Rwanda when she got pregnant, or something."

"Sarah," he said quietly and cautiously. "We broke up about six months before Kaitlyn was born, so it's going to be pretty difficult to argue based on timing alone."

Trust in who you know Ben to be.

And then realization dawned. "You never slept with her," I said, not as a question but as a fact.

His eyes grew wide as he quickly said, "Of course I didn't!"

I wanted to kiss him and I wanted to strangle him. "Why didn't you start with that? Sheesh,

Ben! I'm over here doing the math, and you knew the math didn't matter."

He was silent for a moment, which wasn't the reaction I was expecting. Finally, he quietly asked, "Did you really think . . . I mean, really, Sarah? You thought I slept with her? You thought I'd just drop Maddie off at her house and expect you to mingle with her at my parents' house, and just never mention it?"

"Well, you were with her for years! Why wouldn't you have slept with her?"

He smiled cautiously. "I think you know the answer to that."

I sighed. "Of course I do. I'm sorry. The force is strong in this one," I said as I pointed to him, and then I shook my head, feeling like a complete dork for once again falling back on pop culture in an attempt to deal with life.

"The force?" He suddenly got very tickled and couldn't stop laughing. "So, are you and I Jedi now? Is it time to just own that?"

I groaned.

"In all seriousness, Sarah . . . I am so far from perfect. Please don't think that the reason I never slept with Laura was because I'm this super-Christian. That's not it. I've screwed up. A lot. But that one was honestly never too tough for me. I've had my temptations, but I've only been in love with two women, and Laura wasn't one of them."

He reached out and caressed my hair, and I should have savored the romantic significance of what he was saying, but I was too caught up in the scandal in my midst.

"She did a lot more than kiss some guy in her study group, didn't she?" I gasped accusatorily. "She was already pregnant when you broke up with her! And just think! You were going to propose to that woman. But, wait—" I tilted my head and looked at him in confusion as some gears finally began to shift into place. "If you were never in love with her, then why—"

Ben just looked at me with love, patiently waiting for me to put it all together. And then in one giant moment of clarity, I understood.

"You knew? You knew she was pregnant. That's why you were going to propose?"

"But everything I told you was true, Sarah. Every single thing. I knew about the one time— we had gotten in a big fight when we were both home for Christmas that year, and she stormed out of my family's house on Christmas Eve. I guess she went to a bar and got drunk with some guy. When she found out she was pregnant a couple months later, she told me everything and swore it had been a big mistake. A one-time thing. She didn't even know who the guy was. I thought I was about to do the noble thing, and I suppose I was, but then I found out she had cheated on me a second time. And of course the fact that I ran into Christa about that same time made the choice to walk away even easier . . ."

"Yeah."

I inhaled through my nose and exhaled through my mouth, trying to regain my focus and my equilibrium. I sat back down on the couch, and he sat next to me. We were both facing forward, staring into space.

"Do you remember," I began softly, "when we were driving to your parents' house that evening and I asked you to tell me if there was ever anything about your relationship with Laura that I needed to know, and you said you would?"

"Ah," he said. "So, you meant something like this?"

"Yeah. This would have been good to know."

"Noted."

We sat there for another minute, and then I put my hand out and grabbed his and then rested my head on his shoulder. I knew we'd have to start thinking about what to do next, but right then I just wanted to sit there, loving Ben, trusting in who I knew him to be.

18.

Ethical and Professional Leprosy

Within a half hour, we had discussed all of the nooks and crannies of the situation and all of the potential repercussions, some of which were already in the early stages.

Ben had been immediately placed on unpaid leave while Mercy Point addressed the accusations. The unpaid part certainly presented some challenges, but it was the leave that was devastating to him. To some extent he understood. While he would have preferred his congregation to immediately defend him, call the claims ridiculous, and throw all of their support behind him—and he was hurt that they didn't—he also understood that there was a responsibility to Laura, a member of the body. They needed to be sure they knew the truth before a decision was made.

As hurt as he still would have been, I think he would have agreed that the church was proceeding correctly if it hadn't been for the way Lenore Isaacs had stepped up in the meeting with the leadership committee and valiantly volunteered her husband's services in the interim, before Ben had even left the room.

It was interesting, as we talked, to see just how much his feelings of friendship for Laura had changed. I suppose that was to be expected, but I was still taken aback by the hostility he was expressing toward her. He was much angrier than I was, actually. Then again, that made perfect sense, I guess. As far as I was concerned, she had just lived up to her potential. In Ben's mind, she had undone a lifelong friendship and not only destroyed his career and reputation in the process, but also threatened his relationship with me. Yeah, that was pretty bad.

I, however, just couldn't believe she had acted alone. What was the end game for her? To ruin Ben? To split us up? To ruin me? Perhaps. Those were all things that she most likely believed were well within her grasp. But then what? Why would she do that to Kaitlyn? And did she think Ben would run to her for comfort after all she had done? That seemed a bit unlikely. Tom and Lenore Isaacs, on the other hand, may have had a desired outcome very much in sight.

"How did you end up at Mercy Point?" I asked Ben as we sat on the same couch, resting on each other, taking a breather from our strategy session.

"Well, Christa and I grew up there. It was our home church. So—"

"Hang on," I interrupted. "You and Christa attended Mercy Point together?" I guess I'd just never thought about it, never considered that for Ben those halls could be full of memories with someone other than me.

He nodded. "Vacation Bible School, youth group, summer camp, everything. Her dad was our pastor until they moved to Indiana, when we were in high school. There were so many people there then that I can almost understand how I went so long without really noticing her." He walked over to the bookshelf full of photos and carefully selected the one he wanted and brought it over to me.

I took it and studied it, and while I had previously only noticed the man I loved and the beautiful young woman he was marrying, this time I saw all of the details beyond the tux and the white dress. There was the baby grand piano in the background, just to the left of them, and the steps on which they stood. The built-in baptismal area in the back, and the familiar ornate designs on the pulpit. They'd even been married at Mercy Point.

"When we moved to Connecticut, I think we attended every church in New Haven searching for another church home. I accepted a few positions, but they never lasted very long." He laughed thinking back on it. "My first professional ministry position was as youth pastor at this little church on the outskirts of town— great people, great building, plenty of resources.

The only problem was that the median age of the congregation was seventy-six. Well, until Christa and I joined and threw those figures off slightly." He winked. "They just couldn't understand why I couldn't get teenagers interested in attending there. That one didn't last too long, needless to say."

"I'm sorry." I laughed. "That's awful."

"Oh no. You haven't heard anything yet. The next church was much younger and much healthier. I got hired on as an associate pastor, and everything was fantastic for about two months, and then it all went up in flames."

"Oh no! What happened?"

"The church literally went up in flames," he deadpanned. He raised his hand to cross his heart. "Honest to goodness. But that wasn't even the bad part. It turned out the lead pastor had lost all of the church's money at the horse track, so they couldn't afford to rebuild."

"That can't be true!" I protested.

"It is," he insisted with a chuckle. "I couldn't make that stuff up! There were other stories like that too. We were like a personification of Murphy's Law for churches. I started to think my résumé should come with a warning. But we just kept plugging along, convinced it was what we were called to do. And then Christa was diagnosed, and we moved back to Chicago. There was an opening for a youth pastor at Mercy

Point, so we could have gone back then, I guess. But I just couldn't commit that sort of time and dedication. I needed to save that for Christa and Maddie."

"So what did you do?" I asked, fascinated by this brief period of Ben's history that we had never discussed. "I mean, for a job?"

He smiled. "Lots of prayer, and lots of help." He returned the photo to its proper place and stood there staring at all of the memories for a moment. "Gary and Beth—Christa's parents—insisted I shouldn't work, and that they would take care of us for a while, financially. They wouldn't take no for an answer. For about two minutes I considered that a threat to my masculinity and a lack of faith in my ability to be the breadwinning, independent head of the household I needed to be." He looked back at me, still smiling. "But it didn't take me long to realize what an unbelievable gift it was. I was able to go with her to chemo and steal her away on little trips when we woke up and realized it was going to be a good day. I'll never be able to repay them for providing for us so that I didn't have to miss a moment of those months with her."

My eyes were misty again, so affected by the capacity of his love, and theirs. "I'm guessing they'd never want you to."

He shook his head. "All they want, I think, is time with Maddie." He laughed softly. "I don't

292

know that they were counting on just how much time they would get with me too. I love being around them, and they spoil Maddie rotten, so obviously she's a fan." He smiled. "Gary and Beth understand me in a way I don't think my own parents ever have. Don't get me wrong, I love my parents—"

"I'll be honest," I interrupted, "I expected much worse from your parents."

"Give them time." He rolled his eyes. "But no, they're good people, and I love them a lot. But Gary and Beth . . ."

"They get it." I smiled, remembering his words when I walked out of the sushi restaurant and found him on the phone with Beth.

"Yeah," he agreed. "They always have, I think, but the past few years have really driven that home." He stood up and went to the kitchen to get us both more coffee, and I followed him in. "So after Christa died, I took a little bit of time, and then I needed to get back to work. The lead pastor job was open at Mercy Point, and my mother pushed me to take it. She didn't understand why I couldn't do it. From the time we came back to town, we'd been going to church with Gary and Beth. He's been the pastor of this great little church in Algonquin ever since they moved back from Indiana. And then Christa was gone. I couldn't walk into Gary and Beth's church and face those people and those memories. And I sure couldn't walk back into Mercy Point and face those people and *those* memories. Christa was everywhere. And then I entered my anger stage of grief, and I stopped going to church anywhere for a while."

As I listened to him I understood, without him telling me, that this subject—more than Christa's death or my desire to have children—was actually the one that had never been up for discussion. The things he never discussed and which he had never told anyone were all wrapped up in the conversation we were having. He was telling me about his deepest pain.

"Mercy Point pursued me pretty relentlessly, actually," he continued. "And a few other churches did too."

"Why?" I asked with a wicked grin. "Didn't they know about your track record?"

"I guess everyone thinks they'll be the exception to the rule," he said with a laugh.

Though I teased him, I had no trouble at all understanding why he was in such high demand. In addition to being biblically sound and extremely knowledgeable, Ben is an engaging, charismatic speaker. Of course he's also incredibly sexy, though I highly doubted any of those churches actually put that in their offer letters.

"So you got some pretty good offers?" I asked.

He nodded. "Offers I shouldn't have been able

to refuse. But I was busy wrestling with the Lord, and I just couldn't let go."

We returned to the couch, full cups of coffee in hand, and I did a little mental wrestling of my own. I just couldn't picture Ben falling away from his faith, and I certainly couldn't imagine him as anything other than a pastor. It just always seemed like it was what he was meant to do.

"What is it?" he asked in response to my expressionless silence.

I shrugged. "I don't know, really. I guess it just makes me sad to think of how bad things must have been for you to turn away from God."

He set his coffee cup on the table in front of us and then took my cup from my hands and did the same before wrapping his arm around my shoulders and pulling me close.

He took a deep breath. "I don't think I ever turned from God, actually. It was more that I turned *on* him. I just wanted answers, and I wasn't going to budge until I got them. But I knew it was my battle with the Lord, not Maddie's, so I sent her to church with Gary and Beth every week. And we still read Bible stories and said prayers together. I never lost my love for Christ," he insisted vehemently. "If anything, it grew stronger. But I don't think I'd ever realized how much my faith had been wrapped up in Christa's faith. It was like God, Christa, and I had been on this journey together, and then suddenly it was just God and me. I guess I just had to find out where he and I really stood."

"So what changed?" I asked.

He'd been very serious and focused for the fifteen minutes or so that he had been telling me the story, but as he pulled away to look at me, his face lit up and the smile returned.

"Isn't that obvious?"

I thought really hard, but no. It wasn't. I shook my head.

He sighed and pulled me even closer to him on the couch, and I snuggled into his embrace. "After four years of saying no, the offers pretty much went away. I was teaching some college courses—all thoughts of church work were ancient history—and then I got one last call from Mercy Point. In all that time, they hadn't been able to find a permanent pastor, and they'd lost a lot of the congregation. They couldn't afford to pay me anywhere near what they'd offered originally, but they told me they were sure I was the right pastor to help rebuild the church. They begged me to consider it."

"And you were finally done wrestling?"

"Oh no." He laughed. "I hadn't given up on that yet. But I also couldn't stand the thought of Mercy Point having to close the doors. Especially if I could have done something. So I told them I would think about it. But before I could even give it any serious thought, I knew I had to walk through those doors and see if I could even handle it. So that was the first step. It was a Thursday evening, and no one was there besides the cleaning crew, but I did it. I walked through the doors."

"And it was okay," I said softly, believing I finally saw how God had allowed it all to come about.

"No, it wasn't okay," he corrected me. "It was a lot of things, but it wasn't okay. She was everywhere, and I'd only made it down one hallway. I knew I couldn't do it. I started walking back to the door and pulled out my cell phone right then and there, to call and tell them I couldn't do it. But I started feeling a little light-headed. As badly as I wanted to get out of there and never look back, I had to sit for a minute. I'd had all of these memories flooding my mind and my heart, threatening to overtake me. I just didn't know if I could take any more," he said, still holding me. "I tried to stand up, needing to get out of there, pretty certain I couldn't survive anything else. I wanted to run away as fast as I could, but I couldn't get off that bench."

My tears started falling. "*That* bench?"

"That bench," he confirmed. "So I just sat there, tired of wrestling, having nothing left to give. I screamed out for God to finish me off, once and for all. He won. I was done. I couldn't do it anymore. I made the phone call to refuse the position, but they didn't have anyone to preach that Sunday. They were ready to give up. They were going to close the doors, and all of those people—the ones who had held on and stayed faithful in spite of it all—were going to have to find another church. So as painful as I knew it would be, I agreed to preach one sermon, one Sunday, but that was it. Just to give them one more week to figure something out. Then I knew I would never step foot in that building ever again."

I sat up so that I could look at him. I started to speak, but I had no words, so I just stared at him as he continued.

"That Sunday I was determined to go straight from the pastor's study to the pulpit, and then straight out the door, and yet I found myself walking down that hallway. The music started, you and I went our separate ways, and I wrote a note, accepting the position, and slipped it to them just before I was introduced."

We sat in silence for quite a while, trying to process all of the ways God had worked in our hearts and lives to bring us together, and feeling quite certain that it was something we would never be able to fully comprehend.

I was startled out of my perfect peace and contentment by the shrill ring of my cell phone. I didn't even know that I had it back, but I guess Piper had slipped it into my purse while hugging me. I tried to ignore it, but Ben urged me to at least see who it was, in case God had taken to just calling us directly. We laughed as I stood to answer it, not even worrying about what might await me. After all, Ben and I had discussed all possible fallout, hadn't we?

"Hello?"

"Really, kid? You couldn't have used your best sex scandal material when we were promoting *Stollen Desire*?"

I laughed. "Oh, Joe. You don't even know if this *is* my best material!"

He wasn't laughing. "This is bad, Sarah."

I looked at Ben and rolled my eyes, indicating the call was going to take a little while. He smiled, walked over to me, and kissed me on the cheek, and then picked up our coffee cups and went to the kitchen to tidy up.

"It's not, really," I insisted, still feeling perfectly calm. "This is nothing more than an attempt by Ben's ex-girlfriend to split us up." I still wasn't completely sold on that motive, but it was the one I was going with until I could prove otherwise.

"No, you know what this is? This is *The Thorn Birds*."

Oh, here we go again. "This is not *The Thorn Birds*, Joe. I know where you're going, but the child is not Ben's. I promise you that. There will be no *Thorn Birds*–type situation here. We're not going to have years of Ben mentoring this child like Father Ralph mentored Dane, only to discover with his dying breath that the child was his after all. Besides, Dane was the child conceived in love between Ralph and Meggie, so even if there were other similarities to be drawn—"

Joe cleared his throat. "Well, did it ever occur to you that maybe we had this wrong the whole time? Did it ever occur to you that maybe you're not the Meggie?"

The thought was staggering for one brief moment. For one second—less than a second—I almost let my crazy, pop-culture-obsessed, insecure mind run away with me. After all, what if he was right? And if he was right, and Laura was actually Meggie, then who did that make me? Luke, Meggie's ranch hand husband? No, that wouldn't make any sense. Who was the rival for Ralph's attention and love? Mary Carson, Ralph's elderly, spiteful benefactor who, even after her death, used her wealth and power to try to win Ralph's love away from Meggie? *Stop it, Sarah. Stop it.*

"This is not *The Thorn Birds*, Joe. This is my life, messed up though it may be, and if claiming I'm not the Meggie is the most constructive thing you have to say—"

"They don't want the book, kid."

"What does that mean? What do you mean,

they don't want the book? Who doesn't want the book?"

"The publishers."

"Okay," I said, trying to remain calm. "But it really doesn't matter if they want the book, does it? I have a contract."

There was no chance, none at all, that I wasn't going to be given an opportunity to publish my Christian romance, I tried to convince myself. After all, hadn't that been, at least partially, what God had been directing me to do? Wasn't the Lord giving me an opportunity to put something positive out into the mainstream for a change? Wasn't I the perfect person to do it? Wasn't everything that had happened somehow preparation for the day when I would get to deliver good and light to the masses, rather than the dark, soul-crushing crap I was known for?

"That's right. You have a contract," he said, but it wasn't comforting. "The only problem is they were shaky about it all to begin with, and now they're afraid no booksellers will touch it. And, frankly, they just don't think readers who are wanting to read a Christian romance will consider you a reliable source."

"That's insane, Joe! Because of *this*? Because of Raine de Bourgh, yeah, you bet. That I get. That one was always going to be tricky. But *this*?" It didn't make any sense. "I don't get it, Joe. I just got more free publicity than we ever could have bought in a hundred years. I understand it's not good publicity, but you're the one who said all press is good press, so—"

"Sarah, I would have thought it was Christmas morning if you had given me this sort of PR explosion when we were pushing the other books. This feeds into everything that audience wants to believe you are. But if you're hoping to make a transition to the Christian market?"

I didn't understand anything that was happening. "What they're saying about Ben isn't true, Joe," I said softly. "None of it."

"I believe you." He sighed. "Really. But look at what we're dealing with here, kid. People were already going to have a difficult time disassociating you from *Stollen Desire*. But hey, look, she goes to church now. She's changed. She's marrying a pastor." He took a deep breath. "A pastor whose name is now every bit as connected to sex in the news as hers is."

I stifled my sobs. "We're going to get Ben's name cleared, Joe."

"I'm sure you will. But it's out there. You know? And let's face it—for all the damage he's doing to you right now, that's nothing compared to the damage you're doing to him." He spoke gently, fully aware he was breaking my heart and hating every minute of it—but also not knowing any way around it.

"Because if I'm the person the world thinks I

am, it's not very difficult to think the worst of anyone who would want to marry me."

"Exactly."

I breathed in as deeply as I could, but it felt painfully shallow. "So what do I do now?"

"Like you said, you've got a contract. They don't want the book, but that doesn't mean they don't have to publish it. It just means it might get buried in the bargain bin for a while," he said. "Or you could always go back to what you do best. Maybe it's not time for Raine to retire. Not yet. Maybe it's time for *The Thorn Birds* to merge with the literary community that already loves you. Actually, kid, if you take this story you've been writing, which you know I love, and turn it on its ear . . ." He whistled through his teeth. "And then you reinvent yourself in a few years, when all of this has been forgotten, after you've milked the edgier romance market for all it's worth. Then you have your 'come to Jesus' moment. I can work with that."

He rambled on like that, but I stopped listening. I glanced up as Ben walked out of the kitchen, not saying a word but telling me everything I needed to know. He stood there with a dish towel thrown over his shoulder, the concern evident in his eyes. He didn't need to know what was happening, he just needed to know that I was okay.

"Joe," I said into the phone softly, never taking my eyes off of Ben. "Joe," I said a little more loudly as he continued his rambling. "Joe!" I finally shouted.

"Yeah?"

"How much would it cost to buy out the remainder of the contract?"

He laughed. "You've lost your mind."

"Probably. So how much would it cost?"

"Well, let's see. Of course, there's no chance they'll ever revert the rights to you on the Desire books. And you know how much your advance was for the next book, so we can start with that. Do you still have all of that money sitting around?"

"Well, no," I stuttered. "Not all of it. I bought the house, and I had to pay you and Sydney, and—"

"Sorry, kid. Can't be done. Not realistically."

The tears I'd been valiantly holding in were suddenly released with a vengeance as I began to feel truly hopeless for the first time. Ben walked closer to me, wanting to comfort me but not having any idea what was happening.

"Look, Sarah," Joe said, softening his tone, "you know how I feel about you, and I'm just trying to be up front with you here. There is no chance, absolutely none, that they are going to give up the rights. Ever. But you're the author who wrote those books that have made them so much money, and at the end of the day, I don't think they want to lose you. No matter what they're saying right now. We'll let this blow over, you'll give them something they'll be happy with for this next book, and then when the next contract rolls around, we'll build it around your Christian romance, or even your artistic and inspirational reimagining of the phone book, if that's what you want. We just have to wait a little while. Just be patient. Okay, kid?"

I wiped away the renegade tear as it fell. "Thanks, Joe. I'll be in touch."

I hung up the phone and tried to decide if I was angry or sad. It was difficult to tell, but opening the door and throwing my phone outside, as hard as I could, while making the sound of a wild chimpanzee, seemed to indicate the anger was, at least temporarily, the stronger emotion of the two. The maniacal laughter that followed called it all into question—most notably my sanity.

Ben didn't move from where he stood, but he also didn't gawk at me, or go running from the room, or react in any of the other ways which would have been somewhat justified, considering my crazed state. He just let me have my moment. He'd slammed his hand into the wall, I destroyed a cell phone and howled like a banshee. Everyone handles frustration in their own way. When it seemed that I had dealt with the worst of it, he sat by me on the floor in front of the door, where I had collapsed into an exhausted heap of tears and calamity, his back up against the wall, arms around his propped-up knees.

I don't know how to describe the way I was feeling. In the old days, I would have downed a bottle of wine and gone to bed rather than even try to analyze the emotions. I still felt God's presence, so powerfully, and I knew that, as Piper had said, he had some awfully big plans. My faith didn't falter, and my willingness to follow him had never been stronger, but it sure would have been nice to be given just a little advance peek at what he had in store. Ben was going to continue being the pastor at Mercy Point, where more seats were filled and more lives were changed for the good of God's kingdom each and every week. I was going to use all of my fame and notoriety to inspire others, lead them to Christ, and strengthen marriages. That was the plan, right? Hadn't that been the plan? I'd thought so as recently as morning coffee. To find ourselves contaminated by ethical and professional leprosy, rendering us unclean and untouchable, just a few short hours later was enough to cause whiplash.

I smiled sadly and snuggled into Ben once more. "Remember that time I told you nothing could shatter us? I meant that, but you do realize I only meant our love for each other, right? I think I need to add an addendum that makes it clear that I offer no such guarantees as to our careers, reputations, income, or relationships with others."

He lowered his knees and wrapped his arms around me. "Well, yeah. Obviously. I mean, that was a different time. We were different people then."

I looked at my watch. "It's been about an hour."

He sighed. "Ah, were we ever so young?"

19.

There Once Was a Girl

A few minutes later, Ben and I were preparing to leave Gary and Beth's house, not certain where we were going but convinced we couldn't hide any longer. We were going to run into some reporters or photographers somewhere, we knew, but we were just postponing the inevitable.

"Ground rules?" I asked as we headed toward the door.

"Easy," he said. "Honor God, treat everyone else involved with respect, and don't leave each other's side. Oh, and be honest."

He sure made it sound easy, but I didn't believe he thought it would be any less of a challenge than I did, though I knew we were going to be presented individual challenges. For him, the most difficult thing would be treating everyone involved with respect. He wasn't feeling very respectful toward Laura, I knew, and it would take a lot of prayer and fortitude to avoid throwing her under a bus.

And I do mean a literal bus.

For my part, I wondered if I possessed the spiritual maturity to stick to my guns. Throughout my entire adult life, every speech I had given and every statement I made publicly had been full of lies.

"Well, I'm not saying my sex life is quite as outrageous as that of Alex and Annie, but it has been said we write what we know," I'd said to a national late-night television audience.

"I just couldn't be prouder of him than I am. He deserved this award, not just for who he is in the boardroom, but who he is in life," I'd said to *Chicago* magazine and the entire state of Illinois when Patrick was awarded their "Man of the Year" prize.

"I will," I'd replied to a priest and five hundred people I didn't know when asked if I would be with Patrick McDermott until death separated us.

Though at the time, I'd believed with my whole heart that one was the truth.

As we began to walk out the door, a car pulled into the driveway. I was afraid it was reporters and quickly tried to pull Ben back into the house before we were sighted.

"Relax, it's Beth and Gary," he said, not budging as I tugged on him with all of my strength.

For some reason that was temporarily more terrifying than the thought of photographers. I'd already developed an immense respect for Christa's parents, based on all Ben had told me. They seemed like wonderful people, and I was certain we'd all be fast friends, were I not attempting to fill a void left by their daughter—not only in the life of their beloved son-in-law but also their only grandchild. But as it was . . .

I was hunkered down, squatting just inside the door, under the window so that I couldn't be seen, still holding on to Ben's hand, still pulling on him, a little bit lost in thought trying to come up with an excuse to kiss him.

That had helped the last time I didn't want to meet parents.

"Sarah, what are you doing?" He laughed.

"I can't meet them, Ben," I whispered, still hiding but deciding to go with the honest approach for a change. "I am really uncomfortable at the thought of that. What if they don't like me? I mean, I know they love you, and I'm sure they'll probably support you no matter what, but I want them to like me. I know I can never compare to their daughter in their minds, and that's as it should be, but I want them to think I'm at least okay, you know? And I'm just not sure today is the day that I can put my best foot forward. Can we try another day? Please?"

I heard their footsteps and chatter getting closer, though I couldn't see them from my position near the floor, and I took a deep breath, hoping and praying that this time Ben would understand my heart. I just didn't know if I could stand for him to once again not comprehend how real my fear was, even if I couldn't help but demonstrate it in the silliest and most humiliating of ways.

"Hey, guys." He leaned out the door, still holding on to my hand. "I'm sorry, but would you mind giving us just a minute?"

"Sure," they said in unison. Beth asked, "Do you want us to wait in the car, or . . ."

I saw in Ben's eyes that for a moment he wasn't sure how to answer that question. Should he ask them to leave and come back, or just wait in the car so I could sneak out the back door? But as he looked back to me, I saw a shift—in his thoughts and his demeanor. I didn't know what was happening, but the power I felt between us got very intense once more, and I was worried he was going to tell me how important it was that I meet Christa's parents, and then I would be riddled with guilt and have to go through with it. I would do it, of course, if that's what he wanted, but this time I was hoping he would understand.

"Actually, I'm just going to shut the door for a moment, if you don't mind," he said to them, never taking his eyes off of me. But he didn't wait to find out if they minded or not.

He took a couple of steps into the house, not letting go of my hand. From my mushroom-like position, I was twirled around as Ben got to the other side of me, and I was suddenly facing the inside of the house instead of the front yard as I had been. He used his foot to shut the door behind me and then reached for my other hand with his free hand and pulled me to a standing position.

"Come here," he whispered with a smile.

I was only about a foot away from him, so I couldn't get much closer. But it would have been rude to not even try . . .

"We probably shouldn't make them stay outside," I said as I inched closer. "They might have groceries to put away or something. I'd hate for their ice cream to melt."

He smiled but he didn't respond to that. Instead he released my hands, and as they fell, he placed his hands behind my neck and pulled me to him gently. "Do you realize I had to go three weeks without kissing you?"

The thought had occurred, yes.

He leaned in and tenderly captured my lips with his.

With slightly staggered breath once our lips had parted, I said, "If you're trying to make me forget how nervous I am, it's not going to work." Of course I was not entirely sure that was true. When it came to controlling my emotions, I was pretty sure Ben Delaney could do anything he set his mind to.

"I'm not trying to make you forget anything," he said softly, his lips only inches from mine. "I'm actually trying to help you remember something."

"I knew it. You *are* using your powers for evil."

He didn't say anything in response, but he leaned in and gently kissed me once again.

I sighed. "And also good, I suppose."

He smiled down at me and said, "If you want to go, we'll go. If you want to meet them another day, then that's what we'll do. I'm not going to pressure you into staying, but I do want you to understand that they already love you." He tucked a strand of hair behind my ear. "They were the first people I ever talked to about you. I talked with them after I found out about the books you had written, and I talked with them after I got to the church this morning and saw Laura and all the cameras, and their advice both times was the same."

"What? What did they say?"

"They said, 'The past has absolutely nothing to do with the future God has in store for the two of you.' Our past shapes us and our past prepares us, Sarah, but our past does not define us. In that same regard, Beth and Gary aren't just Christa's parents. They're my friends and my spiritual mentors and my daughter's grandparents. And they love you. They love you for the joy you've brought to my life, and Maddie's. They love you for being a woman dedicated to discovering God's will for her life. And they love you for taking that picture of me running from the goose, because they just think that's the funniest thing they've ever seen."

I laughed and felt all of my worry and fear melt away.

"Mostly," he said with a smile, putting separation between us for the first time but grabbing on to my hands, "they love you because I love you. So you don't have anything to worry about because that's never going to change. Remember that, okay?"

"Well, then," I said, opening the door, "I guess we should let them get their groceries put away."

Thankfully, they didn't actually have any groceries with them, and as they walked into their home their arms were free to hug me.

"This is Sarah," Ben said with affection as Beth wrapped her arms around me before she was even all the way through the doorway.

She pulled away from me and rolled her eyes toward Ben, for my benefit, as Gary swooped in for his introductory hug.

"Of course this is Sarah, Ben," Beth said as she slapped him on the arm before kissing him on the cheek. "I don't know who else he thinks we think he'd be bringing over."

"Plus we saw you on *The Tonight Show*," Gary added as he took Beth's handbag from her and hung it on the coatrack.

My eyes widened and Ben laughed as he draped his arm around my shoulders. "Well, at least we're diving straight into your worst fear, right?" he said to me.

"Worst fear? Are you kidding me?" Beth asked incredulously. "Oh. Because you don't like to dwell on the Raine de Bourgh stuff?"

I blushed. "I guess it's safe to say there are quite a few things I would do differently if given another chance."

"We all have things like that," Beth said. "That's understandable."

Gary walked out of the kitchen with four plates in his hands. "But I don't think appearing on *The Tonight Show* should ever be one of those things."

"Agreed," Beth said as she made her way to the kitchen. "But I have to say, it just hasn't been the same since Leno left."

"I always preferred Letterman," Gary interjected.

"Anyway, who's hungry?" Beth called from the kitchen.

Ben and I looked at each other and shrugged. Lunch with Gary and Beth sounded much more appealing than the media circus we knew awaited us whenever we were finally discovered, so we didn't see any harm in postponing the onslaught just a little bit longer.

As a woman who'd spent almost her entire adult life using the services of caterers and restaurants to prepare everything apart from brownies, I was absolutely no help whatsoever to Beth as she prepared the meal. She and Ben took care of that, and Gary and I set the table, prepared iced tea, and discussed the sermon he had delivered in Algonquin that morning.

A little while later, we were at the dinner table, holding hands as Gary prayed a prayer of blessing over the food. It was one of those prayers in which even though the person is talking to God, you know they're saying things a certain way for the benefit of those present. It was very Maria from *The Sound of Music*, when she thanked the children in her pre-meal prayer for making her feel so welcome, after she sat on a pinecone they'd planted on her seat. Or when she prayed for Liesl by name as Liesl snuck in through the window.

"Heavenly Father, thank you for this meal, for the nourishment it provides, the enjoyment we take from it, and the fellowship we share as we eat. Thank you for family, Father—those in other places today, those who now sit in your presence instead of ours, and especially those sitting around this table. Thank you for Sarah and Ben. Help us to be for them a source of strength, love, and protection, as you are for your children. Amen."

And then, dear Lord, about Liesl . . .

I understood what Ben meant about them getting it. Not only were they kind and so hospitable in a way few other people could have been in their situation, they were also just incredibly cool. We discussed movies and music—Gary has a sincere appreciation for Taylor Swift—and ganged up on Ben when he made the ridiculous claim that *Rocky IV* was actually the best of all Rocky movies. They both knew the Bible every bit as thoroughly as Ben did, but they were somehow less nerdy about it, and I loved listening to the three of them throw passages out there as if there were an applicable verse for every situation in life. They were just comfortably engaged in what was a typical type of conversation for their family, of which I was now a part.

By the time the discussion came around to the call I had received from Joe, I had no qualms about discussing it openly. I explained to them some of the ins and outs of my publishing contract and all of the potential repercussions.

"Well, waiting a little while to get your Christian romance out there isn't really all that bad, is it?" Beth asked over dessert. "And this other book you have to write in the meantime, well, that could be anything, right? So that could be fun. And now maybe the pressure is off. If they're not going to promote the book, you don't have to worry about book tours and all of that. That frees you up to focus on some things closer to home for the next couple of years."

I almost asked what things she was referring to, but Ben's hand suddenly grabbed mine under the table, and I realized that within a couple of years we would be married and it was possible I would finally be a mother. My emotions threatened to overtake me, and while I felt comfortable enough to let them, I also didn't want to get so caught up in my tears that I couldn't eat Beth's homemade coconut cream pie, which was possibly the best thing I had ever tasted in my life. So instead I put Ben's feet to the flames and took a bite. Of the pie, not Ben's feet.

"I guess." I shrugged. "I don't know. Ben hasn't even given me a ring yet."

"Benjamin! Is that true?" Beth asked.

"I'm not even sure it's official until you give her a ring," Gary added.

Ben laughed. "Of course it's official."

"Still, she needs a ring, Ben," Beth added.

I would have felt bad about the lighthearted attack he received from them if I hadn't been so joyfully stuffing my face. Never mind that we'd still only known each other a couple months, and never mind that that day—that horrible, life-altering, exhausting day—was the first time we had seen each other since the day after he'd proposed. And never mind that he was on unpaid leave from a job that didn't pay all that much to begin with. None of that mattered. What mattered was pie.

"She will get a ring, I assure you." He turned to face me. "I *will* get you a ring, you know."

I smiled and winked at him as I chewed and then looked down at his untouched pie. "Are you going to eat that?"

As talk finally came back around to the prospect of unemployment and diverted dreams for both of us, I voiced my frustrations in a way I don't think I had even allowed myself to think on them.

"I know that we don't always get to know God's plan. I understand that. But I'm pretty sure we were right about the basics of the plan. This new book I've been working on, it was like God gave it to me almost fully written. I've been so proud of it, knowing that I was finally going to be putting something positive out there. And Ben . . . I mean, you guys know what a great pastor he is. They've had to add rows of chairs at Mercy Point every week since he's been there, and he's making a difference in the lives of so many. It's not as if we weren't doing good things, right? And now Ben's reputation is damaged, if not ruined, despite the fact that it was all lies. People are still going to have it in the back of their minds, no matter what happens next. I don't know. I just can't understand it."

Beth had been listening from the kitchen as she cleared the table. As she walked back in with a pot of coffee, she said, "This reminds me of a story I used to tell Christa when she was a little girl. There once was a girl who was sickly and poor throughout her entire childhood."

Ben and I looked at each other and started laughing. We just couldn't hold it in.

"Sorry, Beth," he finally said, still laughing as I covered my mouth with my hands. "We know this one, actually. Well, we know separate but equally bad versions of it—though I am really intrigued to hear how you think it could possibly be relevant to this moment. The only thing we learned from it was that our mothers were both horrible storytellers."

"Ah." She smiled. "Well, I'm guessing that's where the problem is. Maybe, if you think you can stand it one more time, you can give me a shot at telling it?"

We stopped laughing and nodded, and she began again.

"There once was a girl who was sickly and poor throughout her entire childhood. She had no one and nothing, except for the ability to sing a beautiful song that possessed healing powers, a gift from her mother. Her father, however, possessed only evil inside him, and he cursed her with the inability to ever sing the song of healing and restoration for anyone outside of their small family, and only within their small hut. He wanted her melody to be only for the benefit of himself and his wife. If she sang the melody outside of the hut, or if anyone entered in as she sang, she would lose the song in her heart—both the gift and the curse of it.

"One dreadful winter, her mother and father traveled far from their daughter, in search of food. Without her song to heal them, they died and she was left alone, with only a song. Night after night, day after day, she lay in her bed, shivering from the cold, singing with all her might. The song was her only friend and her only warmth.

"One day a local trader passed by and heard the song from afar. 'Who is that, singing with the voice of an angel?' he asked. 'Why, it's no one, sir,' the townspeople said. 'It is but only a sickly girl with a song in her heart.' 'Lead me to her,' he pleaded, but the townspeople refused, insisting she would not survive the visit, for they knew of the curse the girl's father had placed.

"Another day, a jester from the court of the king passed by and heard the song from afar. 'Who is that, singing with the voice of a majestic harp?' he asked. 'Why, it's no one, sir,' the townspeople said. 'It is but only a sickly girl with a song in her heart.' 'Lead me to her,' he begged, 'and I will take her before the king.' But the townspeople refused, insisting she would not survive the journey to the palace—for they knew that if she left the hut, she would lose her song.

"Still another day, the prince himself passed

by and heard the song from afar. 'Who is that, singing with the voice of my own heart's desire?' he asked. 'Why, it's no one, your majesty,' the townspeople said. 'It is but only a sickly girl with a song in her heart.' 'Lead me to her,' the prince commanded, 'and I will take her as my wife.' The townspeople, of course, could not refuse the prince, but as they approached the girl's hut, the singing stopped.

" 'She's dead,' the townspeople cried, full of despair and disbelief that the girl was gone, and they would never again hear the song that they'd always believed would someday heal her. That evening, as the townspeople mourned, they heard a melody from afar, and it was more beautiful than any they had ever heard. Even in their sadness, they could not deny its power and they ran to it. Much to their dismay, it came from the hut of the girl, but it didn't stop when they entered. The voice—more beautiful than that of an angel, more majestic than a harp, more than even a prince could ever know to desire— belonged to a beautiful woman they didn't recognize and yet felt they knew.

"They had deprived her of adventure and fame and wealth, and even marrying a prince, but not to be cruel and not to keep her gift for themselves. All of the pain and isolation had been the means to an end—the gift of a village who cared for her, and not just her song."

Gary chuckled as Beth stood and picked up the coffeepot. "Yep, I remember that one." She walked behind him and leaned over and kissed him on the head. "Couldn't be any plainer than that, could it, hon?" He stood and followed her into the kitchen with our cups.

Meanwhile, Ben and I sat, stunned and speechless. What had just happened? Gary and Beth walked back in a few seconds later, and we hadn't budged. They looked at each other and shrugged, and then looked back to us.

"You see, the song wasn't who she was," Beth said, speaking slowly and clearly. "The song was what healed her. It was how she got from point A to point B, but it wasn't her identity."

"She had to go through some pretty rotten stuff, and the townspeople allowed it to happen," Gary added. "They let all of these really good things pass her by, and maybe that seemed cruel at the time, but sometimes we have to pass up 'good' in order to get to 'right.' You know?"

"Yeah," I whispered, still not moving or blinking.

Gary and Beth looked at each other and then back to us once more, I think starting to get a little bit concerned.

Gary spoke softly, as if worried he'd startle us. "The two of you are certainly having to go through some rotten stuff. And you're having to let some really good things pass you by."

"Like this book for you and Mercy Point for Ben," Beth interjected. "And maybe it seemed like they were the ultimate goal, but maybe God has even better things in store. Maybe they are just a means to an end."

Ben finally looked up. "Yeah, we get it. Thanks."

I heard Beth giggle from the kitchen. "Hey, babe, let's give them a minute."

Gary walked behind us on his way out. He patted Ben on the shoulder, and then we were alone.

"How have we been missing that?" I asked.

"Well, in all fairness," Ben said, still in a bit of shock himself, "we never heard *that* story."

20.

Fade to Black

"This morning on Today, *Meredith Vieira sits down with bestselling author Sarah Hollenbeck for her first interview since the scandal that rocked religious and literary communities three months ago. The unlikely love story between a popular Chicago pastor and the queen of steamy fiction was headline-worthy enough on its own merit, but the addition of false paternity claims by a member of the congregation created a story made in tabloid heaven. Today we hear Sarah's side for the very first time, and even get an exclusive peek at her scandalous new project. And believe us, it's not what you think. But first, this is* Today.*"*

"No, no, no! You can't possibly want to watch this again!" I growled at Piper as I searched for the remote.

"Come on!" She laughed. "You were so great! So great, Sarah! Please? Just one more time?" She put her hands together to beg, while pouting and blinking her big puppy dog eyes.

I groaned. "Fine. But that's it. Last time." Oh for the days before DVR, when I could have just pulled out the VHS tape and thrown it away, no remote required. "But I can't watch it again. I'm done. Just let me know when you're through."

"Suit yourself," she said with a smile, clicking play on the remote that I think she had been hiding down her shirt.

What a three months it had been. Not all bad, not all good, but never boring. Come to think of it, I couldn't remember the last time I had been bored. *And you're not bored now, Sarah! Get busy!* Right. I shook myself out of my nostalgic stupor with a mental reminder of all I needed to get done in the next two hours if I had any chance at all of getting a decent night's sleep.

"And that's when Reverend Benjamin Delaney entered the picture. To hear them tell it, love was the last thing either of them had on their minds, but certain forces are just irresistible."

"I thought you weren't going to watch." Piper smiled knowingly as I plopped down on the couch next to her and she handed me the bowl of popcorn.

"I'm not. Just the part about Ben, then I'll get back to work." I stuffed a handful of popcorn into my mouth and then stole Piper's Diet Coke from her hand.

"Who are you kidding? It's all about Ben!"

"True." I nodded. "Let's get shirts that say that."

As I watched Ben tell Meredith Vieira a little bit about losing Christa and being convinced he would never love again, I thought back on the days following Laura's announcement. Ben and I had walked out of Gary and Beth's ready to face whatever came at us. After all, we finally understood that stupid fable. At least we thought so. We both have recurring nightmares of random people coming up to us and saying, "There once was a girl who was sickly and poor throughout her entire childhood . . ."

We knew that everything in our lives was part of a much bigger picture. Before *Stollen Desire* became the bestselling, provocative phenomenon that it is today, it was nothing more than some sheets of paper falling out of my Kate Spade messenger bag, causing a girl who sat across the circle from me to get very grumpy. Without that girl, whom I literally can't remember my life without, there would have been no parking lot salvation and no first Sunday at Mercy Point.

"Laura Bellamy—beautiful, sophisticated— could have had her choice of men, but she had her heart set on one in particular."

"You guys were much nicer than I would have been," Piper said as footage of Laura's publicity stunt flashed on the screen.

I smiled as I watched, so grateful that it had been resolved as peacefully as it had been. And by peaceful, of course I mean it all played out as if written as a sweeps storyline for a soap opera.

The day after Laura had made her accusations, Joanna called Ben and asked if he and I could join her for lunch. As we walked into her house, I felt nervous all over again. Yes, she had been happy about our engagement, and yes, I had been pleasantly surprised that she actually seemed to like me. Nevertheless, I knew how much she cared about Laura, and I couldn't imagine that the timing of our lunch visit could possibly be unrelated to Laura's claims.

We walked to the door, and Nate greeted us outside. "Listen, kids. You need to hear her out, okay? This is as tough for her as it is for you."

What in the world could possibly be so difficult for Joanna? Was it going to be difficult for her to ask Ben if Laura's accusations were true? Or was she assuming they were, and she was going to give a lecture about responsibility? Maybe she was just going to disown Ben altogether so she could adopt Laura once and for all.

Ben and I looked at each other, and we saw the confusion in each other's eyes.

"Of course we'll hear her out, Dad." Nate walked through the doorway, and then Ben held the door open for me as I entered. "But you also need to know that there's a lot more to the story than—"

I stopped in my tracks as I turned the corner to enter the living room behind Nate, and I put my hand behind me to grab Ben's hand. It was then that he saw what I had seen just a split second before he did—Joanna sitting on the couch, Laura by her side.

"What's she doing here?" Ben asked angrily as he looked from Nate to Joanna, and then back to Nate. He stepped in front of me, as if to shield me from whatever was happening. "You want us to hear *her* out? You think this is as tough for *her* as it is for us? Really, Dad?" If he was trying to hide the contempt he felt for Laura, he was failing horribly. It was evident in every word, through every expression. "Come on, Sarah, let's go." He held tighter to the hand I had offered him and began to pull me out of the room.

"Ben, wait. Please," Laura pleaded.

He was already halfway out the door, but I planted my feet. He turned to face me as we stopped moving, and I softly said, "If you walk out right now, you'll always wonder what she was going to say. Stay for that reason, even if it's the only one."

With his eyes he implored me to reconsider my stance, but I didn't. Finally he sighed. "Okay," he answered me gently, before leading me back into the living room. "Make it quick," he instructed Laura, though he only looked in her general direction.

"Don't you want to sit, Ben?" Joanna asked, a little bit nervously.

"No, Mother, I don't. Come on, Laura. Get on with it."

She cleared her throat. "First of all, let me just tell you how sorry I am."

"Sorry?" He laughed bitterly. "Oh, good. You're sorry. Well then, let's just forget it ever happened."

"Excuse us a moment." I smiled uncomfortably at everyone. "Ben, can I see you outside for a second?"

"No, actually. I'm kind of in the middle of some—"

"Ben!" Nate shouted, and then spoke in his usual quiet tone once he had his attention. "The woman you plan to marry just asked to see you outside. I think you'd best see what she needs, don't you, son?"

I suddenly understood very clearly what the Delaney family dynamic must have been like when Ben was a kid. Mom called most of the shots, but when Dad meant business, you knew better than to disobey.

"Yes, sir." Ben sulked as he walked outside. If the situation hadn't been so dire, I would have had to laugh at the grumpy little boy in front of me.

I nodded my appreciation to Nate, and he nodded his back, and then I ran out after Ben. When I got outside, he was pacing and, I think, looking for something to punch.

"You need to go to a boxing ring and punch something," I said, not really having a clue what I was talking about. All I knew was that Ben had years of pent-up frustration that, overall, he managed pretty well. But I couldn't shake the feeling that he would feel really good if he could just punch something. "You know," I continued, in a feeble attempt to lighten the mood, "like in *Rocky IV*. Because when I think boxing, I think *Rocky IV*."

"I'm sorry, Sarah," he growled, still pacing. "But I wasn't prepared to see her here today. If they'd just warned us . . ."

"If they'd warned us we probably wouldn't have come," I said, inching closer to him, wanting so desperately to comfort him.

He noticed. "I recognize that look in your eyes. If you kiss me right now, I'm going to start thinking we have a problem, you and I. Always kissing at parents' houses." A smile broke through, no matter how hard he tried to not let it.

"I'm not going to kiss you." I smiled, still inching closer.

"You're not? Why not? I was just kidding about having a problem. Personally, I think we're just fans of opportunity. And this moment seems to be as opportune as any other."

"Three months from today," I stated matter-of-factly.

"No, I'm sorry," he scoffed. "I refuse to wait three months to kiss you."

"Oh no. You misunderstand me. The way I see it, three months from today you could be doing a whole lot more than kissing me."

He gulped and swallowed a little too much air, which made him cough and made me laugh. I was so intrigued and fascinated by his attraction to me.

"Are you suggesting we set a date, Ms. Hollenbeck?" he asked once he finally got his breath back.

"No, Mr. Delaney. I'm telling you I just set it. Three months from today. Be there."

With that I turned around and started walking back toward the house, which left him confused and laughing.

"Hey, where are you going?"

I ran over to him and gave him a quick kiss and said, "I'm going back inside to face something that really doesn't matter in the least. After all, I get to marry you three months from today. What else is there?" I smiled and grabbed his hand, and together we went in to face something that didn't matter at all.

"Sarah, would *you* like to sit?" Joanna asked once we were back in the room. She'd given up on Ben, who was standing, leaning against the wall, seemingly determined to keep as much distance as possible between Laura and himself.

"I'm fine." I smiled at her and held tighter to Ben's hand. I needed to make sure he knew I wouldn't leave his side. "But thank you."

"Laura, I believe you were telling us how sorry you are," Ben said, unable to make himself less angry in her presence, no matter how much we told ourselves that none of it mattered.

"I am, Ben. I'm so sorry. I never meant to hurt you—"

"Oh, come on!" he shouted, letting go of my hand and walking a bit farther into the middle of the room. "You never meant to hurt me? Really, Laura? What did you think would happen?"

She blew her nose and kept her head down as she said, "It was really more about hurting Sarah."

I suppose I shouldn't have been surprised by that, and I wasn't really. But it still felt strange to hear.

"And you didn't know that hurting her *was* hurting me?" Ben fumed. "And you didn't think that it might do a little bit of damage to my job? My reputation? My ministry, Laura. You didn't think *that* might hurt me?"

"I don't know!" she shouted back as she buried her face in her hands. "I didn't think. I panicked. I was so stupid when we were kids, and I didn't realize what I had with you until it was gone. But I never got over you, Ben. I never stopped loving you." She raised her head and for the first time looked straight at me. "I'm sorry you're having to hear this, Sarah."

I opened my mouth to respond to the apology, however insincere I believed it to be, but Ben spoke before I could say a word.

"You're not saying anything Sarah didn't already know. She saw it from the beginning." He ran his hand through his hair and began pacing the room. "But I didn't believe it. You were my friend, Laura. I was sure of it."

"I *am* your friend, Ben!" She stood and rushed over to him, but he quickly backed away and rejoined me along the wall.

"No," he stated firmly, once he had grabbed my hand again. "You're not. But that's not what matters right now. What are you going to do about it, Laura? How are you going to clear this up?"

She sighed as she returned to her place beside Joanna. "Well, it's complicated."

"Actually, it's not," Ben argued. "I mean, damage has been done, but we'll deal with that." He released my hand and then placed his arm around my waist and pulled me closer—as if wanting to make sure she understood that she was not a part of "we." "Sarah and I are getting married—"

"In three months," I chimed in, perhaps unnecessarily—although the slight trace of a smile that appeared on his lips made it feel pretty necessary.

"And everything else will work out some-how," he continued. "But you've convinced some people at Mercy Point that I'm Kaitlyn's father, and it's just a matter of time until that lie spreads. The reporters are going to dig deeper into your generic claims, and someone at Mercy Point is bound to fill in the rest of your story. You need to clear that up."

"Well," she muttered softly, "that's the part that's complicated."

"Are you sure you don't want to sit down?" Joanna asked one more time, I suppose to the room at large.

"Why is it complicated, Laura?" Ben prodded, ignoring his mother. "Don't you know who Kaitlyn's father is?"

"Of course I do," she replied, stung. "But it's complicated because . . . well, I mean . . . we have to look out for Kaitlyn."

"I agree. And I really wish you'd thought of that before you ever created this mess, but that doesn't change the fact that—"

"She is your family," Laura said, sobbing.

"How *dare* you turn this around on me, as if I'm the one dragging Kaitlyn into this? Yes, she is a great kid, and we all care about her. I'm not suggesting for a minute that we do anything that would—"

He looked quickly at me and I greeted him with a deer-in-headlights look. I figured that I understood less than anyone else in the room, having missed out on the first thirty-plus years of history between the Delaneys and the Bellamys, but even I could sense from Laura's tone, and the flood of new tears that accompanied it, that we had finally gotten to the heart of the matter.

"She's my family?" he repeated. "As in . . ."

"She's your niece," she wailed as she buried her head in Joanna's shoulder.

"Wow," Ben said as he sat down at last, more out of necessity than anything else. Anger had, at least temporarily, been replaced by complete and total shock. "I mean, I knew you and Jeremy dated for a little while after we broke up, but I never realized there was anything going on earlier. Wow. Does he know that she's his?"

"Actually . . ." Laura began.

"No, there's no way he knows," Ben continued. "He couldn't have kept this from me, and he certainly would have wanted to be a part of his daughter's life. Does Kaitlyn know?"

"Actually, Ben," Laura tried again.

"She's been around him her entire life. To think—"

I saw Laura struggling, needing to say more but not knowing how. And Ben's ramblings weren't helping.

I walked around and stood behind the chair where he sat, and placed my hands on his shoulders. "Ben," I whispered. When he looked at me, I motioned for him to look at Laura, and then he saw her pain and stopped talking.

"Actually, Ben," she whimpered, "it wasn't Jeremy. It was Jacob."

You could have heard a pin drop on the plush, outdated carpet as Ben took in the information. You could see his train of thought, moment by moment, and it wasn't difficult to predict where the train would stop. But I couldn't take my eyes off of Joanna, to whom none of it was a surprise. It all made sense—her dedication to Laura, her insistence that Laura and Kaitlyn be included as part of the family. It had never been about Laura. It was about Kaitlyn. And Jacob.

Ben's mental train pulled into the station, and it desperately wanted to be anywhere else. "He was a kid, Laura! You slept with my baby brother? How could you do that?"

"Your 'baby' brother was a couple months past eighteen, Ben," she argued.

"Exactly! Legally an adult, but still a kid! He was a kid who always had a crush on you, and you took advantage of him to get back at me. Because we had a fight? That's when it happened, right? That Christmas?"

"Yes," she whispered, making no attempt to deny or defend. That surprised me, and Ben too, I think.

"Does he know?" he asked, much more quietly.

Laura shook her head. "No. It was bad enough

that I was single and pregnant. I didn't want to ruin him too."

"She didn't make that decision alone, Ben," Joanna spoke up. "She doesn't hold all of the blame."

I wanted to wrap my arms around Ben, but he was no longer within my grasp as he stood from the chair and walked back toward the wall. As he passed me I saw the redness in his eyes, and I had to quickly wipe away the tears from my own eyes—a result of seeing so much pain in his.

"How long have you known, Mom?" he asked through raw emotion he was struggling to contain. "Since the beginning?" Suddenly he laughed, but the laugh was full of nothing but agony and betrayal. "You knew I was going to propose . . ."

"I didn't know then, Ben," Joanna cried. "I promise you, I didn't know then. I never would have let that go on, sweetheart. Not without you knowing. She told me a little after that. I should have told you. I know that now, and I'm sorry. I didn't know what to do. But I promise, I didn't know until after the two of you broke up. By then you were with Christa, and I didn't think—"

"Hold on a minute," Laura spoke up, as all of the color drained from her face. "You were going to propose . . . to me?" The soul-level despair had been replaced by the pouty-lipped countenance I was much more used to from her.

I certainly felt no obligation to assist Laura, but right then I felt like offering her some unsolicited advice.

Learn when to keep your mouth shut.

"When were you going to propose to me, Ben?"

I knew that there were so many more things Ben wanted to say to his mother, and I knew that eventually he would, but Laura's badly timed statement of disappointment helped turn his attention back to her.

"So you didn't want to ruin Jacob, but you had no qualms at all about ruining Sarah and me?"

"I love you, Ben," she said through her tears.

"What do you think saying that is going to accomplish? Who do you think you're fooling?" Ben started pacing again. "You don't love me! This isn't what you do to people you love, Laura."

"Ben . . ." Nate said, trying to calm him down.

I, on the other hand, did not try to calm him down. He wanted to punch something, but it wouldn't be Laura. He had, however, earned the right to say his piece.

"Nate, Joanna . . . these two have about fifteen years of history they need to deal with. And I think Ben deserves a chance to say what he needs to say. So we're going to let him say it. If that's not something you feel comfortable being present for, it might be a good time to step outside."

I don't know who was most shocked that those

words came out of my mouth. Joanna wasn't sure if she should stay or go, Nate wasn't sure he liked me telling him what to do in his home, Laura didn't seem to like the fact that I, for one, was staying put, and Ben fell even more in love with me. Nevertheless, no one moved.

Ben grabbed my hand. "Actually, I'm good. I forgot it doesn't matter." He looked at me with overflowing amounts of affection, and the pain and sadness in his eyes made it very clear that it actually mattered a great deal. "But thank you," he whispered to me as we walked to the door.

"You're just . . . *leaving?*" Laura asked in disbelief.

He tightened his grip on my hand, but he didn't turn back and he didn't say a word.

"Mercy Point Church has since closed its doors, the victim of much more than an age-old sex scandal."

"Aww, this part makes me sad," Piper said as we finished off the popcorn.

It made me sad too, but I couldn't help but get this little, tiny bit of glee whenever I saw the footage of Lenore Isaacs being escorted out of the church building in handcuffs. In hindsight it all made perfect sense.

Tom Isaacs was guilty of nothing more than being an idiot who would do whatever his wife told him to. It was Lenore who had a problem with my tithe check, but only because she thought her husband could come out on the winning side of a fight against immorality. She'd soon learned that Ben and I were a couple, which originally seemed like an opportunity to not only make Tom look good but get rid of Ben in the process. But then she realized the plan she liked even more was the one in which she embezzled the additional funds coming in from the pastor's new girlfriend.

I hadn't been at all surprised to learn that Laura and Lenore had in fact been in cahoots. Laura had first taken her claims to the church board, and from what we could tell, she hadn't originally planned to take it any further. As a member of the board, Lenore had been handed everything she needed. What was surprising, however, was the revelation that Sydney had been the one to put them in touch with the appropriate media outlets. She took her job very seriously, I suppose, and she saw Ben as something standing in the way of her doing her job effectively because, as she said in court, he kept me from doing my job effectively.

And of course if I was kept from doing my job effectively, Sydney might be kept from the sizable bonus she was to receive each time one of my books hit the shelves.

Mercy Point hadn't closed immediately—that didn't happen until after they had begged Ben to come back. But we knew, despite our deep love and appreciation for the church and its people, that Mercy Point wasn't part of the bigger plan. Laura had confessed, Lenore had been arrested, Sydney had been fired. We had reached a point where we could pretty much allow life to get back to normal. Of course, no matter how normal everything seemed, we knew that everything had changed.

"And what of the Christian romance that Sarah had planned to write? Scandal behind her, could the project be saved?"

Piper plopped down on the couch with a refilled bowl of popcorn and asked, "Didn't Meredith Vieira leave this show? Why did she do your interview?"

I smiled, feeling very powerful. "Because I asked for her."

"Oh. Well! Aren't you something special?"

My publishers certainly seemed to think so. Once Ben's name was cleared, and it became clear that public opinion was much more on our side than perhaps had been anticipated, they couldn't wait to get their hands on my Christian romance. I gave them the story that Joe loved so much, complete with a loving, realistic-though-more-dramatic-than-most, sexy Christian relationship. But when contract time came around again, I decided it was time to move on.

Ben and I started Means and Ends Ministries,

and a division of that is Song in Her Heart Publishing. Our first project is a memoir written by an up-and-coming author by the name of Sarah Hollenbeck. Actually, I guess she'll be Sarah Delaney by then, not that the name matters—as long as the name isn't Raine de Bourgh.

"Tomorrow, Sarah and Ben will be married in a private ceremony in Algonquin, Illinois. When asked what they're most looking forward to in this new life they are beginning, this seemingly perfect couple disagrees for the first time."

"Oh gosh!" I groaned. "Turn it off! Turn it off!"

"Shh!" Piper laughed. "This is my favorite part! Ben goes first. So sweet!"

"Probably babies. She's wanted to be a mother for so long, and she's so fantastic with Maddie, and I just feel so blessed to be the guy she'll raise a family with. We intend to have a pretty large family. I mean, not von Trapp large, but large."

"It does get me pretty hot whenever he references *The Sound of Music*," I said to Piper.

"Shh! You're going to miss it! Okay, so Meredith asked, 'And what about you, Sarah? What are you most looking forward to?' and you said . . ."

I buried my face in a pillow as she hit play once more.

"Truthfully? I think, after all this time, what I'm most looking forward to is the part where we actually get to make the babies."

"That is so stinking cute!" Piper laughed. "Just look at you blushing. I love it! Let's watch it again!"

I snatched the remote out of her hands and turned it off, unaffected by her pouts this time around. "No. We have so much to do!"

"Fine," she said, finally standing up. "Geez, you act like you're getting married in twelve hours or something."

Eleven hours later I was in the basement of Gary and Beth's church in Algonquin, surrounded by more mothers than any one girl needs. Beth was fantastic, and Joanna was okay.

My mother was, well . . . my mother.

"Are you sure you want to go through with this, Sarah? It's not too late to change your mind."

"What?" I laughed. "Yes, Mom, I'm sure."

"I mean, it's not that Ben isn't a nice boy. He is." That was said to Joanna, I think. As if she needed reassuring. "It's just that I know you're trying the Christian thing, and that's lovely. But the last thing you want is to be unprepared and get stuck with someone you aren't sexually compatible with. That can make for such a miserable marriage while it lasts—believe me." Though I certainly didn't want to linger too long on the thought, I couldn't help but wonder which of her four husbands my mother was referring to. "I just think it's very risky, that's all."

Oh, shoot me now. "Mom, first of all, I'm not 'trying the Christian thing.' I am a Christ-follower. It's not some fad I'm testing out, like the Atkins diet or my 'Rachel' hairdo from a few years ago."

"Second of all," Joanna stepped in, "my husband and I were not intimate until our wedding night, and I assure you—"

"Okay, Joanna," Beth interrupted, mercifully. "I think it's best we don't hear how that sentence was going to end."

"I would like to go find a poufy dress-sized hole to climb in now," I muttered softly.

They all—with the exception of my mother, of course—got lost in a fit of giggles that didn't stop until there was a knock on the door. I looked at the clock on the wall—I still had twenty minutes. "No! I'm not ready yet!"

"I'll get it," Piper said, despite the fact that with my eyes I threatened to never speak to her again if she left me alone in mom hell.

"Ben can't see me!" I called out. "Make sure it's not Ben!"

"Um, it's not Ben," she said a second later.

Before I could even turn around to see who it was, my mother's excited squeals gave me a pretty good idea. "You're saved!" she said to me in a way I think she genuinely believed was discreet, and then she ran to the door to hug my "savior."

"Sarah, you look beautiful."

No. No, no, no.

I turned around, not that I needed further evidence that the man at the door was most certainly not Ben.

"What are you doing here, Patrick?"

"Patrick?" Piper screamed. "Oh no. No, no. You will not be here right now. You *are not* here right now. I refuse to accept that you are here. Shoo! Get out!"

"Hey, Piper, it's okay." I smiled. "But thank you."

"What do you want us to do, sweetheart?" Beth asked softly and sweetly.

"Who's Patrick?" Joanna inquired naively.

I grabbed Beth's hand and squeezed it, while smiling at her reassuringly. "Could you maybe occupy those two for a few minutes?" I nodded my head toward the two moms.

"Of course." She winked before giving me a quick hug. She crossed the room to them and looped her arms through theirs. "Did you see the gardens on your way in? You just have to see the gardens."

My mother bounded out, leading the way, before Beth had finished the sentence, confident that Patrick would ravage me as soon as everyone left and all would be right with the world once more.

Piper walked over to me, though her wary eyes

never left Patrick. "Would you like for me to stay?"

"Are you really giving me a choice?"

"Of course not."

"Good." I laughed quietly before turning to Patrick. "So what do you want?"

He looked from me to Piper and then back again. "Well, I was hoping to speak to you alone for a minute . . ."

"This is as close as you're going to get. So what do you want?" I repeated.

He cleared his throat and shuffled his feet as he adjusted his tie. His *tie.* Did he come dressed for the occasion, expecting an invitation to stay? Or was he just still the same pompous, uptight man he'd always been?

"I don't believe we've met." He smiled as he put out his hand and approached Piper. "Patrick McDermott."

Piper kept her hands to herself as she raised her eyebrow and said, "Oh, believe me. I know who you are."

It didn't take him very long to realize he was interacting with one of the few women on whom his charm would have no effect, so he made his way back to me.

"You really do look beautiful. Even more breathtaking than the day we met."

I was amazed to discover I felt nothing for him. I already knew I wasn't in love with him

347

anymore, of course, but even so, you would almost expect there to be a touch of nostalgia or a fondness associated with all we had shared. But there was nothing. I didn't even find him attractive. He was taller than Ben, which meant he was too tall; he wasn't as muscular as Ben, which meant he was too skinny; he wasn't Ben, which meant the sight of him did absolutely nothing for me.

"You have about one more minute, so you should probably cut to the chase," I insisted impatiently.

He took a step toward me, but I put my hands up to indicate he shouldn't come any closer, and he stopped. "I saw you on television and I just had to make sure you're happy."

"I am, thank you. Now if you don't mind, it's probably best that you—"

I tried to usher him to the door, but he didn't budge. "I just can't help but think there are still some feelings between us which need to be addressed."

"Does Kiki know you're here, Patrick?" Piper asked.

He looked extremely confused by Piper—what she was talking about and why she was in the room.

"I'm sorry? Kiki?"

"I believe she is referring to the mother of your child," I clarified, biting my lip so that I could focus on the seriousness of the moment rather than how tickled I was by Piper.

"Oh. Her name is Kimberly."

She shrugged. "Whatever. Does she know you're here?"

He sighed and tried once more to step closer to me, and we repeated our dance. "This doesn't concern her."

"Of course not," I said, shaking my head. I quickly thought back to when he had first called me to tell me about Kimberly and the pregnancy. "Isn't she due any minute, Patrick?" I looked at the clock on the wall. "I mean, if my math is correct, you could literally be a dad before I'm a wife. And yet here you are . . ."

"She doesn't understand me like you do, Sarah," he whispered.

Oh, how I laughed at that line. "Really? That's the best you can do? Do women really fall for that? Oh, wait. They probably do, because they *don't* understand you like I do. I understand that you will always want what you don't have and it's just a shame. You had me, Patrick, and you didn't want me. You sure don't get to have me now."

"That's not it at all," he replied earnestly. He glanced at Piper again before turning his face away from her and saying, as discreetly as he could, "You're the only woman I have ever loved, Sarah. Don't you know that?"

I was sad, for just a moment, as I realized

that was probably true. And for just a moment I thought about the type of guy he had been before money and success became a part of our lives. Whoever he had become, if that guy who drew beautiful sketches was still in there somewhere, I was sad for him.

But all of that went away when he leaned in as close as he could—as close as I would allow—and said, "Come on, Sarah. Let's get out of here. For old time's sake."

"All right! That's it!" Piper stated with authority. "Time for you to go."

But I wasn't quite done yet. I couldn't help but chuckle as I said, "I'm sorry, I just can't even take you seriously. Do you know what I've been through the past few months? Oh, of course you do. That's the only reason you're here, right? You saw me on TV and couldn't stand the thought of me being happy? What I just find so pathetic is that you think that you still have the ability to affect me in some way. You think I'm going to 'get out of here' with you? Well, let me tell you something. Ben is my everything now. *We're* everything, Ben and I. You and me? We're done, Patrick. Now if you'll excuse me, I'm getting married in a few minutes."

I glanced at Piper, who was furiously dabbing at her eyes with a handkerchief so that her makeup was not ruined by proud tears. She smiled at me and rushed over to stand by my side.

"Allow me to show you out," she said, the scary "don't mess with Piper" expression returning as she faced him.

"I'll go with you," I said. "I want to make sure he's really gone."

Patrick raised his hands in defeat—and even in defeat he was smug and disgusting. "That won't be necessary."

Piper and I looked at each other and rolled our eyes. We wouldn't trust him as far as we could throw him, so we knew it was very necessary. Piper led the way, and I pushed Patrick along to follow out after her. As we reached the door, we passed Beth and the mothers making their way back in.

"Everything okay?" Beth asked with concern.

"Where are you going?" my mother asked, true to form. "Sarah, where is Patrick going?"

He turned to face me one last time—and I felt nothing but relief, confident that it would, in fact, be the last time. "You're making a mistake, Sarah."

"Good-bye, Patrick." I smiled as I gave him one last little nudge to get him to the other side of the doorframe.

"I hope you and Kiki are very happy together," Piper added as she slammed the door in his face.

Less than an hour later—after Maddie had laid her trail of flowers and Joe had walked me down the aisle, after Piper had read from Song of Solomon and Gary had asked us to repeat after him, we were pronounced Mr. and Mrs. Benjamin Delaney, and Ben finally kissed his bride.

We mingled for a couple of hours, acting like we cared more than we did at the moment about well wishes from family and friends and things like cake and punch.

"I'll be back," I said softly at one point. "I'm going to change into my traveling clothes."

"I'll go with you, to help you get out of your dress," Piper said, standing up.

"Actually," Ben said, playfully pushing her back down, "I think that's my job now."

I felt at least two-thirds of the blood in my body rush to my cheeks as we walked out of the room together.

"Ben, so help me," I whispered as he actually walked into the ladies' room with me. "After holding out this long, we cannot—I repeat, cannot—make love for the first time in your first wife's dad's church's ladies' room." I talked a good game, but I was really just lecturing myself, knowing that the desire for romance was now the only thing stopping us.

"I heard you had a visitor earlier," he said as he locked the door behind him.

I groaned. Which of the mothers had thought immediately following our wedding was the perfect time to tell him about that?

"I'm sorry I didn't tell you yet. In all fairness, I've barely had time to say two words to you."

As he stepped closer, slowly, he smiled an oh-so-sexy smile and said, "Well, if you only had time for two words, I'm very glad you chose 'I do.'"

"Seemed like the right thing to say."

He sighed. "Well, be that as it may, I'm very disappointed I didn't get a chance to meet him."

"Are you?" I asked with a tilted head as he continued his agonizingly slow walk to where I stood.

"A little. There are a few things I might have liked to say to him. But from what I hear, you handled it pretty well without me."

Ah. Piper was the informant. That didn't bother me nearly as much, as I was certain she'd not neglected to tell him how awesome I was.

He finally reached my side, and the nearness put my senses on high alert. "Look at me," he whispered as his hands framed my face.

I didn't have to wait long before I felt his hands envelop my waist and his breath on my neck.

"I thought I was prepared for how beautiful you would look today," he whispered, "but I hadn't even begun to imagine. When I saw you, all I could think was, 'Seriously, Lord? She's mine? Are you sure?'"

I laughed for a second, but I stopped when he moved his hands from my waist and started the task of unbuttoning a couple tiny buttons at the top of the back of my dress. Then he stopped, gently caressed my hair, and slowly and excruciatingly moved his hand down my neck, across my collarbone, down my arm, across my waist, finally landing on my hip. I was completely powerless, and all I could think about was how silly my little "no first time in the bathroom" rule was. Thankfully, he wrangled up more willpower than I.

He cleared his throat, backing away slowly. "Now that I think about it, do you want Piper to come help you from here?"

"Yeah, that's probably a good idea."

"Check," he said as he struggled to get the door open. He finally succeeded, and then ran the right side of his body into the doorframe as he tried to leave. He turned back around and offered some sort of dorky little salute thing, and then he left. Immediately, he rushed back in and said, "That can't be my parting move. Unacceptable." With the door still wide open, he threw one arm around my waist while the other hand got very intentionally tangled in my hair, and then he dipped me and bent over to match my curved form as he captured my mouth with his. "Better," he said as he tore himself away and left before I had even opened my eyes.

It would have been the cool and sexy exit he was looking for if I hadn't heard him say

"Ouch!" as he ran into something in the hallway.

Piper came running in a few seconds later and shut the door behind her. She quirked one eyebrow at me in suspicion, and I just smiled and shook my head.

I turned to the mirror to check my makeup. "Your last official duty as maid of honor is to help me get dressed as quickly as possible so we can get out of here. I'm not sure we can hold out much longer."

She laughed. "Yeah, I kind of got that impression when Ben asked Gary to go start the car already."

Ten minutes later we were saying our good-byes to everyone, but especially Maddie.

"You have a good time with Grammy Beth and Pawpaw, okay?" Ben said as he gave her a third hug. "We'll call you lots."

"My turn!" I squealed, squeezing in between them.

As I hugged her, I couldn't help but think I really needed to have a *Sound of Music* moment with her. She'd ask if she could call me Mother, and I'd impart to her all of the knowledge passed on to me from the Mother Superior, and then we'd sing. But in the end, the reality was even better.

"I love you, Applesauce," she said, hugging me tightly.

As the tears flooded my eyes, I said the only

thing I needed to say. "I love you too, Maddie."

I was starting to think I would never get Ben out of there—after all, it was one thing to say good-bye to decorum and propriety. Saying good-bye to his daughter was another thing entirely. Ultimately I decided the time for playing fair had passed, so I whispered in his ear, "My dress is coming off in thirty minutes, regardless of where we are. The rest is up to you." Then I blew Maddie a kiss, waved good-bye to everyone, and turned around to walk away. Not surprisingly, he was with me before I got to the door, and twenty minutes later we had checked into the honeymoon suite, right there in Algonquin.

"Where do they all think we are?" I laughed as I looked out the window from our top floor viewpoint and spotted the church where we had just been wed.

"Far, far away," he said as he tipped the bellhop.

Ben escorted him to the door and then closed and locked it. By the time he turned back around, I had drawn the curtains and was sitting on the edge of the bed.

"Do you realize," I began as I bent over to take off my heels, "that this is the very first time we have been in a bedroom together?"

He started walking slowly toward me. "I'd say there is a good reason for that."

"And do you realize that we've never so much as sat on a bed together?" I finished with my shoes and threw them carelessly to a far corner.

"I'd say there is a very good reason for that," he said, closing the gap further.

I patted the bed next to me, but he shook his head. "Now, you see, there isn't a good reason for it anymore," I argued. "You can sit."

"Well, I would," he said as he took my hand and pulled me up, "but I believe this dress has reached its expiration date."

"Wow. Has it been thirty minutes already?" I laughed softly. "Well, okay. A promise is a promise." He reached to start unbuttoning me— but I stopped him. "Actually, let me this time."

"If you insist," he said, and then he leaned in to kiss me. I only let him kiss me for a moment before I began unbuttoning the dress slowly.

We tried coy and seductive. We really did give it the old college try, but we couldn't take it anymore. As he scooped me up to take me to the bed, my eye caught a glimpse of a lamp on the wall, which, in my imagination, was shaking from the motion of the train.

Fade to black.

Acknowledgments

There are so many who have made it possible to get to this point—in writing, in life. I can't possibly name you all, but please know that you are loved and appreciated.

Special thanks to my dad, who has read more romantic comedy than he probably ever cared to, just because he's awesome and supportive like that; to my mom, who was my first editor and has helped my writing click into place for most of my life; and to my sister Missy, who seems to think I'm funnier than I actually am (but not funny enough to make her want to read what I write). I love you guys!

To Jenny, my BP, who was the first to ever read Sarah's story. Every word I have written and will ever write goes through the filter of "What will Jenny think?"

So much love and thanks to LeeAnn, who made a life-altering journey with me and who encourages me to write like I'm running out of time.

Much love to Secily, who has helped me embrace my unicorn status. Without your glitter, the world would be a darker place.

Thanks to Anne, who said, "I want to be a

friend like Piper," and to whom I replied, "Who says you aren't a friend like Piper?"

Gonzo once sang, "There's not a word yet for old friends who've just met." Zaida, Annaliese, Maureen, and Mikal—I may not have a word for you, but my life is better because you're in it.

Thanks to my agent, Jessica Kirkland. Your encouragement is priceless!

So much appreciation to Hannah, Jen, Michele, Karen, Kristin, and everyone at Revell. I'm still pinching myself that you're the team I get to work with!

To my friend, editor, and spirit animal, Kelsey Bowen. I don't know that I have words enough to thank you. I didn't really know what I was praying for . . . turns out it was you!

David, you've helped me find my direction countless times, and I'm so glad you know me well enough to point me right or left, never east or west.

Jacob, I'll owe you forever for a million things, but I'm most in debt to you for the way you believe in me. Well, that and the Hogwarts Express.

Ethan and Noah, I am so immensely proud of who you are. All of my other creations will always pale in comparison.

Kelly Turner, you are my favorite.

Bethany Turner is the director of administration for Rock Springs Church in Southwest Colorado. A former VP/operations manager of a commercial bank and a three-time cancer survivor (all before she turned thirty-five), Bethany knows that when God has plans for your life, it doesn't matter what anyone else has to say. Because of that, she's chosen to follow his call to write. She lives with her husband and their two sons in Colorado, where she writes for a new generation of readers who crave fiction that tackles the thorny issues of life with humor and insight. Visit Bethany online at www.seebethanywrite.com.

Center Point Large Print
600 Brooks Road / PO Box 1
Thorndike, ME 04986-0001 USA

(207) 568-3717

US & Canada:
1 800 929-9108
www.centerpointlargeprint.com